UNDER ORDER

Sadey Quinn

Dedication

To N.
For waking up with me before the crack of dawn to work.
For helpful editing and invaluable suggestions.
And most of all for loving me.
This book is for you.

"I do not want to be the leader. I refuse to be the leader. I want to live darkly and richly in my femaleness. I want a man lying over me, always over me. His will, his pleasure, his desire, his life, his work, his sexuality the touchstone, the command, my pivot. I don't mind working, holding my ground intellectually, artistically; but as a woman, oh, God, as a woman I want to be dominated. I don't mind being told to stand on my own feet, not to cling, be all that I am capable of doing, but I am going to be pursued, fucked, possessed by the will of a male at his time, his bidding."

-Anaïs Nin

Other Titles by Sadey Quinn
Social Service
Spanktastic
Slaves on Pertz

Chapter One
SEEDS OF CHANGE

I passed the bar exam and was a real lawyer. I rushed to my apartment after I received the notice. It was well before noon, so I sat waiting anxiously. It was a chilly morning, but I barely cared or noticed. I was just so excited about my good news. I heard the key in the door and rushed to it, paper in hand, nearly bursting out of my skin with joy. Ryan would be the first to know.

He didn't open the door fast enough so without further thought, I swung it open, ready to jump into his arms.

"Eeeeeeeeeeeeeee!" I was squealing, bubbling over with happiness. "Ryan – I did it!"

Then, I looked at who was standing outside on our porch entrance. Ryan, my fiance, was embracing a small, blonde woman wearing a smart business suit. She was holding a beautiful bag. It was Prada. I remember the bag more than I remember her face. I also remember the weather, because at that very moment it began to rain.

Ryan looked at me, startled. I wasn't supposed to be home. After three years of law school I passed the intimidating bar exam on my first try. When I got the good news, I left work. I just couldn't wait any longer to tell him.

"Heather," he said. *Heather.* No explanation, no excuse. No show of remorse or really emotion of any kind. Just, *Heather.* My world went black around me; my emotional high meeting an all-time emotional low as I learned that my fiance was a cheat and a fake. And he didn't love me. I walked back inside and closed the door.

Ryan packed his things within 24 hours and was out of my life. Who was that woman? Ryan didn't say, and I didn't ask. My friends surrounded me to show support, knowing how much I depended on him and wanting to console me and help me. But I found myself strangely needing no help or consoling. I was at peace with the lying, with our break-up, with Ryan, and with the small blonde woman. I didn't mind when his friends called looking for him, forgetting to change his number in their phones. I mailed him his favorite shirt when I discovered it behind the washing machine. I didn't feel bitter, or hurt, or really anything at all.

I went on with my life as a bit of a zombie, keeping my appointments and current friendships but staying away from anything new. This irritated my friends, who after a few months became determined to set me up with their new co-worker, or their hot gym buddy, or even in one case, my former high-school history teacher. I turned them down systematically, and avoided my friends when I could. The pressure to date wasn't anything I was interested in facing.

I focused instead on work at the law firm of McLaughlin,

Richards, and Kingston. During law school I worked there as an intern. Passing the bar exam automatically gave me a sizable pay increase. I had never before been so completely devoted to anything besides Ryan, and with my new found ability to rabidly focus on work, I quickly found myself advancing. Not having a relationship proved very advantageous. Within a few months I was taking on my own cases. They were small cases, but I felt so *good* about myself when I could pull away with a victory. I spent most of my time in the office or in court. When I made it back to my apartment I would flop down onto the couch in exhaustion. On good days, I poured myself a glass of red wine and watched the news before sleep beckoned me into the world of the unconscious. Even my dreams were about work.

My direct boss, Mr. Richards, commended me for my hard work but after a few months he began to show concern. I had lost a lot of weight, mainly due to forgetting about meals, and I occasionally nodded off in the office. Perhaps this is fairly typical behavior for young, eager lawyers, but I couldn't argue with him when he told me I needed to take a break. One Tuesday morning he sent me home from work, warning me not to come near the office until the following week.

So, I went home. And I slept all day and most of the next.

Then, I got bored. *Really* bored.

And then, I got horny. *Extremely* horny. I realized that I had barely thought about sex since Ryan left, and that was nearly four months ago.

I turned on my computer and looked up sex stories and videos. I used headphones to listen so no one could possibly know what I was doing inside my apartment. I watched all the free videos I could find: men fucking women, women fucking women, anything involving sex and orgasms. And I came. I fingered myself for so long, I came at least four times. I slept peacefully that night.

The next morning I woke up in the leisurely way I did when Ryan and I were together. I put on coffee, read the news and tidied up a bit. My apartment, though now barely lived in, wasn't exactly a model home for cleanliness. I threw off my robe, put the music on loud and danced around the apartment in my panties as I cleaned. I felt sexy.

When I was changing the sheets on my bed I caught a look of myself in the mirror and paused to study my body. Mr. Richards was right; I had changed a lot in the last few months. I always had a nice body, but losing the extra weight made me look *really hot*. I usually wore pantsuits to work, and only spent enough time in front of the mirror to put on a quick layer of makeup. I hadn't really *looked* at myself in a long time.

I turned around to peer at my butt. *Not bad*, I thought. Though the previous night of solo entertainment had been fun, I wondered if I should go out and try to get laid. In real life. By a man.

I giggled to myself. I had other boyfriends before Ryan but nothing very serious. Never in my life had I even considered a one-night stand. But a relationship just wasn't a possibility at this point in my career. This could be my last chance for a long time to have any time at all for a quick fuck.

It was Friday, so it would be a perfect night to go out. Before I could think about it any further, I called an old friend of mine, Rebecca. We had gone to under-grad together. Though I hadn't heard from her in years, I had received a message from her last week. I originally decided to ignore her call. But considering my goal, and Rebecca's open attitude about sex, I figured she wouldn't disapprove if I started the night with her and ended it with some guy from a nightclub. She sounded surprised to hear back from me, but as always, she was ready for a night out. When I told her I wanted a really fun night, she said she knew of a great spot.

Rebecca came over early as I was getting ready. She sat on my bed as I threw pantsuit after pantsuit out of my closet, looking for anything even remotely sexy from my college days. The weight I had lost proved to be a bit of a problem. My hottest black dress didn't quite fit right anymore. Rebecca walked over to my closet, and spent about five minutes rummaging around in drawers and through the hangers. She pulled out three items: a metallic silver halter-top, a black miniskirt, and 4 inch black heels.

"I have no idea how you just did that," I said, seriously amazed. The silver top was from a Halloween costume I wore in high school – I was a robot, my then-boyfriend was the robot controller. The heels were an impulse buy when I just started dating Ryan and wanted to impress him. I had absolutely no idea where the black skirt came from.

I put on the outfit and stood back to look at myself in the mirror. Rebecca gasped, "Oh-my-god Heather. You look slutty. And *hot*."

She performed a six-minute magic trick on my hair, putting it up into a messy ponytail that somehow resembled what my hair would look like if I were, in fact, getting fucked. I touched up my makeup and we were out the door.

I prayed that I wouldn't run into any of my coworkers. Not that they would recognize me.

Rebecca recommended a nightclub, Dynamic, in a somewhat nice part of town. We took a cab since neither of us wanted to be responsible drivers that night. The bouncer waved us in, in front of maybe twenty people in line.

I raised an eyebrow at Rebecca, "You have friends here, huh?"

She grinned at me. "Let's dance!"

Dynamic had two floors. The first floor was the basic dance and party scene. Loud music, flashing lights and lasers. The dance floor was filled with a nice looking crowd in their 20s and 30s and Rebecca and I worked our way into a spot near the DJ. I danced with Rebecca, sometimes brushing against other dancers, while eying the masculine options around me. We kept up with the high rhythmic energy of the music and I felt a light sweat on my skin. I could smell the salt and pheromones in the air. None of the men caught my eye and none turned their focus to dance with us. Maybe they thought Rebecca and I were a couple of lesbians. I closed my eyes and let the music control my body. The pounding rhythm and waves of dancers surrounding me could not quiet my mind. Soon I was bored and impatient. I was on a mission to get fucked, and I had very little time to accomplish my goal. I left Rebecca dancing and climbed up the wide stairs to the second floor.

The upstairs was a dark lounge, lit with candles and and red lights. It was quieter, except for the loud thumping of the music from down below. A video screen provided a flickering eerie light. Part of the room was blocked off by a thick black curtain. Several men sat at the bar, and a few couples sat at the tables and deep blue velvet couches spread around the room. I felt nervous and alone, and a bit out of place. As I turned to go back downstairs, a waiter intercepted me.

"Miss? Would you like to sit and have a drink up here? It can be a nice break from the chaos downstairs."

I looked at him. About my height, and maybe a few years younger than me. He was being genuinely kind. "Actually, thanks, yes that sounds lovely. I could use a break from the music." He was good enough looking to be an option for the night, but he would probably be working too late to serve my needs.

I sat down at a small table and ordered a glass of house red wine. I felt awkward and shy, suddenly not so confident with my slutty outfit. I should have had a drink before getting to the club. Glancing around I noticed the other women, who were all very attractive and dressed with a bit more class than me. I resolved to drink my wine as quickly as possible before going downstairs where me and my outfit belonged.

The waiter brought the glass of wine and set the bottle down on the table as well. I looked at him, surprised. He shrugged and walked away, not saying a word.

One sip of that wine and *ooh* it was heaven. I knew this was not the house wine I had ordered. I looked around and caught the eye of one man across the dark room. He was looking directly at me. He raised his glass to me. I blushed and toasted him back, then looked shyly away. The video screen showed people dancing and then I realized that it was showing the dance floor below. I tried to pick out Rebecca but couldn't see her in the writhing mass of bodies.

I glanced back to the man across the room. He spoke with his table companion, a blond woman in a white dress, then stood, excused himself, and walked towards me.

Could this be happening? I thought. *So easy!* My cockiness returned and I confidently sipped my glass until my handsome stranger appeared at my table.

"Are you enjoying your wine?" he asked, looking down at me. I looked up and nearly gasped out loud. He had very strong features, bright green eyes, and slightly curly dark brown hair. He was easily the most beautiful man I had ever seen.

"Y..yes," I stammered. "Although it isn't what I ordered."

"I didn't think you made the correct choice," he replied, smiling slightly.

"Oh." That was all I could think of to say. He continued standing there, watching me. Waiting for something.

"May I join you?" he finally asked, looking at me expectantly.

"Oh yes, of course, please sit down," I said. I was hoping he didn't notice my total lack of proper social etiquette, or that at the very least he found my social awkwardness to be endearing. As an attempt to recover, I offered him a glass of the wine. From the bottle he had bought. He accepted, and the waiter brought over another glass, setting it down without a word.

"Does he... does he know you?" I asked my new friend.

"He does."

"Does he not like you or something?"

"He does not."

OK, I thought. *Obviously not the type to chatter on or gossip.* I tried something simpler. "What's your name?"

He turned to me, smiling slightly. "My name is Mark. What's yours?"

I giggled. "Heather. It is very nice to meet you, Mark."

We shared the bottle of wine and talked. It felt very natural to chat with him. He led the conversation, asking me about friends, family, and work. When I got past my initial awkwardness and got over thinking about his gorgeous face, I relaxed into the social-Heather I was before I got so wrapped up at the office. When the topic turned to work I was brief; I knew if I started talking about work I probably wouldn't stop. Mark also glazed over information about his job. I assumed he, too, thought it best to keep work away from social chit-chat. When the topic turned to my friends, I pretended I was living in my pre-lawyer days. When I actually had friends. And when Mark asked me about my family, I surprised myself by telling him more than I usually reveal. I'd been raised by deeply devout Mormons, and had happily left them and their lifestyle behind when I went to college.

As soon as our bottle was empty, the waiter brought another without being asked. I must have looked surprised, and Mark explained.

"I'm a regular. He knows what I want."

I wanted more than to share a bottle of wine with this man. I felt a bit tipsy and bold. I scooted up next to him and put my hand on his leg. I was making my move.

He took my hand in his and held it, away from his leg, but not rejecting my advance.

"Heather," he said calmly, looking me in the eyes.

"Yes?" I said, my stomach fluttering a bit, hoping he would kiss me.

"I am not going to be sleeping with you tonight."

Blood rushed to my face and I turned away from him. *Fuck*, I thought. I had been wasting my time. And I actually liked him. I felt rejected and became sad, and a bit angry. I was ready to protest that I had not been thinking of sleeping with him that night and that he was being presumptuous. But my protests would have been a lies so I just sat looking at the video screen of the dancers on the floor below.

After thirty long seconds, to my surprise, a tear rolled down my cheek. I recalled that in just a few days I would be back at the office, working hard and not getting any sex. My only chance for relief might be tonight. How could Mark not understand this? Doesn't any man want easy sex? I looked at the woman in the elegant white dress who waited patiently at Mark's table. Was she better looking than me? Was she his wife? Instead of being sexy, did I look trashy in my silver halter top? I realized I knew nothing about Mark. Perhaps he was even the owner of the club just making a new customer feel welcome.

I wiped the tear away and looked back at Mark. He smiled at me with a very calm and rational look on his face. I supposed he lived in a world where sex just *happens*, and isn't a once-a-year opportunity. My mixed emotions silenced me and then he spoke.

"I would like to sleep with you eventually. It would please me, I am sure, to have you in my bed."

"Well *that's* forward," I shot back, annoyed with the situation. "Look, Mark, you don't understand. I am a very busy woman. I have one week off from work, and at work I have *no time at all* for relationships or dinners or dates or even sex."

"You'll make time," he responded.

"I can't just *make time*," I said, irritated. I stomped my foot on the ground, not really realizing what I was doing until after it was done. He chuckled. Which was infuriating.

"Trust me, you'll make time. Would you like to meet me for dinner tomorrow evening?"

I paused, looking at him, wondering if he could possibly know how insanely horny I was at that moment and exactly how pissed off I was at him for not wanting to take me to his place and fuck my brains out.

"OK," I agreed, surprising myself.

"Give your address to the waiter. I'll pick you up at seven. Be ready to go on time, please."

"OK," I said again.

"The waiter will arrange for you and your friend to take a taxi home. Goodnight, Heather. I'm happy to meet you." He leaned over and pecked me on the cheek.

Before I could say goodnight, he got up and returned to the woman in the white dress. I sat and watched the dancers on the video screen and finished the last of the wine. Rebecca and I left in a taxi. At home, I took off my slutty clothes and curled up, naked in the bed. Exhausted and unsatisfied, I cried myself to sleep.

Chapter Two

FRESH SKIN

The next morning I lay in bed longer than usual, lazily fingering my cunt and thinking about my Prince Charming from the previous evening. Mark. Maybe he was more Mysterious than Charming.

I replayed the events of the evening and imagined that my advances had worked, and Mark took me to his apartment... another glass of wine, perhaps, before we moved to his bedroom. I pictured a large bed with fluffy down pillows, where he would have laid me down and began to fuck me... slowly, at first, teasing me with his hard cock. Then faster... thrusting quickly, in and out of my cunt. I imagined myself groaning and begging him to fuck me as hard as he could. My fingers worked hard, I was fucking myself with one hand and frantically rubbing my clit with the other. Just... about... to... cum....

A knock at my bedroom door threw me out of my imaginary fuck session.

"Dammit," I muttered to myself.

"Hey Heather! Are you awake? I made us some breakfast. Come on, get up, I gotta go soon." It was Rebecca. I'd completely forgotten that she crashed on the couch last night.

"I'm up. I'm coming." Not *cumming*, I thought to myself as I, once again, pushed my sexual frustration aside. I threw off the covers and pulled on some sweatpants and a tank top over my naked body. My nipples were hard and excited, poking through the tank top, making my arousal obvious. *Whatever. Rebecca wouldn't care.*

She was in the kitchen, humming to herself and working at the stove.

"Coffee?" she asked.

"Please," I said. Rebecca slid a mug across the counter in my direction and pointed to the carafe.

"I'm making you an omelet. How many eggs?"

"Two." I was starving. And a bit hungover. I sipped the coffee and watched Rebecca work. Despite my questionable reasoning for choosing her, of all people, to go out with last night, Rebecca was a pretty amazing person. She studied art in college and since then started her own graphic design business to supplement the income she got from her paintings. She worked really hard and had a unique set of skills. Cooking, I remembered, was one of her strong points.

She flipped the omelet onto a plate that was ready to go with strawberries and a scoop of yogurt.

"I already ate. Dig in." She poured herself another cup of coffee and sat at the counter across from me. "So," she began, "who's Mark?"

Straight to the point, as always. "I don't actually really know," I said, taking a bite. "He just approached me. Bought some wine to share. Seemed to know the club well. We're going out tonight."

"You told me that last night."

"Yeah. We shared a *lot* of wine. Wow, Rebecca, this is *amazing.*" I took another huge bite of the omelet. "What did you put in here?"

"Secret." She looked at me. "There are a few regulars at that club. Some are great. But, I don't know, Heather. I don't know if you should go out with him tonight. I mean, he's probably great. You evidently think so. But... he could be trouble for you."

"What do you mean?" I asked, barely willing to look up from my food. I was hungry.

She sighed. "I don't really want to get into it. Just, if you go, be careful. Take your phone, I'll call you around eight to be sure you're all right. Do you know where you're going with him?"

"No, he didn't really cover that."

"Do you have his number to call and ask?"

"No. He didn't leave a number."

"Heather..."

"He seems fine, Rebecca. And I'm pretty independent. I think I can handle it."

"I know you can. I just worry. I'll call you at eight. I gotta run now, though."

"OK. Hey..." I paused from my studious effort at demolishing every last bite on my plate. "Thanks for coming last night. And thanks for breakfast." I smiled at her as she pulled on her coat.

"I had fun too. Don't be such a stranger. I've missed you." She leaned over and kissed my cheek. "Bye for now!"

The omelet and coffee pulled me out of my hangover, and I started thinking about my upcoming date. And my pantsuits. *Fuck* – I needed to go shopping.

I brushed my teeth, didn't bother changing out of my

sweats, and pulled out of my apartment's small parking lot. It had been a long time since I had thought about how to make myself look good for a date. I thought about my outfit from the previous night, in contrast to the outfits worn by the other women on the second floor of Dynamic.

I resolved to find something sexy yet *appropriate.* I drove to Second Skin, an upscale clothing store. I used to go there just to gawk at the clothing and accessories, but never considered purchasing anything. While my first four months of working hadn't made me rich, the fact that I didn't spend any of my earnings on a social life meant that I could *finally afford nice clothes.* I took a deep breath before entering the door with a shiver of excitement.

There were two women working. One of them, a tall, pretty red-head, looked over at me, and then went back to what she was doing. The other one, a short, dark skinned, beautiful woman was busying herself flipping through a catalog at her desk. She didn't even look up as I stood waiting. I looked down at my current outfit and grinned at them. It was understandable that they would ignore a sloppily dressed woman with last night's makeup on her face.

I approached the red-head. "Excuse me. I need to buy a dress for a date this evening. And some... night wear as well."

She looked at me. "Ooookay, honey," she sang, as if she had dealt with my kind of people before. "Do you know what your price range is?"

"I'm pretty flexible, but I also find spending exorbitant amounts of money on clothing to be a bit silly. But this is a pretty important date for me."

She smiled. I had said the right thing. "My name is Rose. Where's your date taking you?"

"Oh," I paused. "I... uh... I don't know that. We're eating...

we're going to eat. We're going to dinner." My confidence quickly vanished and I felt very out of place.

"Oooookay." Rose looked me up and down. "Well, what do you *think*? Casual dinner, fancy restaurant, dinner at his place, dinner and opera? What's your best guess?"

I paused again. I hadn't really considered anything beyond how I hoped the end of the evening would go. I thought about his outfit last night and the expensive wine. I remembered how the other women were dressed. "Fancy restaurant. I think I'd like to go with something simple. But elegant. Sexy but not obviously so."

She smiled. "OK, honey. Why don't you step into the changing room and take off those sweats. I'll be there soon with some outfits to try."

"OH!" I exclaimed. *Fuck*. "I'm.... uh.... can we maybe find some panties first?"

Rose looked at me as if I were speaking a different language. "You don't shop much, do you hun?"

I blushed. "No... I just... I'm a very busy woman. I haven't shopped in months. My name is Heather, by the way."

"Nice to meet you, sweetie. Go on in and take off the sweats. I'll bring in dresses *and* panties. Relax, we'll find something that will make you *so* beautiful."

I walked into the dressing room – the one area of this store I had never had the pleasure to be in. It was beautiful, spacious, with couches, cut flowers set on the end tables, and mirrors on every wall. I suddenly felt very self conscious. I only had, at that moment, two articles of clothing separating my naked body from what seemed like a hundred mirrors.

But, what could it matter? Rose had probably seen many naked women before. I slid out of my sweatpants and pulled off my tank top, folding each piece carefully as to not disturb the beauty of the room. Then, I was naked. There were a *lot* of naked me in that room due to the mirrors. I shivered a bit, and looked around for somewhere to put myself. I couldn't sit *naked* on the couch. I opted for standing in a corner of the room where only a few mirrors could reflect my body back at me.

The door opened, and in came Rose with an armful of clothing. She looked at me and smiled. "You really do need to invest in some panties, huh sweetie?"

I wasn't sure whether or not to be grateful for her forwardness.

"Hey Jasmine," she called through the door. "Can you bring in some of our panties, get some of the small g-strings for Heather to pick out."

Well, all right. I was definitely *not* grateful for her forwardness.

"Heather are you planning on getting waxed or anything before your date?" Rose was looking directly at my cunt, which, while I had taken care to trim well for last night, was not really ready, hair-wise, for a skimpy g-string.

I blushed. I had become used to being strong and having great responses and solid comebacks in court. But being asked point-blank about my pubes was not something I was used to. "I hadn't really thought about it..." Now I wondered if that was what I was *supposed* to do. "What do you think?" I asked her, before really evaluating whether or not I wanted the advice of a complete stranger.

"Well, I think about ninety percent of our regular customers keep their hair pretty well-maintained. Not to say they shave completely, that'd be maybe..." Jasmine chose this ridiculous moment to join us. "What do you think Jasmine, maybe forty percent go completely bare *down there*?" Rose asked.

Jasmine agreed with a short nod. She glanced at my cunt

and set down her armful of underwear, then stepped back to look at me. "You need to choose some panties before you try on our dresses."

I nodded, feeling very meek and ashamed. I wanted panties on *as soon as possible.*

"Come on then," said Rose. "Why don't you pick some out. If you want to keep your hair, you'll need to go with something a little less revealing, though."

"No... I think... I think I'll just trim it."

"Are you sure you don't want to be waxed? It's much easier, and lasts longer. And it only hurts for a split second."

"No no. I don't think... I'll just shave a bit. Thanks." I quickly examined the pile of underwear and picked out a pair of black panties, bikini style, with lacy straps, to cover me up during this humiliating process. I slid them on as fast as I could, ignoring the smirk from Jasmine. I picked out a few more pairs; they were all beautiful. I thought about my own collection of panties, which was pretty sad and prudish. Maybe if I felt a little bit sexy underneath my pantsuits at work, I'd at least enjoy a little bit of thrill now and then when I returned to work.

"OK," I said. "The dresses."

Rose stood up and walked over to the collection of dresses she had hung by the door. "You know, I picked out seven dresses for you to try. But now that I've been watching your body, I think I have it narrowed down to two."

Well, at least my humiliation had caused a bit of efficiency, I thought to myself.

"Are they by Rachel?" Jasmine piped in.

"Yes, actually. Both of them." Rose turned to me, holding a dark green dress. "We've been working with a new designer, who is *great*. Your body is exactly the shape she is designing for. All right, hands up in the air. Close your eyes."

I felt like a child. I closed my eyes and raised my hands into the air and Rose slipped the dress over my head. She moved behind me and put the dress into place, zipping it up at my side from my waist to my armpit. The silky fabric felt exquisite on my skin.

"Open up," Rose said cheerfully as she turned me directly in front of a mirror.

I opened my eyes and inhaled sharply. I looked *gorgeous*. The breast-line cut was low enough to show just enough to be revealing, but still be classy. The dress was long to my right ankle, but cut up to my left calf, with a slit up to my left thigh. The back was cut very low, just an inch or two above the crack of my butt.

"I love it," I whispered, twirling around in front of the mirrors. "It's perfect."

"Wait, you still have to try on the other one, so don't get too attached," said Rose, as she went to get the second dress.

The second dress was a deep burgundy, and made me look equally amazing. It was definitely sexier, but slid on the edge of being classy. I loved it, and wanted to take them both.

The total price, though, I did *not* love. With the panties, the dresses, and two pairs of heels, I was nearly at $2,000.

"Can you just hold the burgundy dress for me? If I decide I want it, I can come back and get it?"

Jasmine responded curtly. "We hold dresses for five business days. Any more time and you lose your opportunity."

"Yes, but Jasmine, don't you think we should speak with Rachel? She might want to use Heather as a model, or assistant." Rose turned to me. "Heather, your body is absolutely perfect for Rachel's line. I imagine she wouldn't mind working out a trade with you on occasion. She does undergarments as well." She winked at me.

"I.. I don't really have time for that kind of thing."

"Well, if you change your mind, come on back. We can set up a meeting."

I thanked Rose for her time, ignored the rude Jasmine, and collected my purchases. Walking outside, I felt so wonderful; attractive, even. And ready! I would look beautiful and sexy for my evening with Mark.

Chapter Three
HIS WAY

As the evening approached, I prepared myself. A long soak in the tub eased my nerves. Using small scissors I trimmed my cunt as best I could, but I could not see the hairs back between my legs. I propped a mirror against the wall and crouched down so I could see. I wondered what Mark would think if he was watching at that moment.

I dried my hair and put on makeup. Not excessive makeup, just a bit of foundation and mascara. I wore small, silver earrings. My hair, I kept down. My hair was thick; dark brown with a bit of a wave. It fell down to below my shoulders. In college I had kept it shorter, and now at work I always wore it up. Looking in the mirror at the way my hair fell alongside my face, I felt more feminine than I ever had in my life.

Then, the dress. I slid it on, zipped up, and studied myself in the mirror. *Not bad.* I hoped with my whole self that he wasn't planning on taking me somewhere cheesy where I'd be terribly overdressed.

At six fifty I was ready, pacing, and nervous. I poured myself a glass of white wine. Though I preferred red, I feared that in my nervous state I'd spill all over my gorgeous new green dress. I drank it quickly. Six fifty-nine.

Breathe. I stood looking at myself in the full length mirror in the hallway. "Breathe," I commanded out loud. My reflection didn't even look like me. I wasn't this fancy. My heart was racing – was I trying to be someone I wasn't? Would Mark see through me and find me silly for trying to be someone glamorous?

At exactly seven o'clock, I heard the buzzer. I buzzed him in the gate and within seconds I heard a knock at my door.

How could I quell this nervousness? I took two deep breaths and went to open the door. I used the peep hole to see him first. There he was, beautiful Mark.

"Hi," I said as I opened the door a bit.

"Hello, Heather." He smiled at me. A friendly smile. He waited.

I waited.

"Heather, may I come in?"

Dammit! Why was I such an idiot around him? I held open the door and stepped aside as he entered. He looked at me and chuckled. In one fluid motion, he clasped my upper arm and pulled me towards him. He pressed my body fully against him and gave me a strong quick kiss on my lips and released me just as suddenly. He shut the door behind him.

"Relax," he said. "I don't bite without permission."

"OK. I'll try." At least we had acknowledged my nervous awkwardness, and it was out in the open. No need to try to hide my state anymore. "Would you like a glass of wine?"

"That would be lovely," Mark said. "Just one, we have reservations in an hour over by the park. You look incredible, by the way."

"Why, thank you," I responded, leading him to the kitchen. I pulled the open bottle from the refrigerator and grabbed another glass from the dishwasher. Pouring the white wine, it occurred to me that this wine was *cheap*, and I was pouring Mark, who had obviously shown his interest in good wine last night, a portion of *crappy wine* in a *juice glass*.

I decided to ignore this, and with all the confidence I could muster I handed him his wine.

"Thank you, Heather." If he cared, he didn't show it. He stood very close to me.

"Did you know that vampires have to be invited into the home before feeding on their lovers?" he asked. As he placed his hand on my cheek, he put his face so close to mine I expected another kiss, or to see fangs ready to penetrate my neck. His green eyed gaze was intense. "Relax all of you," he said in a hypnotic voice, "tonight will be pleasant." All I could see was his eyes until he released me from his gaze. I remembered Rebecca's warning about this man.

We sat in my living room. Actually, *he* sat in my living room. I felt like a teenager. He took a seat on the couch and I wasn't sure if I should sit next to him or sit across the room from him. I resorted to pacing about, pretending to pick things up and move them to their appropriate location, though I was actually just moving random objects around my living room. He watched me for a few minutes, as I babbled on about this object or that book.

Finally he interrupted me. "When I told you to relax earlier, did you understand what I meant?"

I laughed. "Yes. I just have trouble relaxing."

"Sit down, next to me, and stop talking. Not another word until we are out the door."

I weighed my two options. *Not* talking, and the

awkwardness that comes from silence, seemed much better than continuing on my blathering about nothing. "OK." I said, and sat down next to him.

Mark put his arm across my back, then down to my butt, using his hand to scoot me towards him until our thighs met. Then he just held his arm there, holding me and pressing me towards his body. I sighed, and I relaxed. I realized I had missed this – physical closeness and the comfort that comes with it. He kissed the top of my head as I leaned into his shoulder.

"The next time I tell you to relax, at least *try* to relax."

"OK," I responded.

"No talking from you," he said.

I realized that Mark was trying to tell me what to do, but then, just as soon as I had that revelation, I remembered that I was a nervous wreck. At least Mark was helping me by getting me to shut the hell up. It was oddly comforting.

Mark finished his wine and looked at his watch. "Up you go, time to leave. I hope you're hungry."

"I'm famished," I said, getting up off the couch. I hadn't eaten since Rebecca's omelet.

"Heather." He grabbed my arm and turned me towards him. "I didn't want to hear a word from you until outside your door. Did you forget?"

I laughed. "Come on, I was just responding to you..."

Mark looked at me. His green eyes really *looked deeply* into me, penetrating my eyes, and for a moment I felt a bit scared. "Let's go," he said.

He drove a dark blue BMW. As we pulled out of the driveway, I mentioned that Rebecca would be calling me around eight o'clock, just to check on me. Mark smiled.

"Don't trust me yet?" he asked.

"No... it was just... it was her idea. She said sometimes the guys at that club can be trouble."

"She's right," he said. "Guys anywhere can be trouble. She'll be calling soon, so you can tell her where we are going. Our reservation is at Haven. My phone number is here; give her that as well." Mark handed me a card with his name and number. Glancing at the card, I realized I hadn't even bothered to get Mark's last name. *Mark Doston.*

Mark continued, "You probably shouldn't tell your suitor about your security phone call, lest you lose the opportunity to use it for your security."

My mind raced as I thought to myself, *Who uses the word 'suitor'? Was he trying to scare me or was he just kind of scary?*

He was quiet for the ride to the restaurant, and didn't say a word during or after my quick phone call from Rebecca. I felt like he might be mad in some way, but I couldn't get a read.

As we pulled into the parking lot, Mark slid his hand under the slit on the left side of my dress. I tensed up a bit, then tried to relax, remembering that my whole goal with him was to just get myself fucked, to get me through a few more months of all-work with no-play at the office. I parted my legs a bit and enjoyed feeling his hand rub my thigh. He slid his fingers up to feel my panties, and then through them gave my clit a quick squeeze. He pulled into a parking space, and said, as if he was asking me to pass him a tissue, "Give me your panties."

"What?" I asked, surprised.

"You heard me. We will continue this date when I have your panties." He put the car in park, shut off the engine, pocketed his keys, and waited. Watching me.

I was conflicted, not used to being told what to do. Though the request wasn't totally unreasonable – after all, my whole hope was that this date would be all about sex. Sitting with him at dinner, without panties, would remind me about this and it actually seemed kind of exciting. I realized I was getting wet and my decision was made.

I pulled up my dress as little as necessary to allow myself to hook my fingers into my panties and pull them down. I handed them to him and straightened out the fabric of the dress.

"Good girl," he said, pocketing the panties. "Let's continue."

He opened my door for me and led me into the restaurant. I had never been to Haven before, though had heard about it from co-workers. It was the newest place in the city, and ever since it was written up in several national newspapers as a four star restaurant it had become exceedingly difficult for locals to get reservations. Mark made our presence known to the host and he was greeted warmly; obviously he had been here before. Being with a man who can go where he likes made my pussy a little wetter.

We were led to our table. He guided me, placing his hand on the bare skin of my lower back, occasionally grazing my ass. We were seated in a small alcove near the back of the restaurant; a half circle booth that was a bit hidden, yet offered a view of nearly the entire dining area through the flowering vines and large leafy potted plants.

"This is... this is incredible," I stammered. I had never visited a restaurant this fancy, and certainly not with anyone who apparently had dibs on one of the best tables in the place.

"*This* is not incredible. *This* is a room, with people. The *food* is incredible," Mark stated frankly. "The chef here is my best childhood friend. If I give him enough notice, he always makes sure I have a spot to dine here. I called him yesterday, and as luck would have it, even though Saturdays are typically packed, they had space for me tonight. So, Heather, you're in for a treat."

A waiter came to greet us and Mark ordered a bottle of

wine. "Please have Chef James serve us what he suggests for tonight."

"Of course, sir."

He held up a finger to hold the waiter's attention and asked me, "Do you have any dietary restrictions?" It took me a moment to realize he wasn't asking me that as a doctor, but rather gauging what I wanted to eat. What did I not like to eat? What was I allergic to?

I said, "No restrictions."

"Good," said Mark, and dismissed the waiter.

He turned to me. "How do you feel?"

"What do you mean?"

"Well, does it feel normal for you to be wearing an expensive dress, in a nice restaurant, with no panties on?" As he said this, he used the damned slit in my dress to his advantage again. I didn't mind; I liked the touch of his hand on my skin. His hand slid between my legs. One of his fingers flicked up and down lightly on my pussy lips before entering me. "You're wet," he stated.

I blushed. This day had been full of uncomfortable moments. There was the first-date stress and excitement, the women at the clothing store and the humiliation of being completely naked in front of them while they thought about my body and what dress and panties would work for me, and now Mark. He knew my inappropriate state of arousal while we were sitting at a restaurant waiting for our dinner.

Mark began fucking me slowly with his finger, watching me. I wanted to crawl underneath the table but my back arched and my thighs parted a little more. Not knowing what to do with myself, I just put my hands in front of my face, trying to hide at least part of myself from the current situation.

He laughed and with one hand grabbed both of my wrists

to pull my hands away from my face. He gave me a kiss, then pulled his fingers from my cunt.

"Open," he said.

I opened my mouth and sucked my own pussy juices off his fingers. I looked around to be sure no one was watching, and then relaxed into the booth. I was so horny and no longer had any idea where this evening was going. I certainly had no idea what to think of Mark, but my body had all the voting power to determine my actions now.

"Good girl," Mark said.

The waiter came with the wine and small appetizers. I accepted my glass eagerly, relieved to have something in my hands to hold. Mark kept his hand on my thigh while we drank wine and enjoyed the mildly marinated assortment of mushrooms, sweet peppers, and olives. I wondered what I was having for dinner. Mark led the conversation, and I felt comfortable with him and as calm as I had the night before. I looked at his mouth and his eyes as he spoke. Those lips had already kissed me. Those lips would kiss me again. There were slight dimples on his cheeks and I could see a shadow on his chin of whiskers. I imagined him shaving in the morning after his shower.

I wondered if he was lonely. Who was I to him? Was he reciting the lines he speaks to everyone? My mind wandered with one thing he would say and then I would realize I wasn't listening anymore but just hearing the gentle cadence of his voice. Then I would refocus on what he was saying and wonder if he noticed my attention had wandered.

"The chef is too busy to come out and greet you, sir, but sends his regards and invites you back to say hello after you dine," the waiter said, interrupting my thoughts. "Your first course: Squash blossom soup topped with fresh croutons and a cilantro pepita pesto."

"Thank you," said Mark.

The waiter quickly disappeared.

"What's pepita?" I whispered.

"Pumpkin seeds," he said, placing his napkin on his lap. He reached for the large spoon set beside his plate and I mimicked him, unaccustomed to having such a selection of silverware to choose from.

Throughout the meal he helped me know what I was eating, how it was prepared, and spoke very highly of his friend, the chef. From the beauty of each course to the exquisite taste, it was obvious that his friend was truly gifted. I could see now why it was so hard to get a reservation at Haven.

For our main course, we were served grilled ocean scallops with a sauce made of morel mushrooms, garnished with radish sprouts. The plate was beautifully decorated. The sauce was drizzled artfully around and on the seafood, and a crisp side salad kept the scallops company on the oval white plate. I completely forgot about my nervousness and enjoyed the intense and varied flavors.

When we finished with the main course, the waiter brought us two desserts and two small glasses filled with a dark purple liquid.

"What is it?" Mark asked, pointing to the glasses.

"Loganberry liquor, from an island vineyard. A new selection on our menu, and complements of the chef, sir," he replied. "The desserts tonight are tiramisu and cheesecake prepared with goat cheese. I brought you a bit of both, to share."

"Thank you," said Mark.

When the waiter left, Mark leaned towards me and whispered into my ear, "Close your eyes."

I did as he said. Soon after, he whispered, "Open your

mouth."

I opened my mouth and felt the lip of the glass. Mark pulled gently at my hair, moving my head back. The liquor spilled slowly into my mouth and I savored the sweet taste before swallowing.

With my lips parted Mark fed me bites of both desserts. The entire time he kept a hand on my thigh, caressing me occasionally, teasing me with his touch.

It was romantic, and very intimate.

After dessert, Mark excused himself to greet the chef and left me at the table, where I sat anxiously in my aroused state. When he came back, *finally*, I was more than ready to move on with the more... physical... part of the evening.

On the way out to the car, Mark held my hand and spoke softly. He opened my door for me, and crouched beside me as I buckled my seatbelt.

"Heather," he said, looking at me carefully.

"Yes?" I asked.

He ran his hand over my legs, making me moan. I needed him so badly. I couldn't remember a time when I was so wanton, so aroused.

"I'm going to take you back to your apartment now."

"Please, Mark," I whispered. He knew how aroused I was. He had been feeling my wet cunt all night.

"We will go out again next week." Mark closed my door and walked around to his. He was calm, almost professional in his manner.

On the way to my apartment, I wondered if I could invite him inside. If I could seduce him into taking me tonight rather than waiting another week. I shifted in my seat, uncomfortably reminded that I was naked under my dress. Naked and so wet.

"Mark," I began softly, reaching over to put a hand on his leg. "Can I invite you inside for a drink? For wine, or coffee?"

"No, my sweet," he said as we pulled in front of my apartment building. He put the car into park and turned to face me. "I had a very nice time with you tonight. Let's meet again next Sunday. You'll come over to my apartment for dinner. I'll have a car pick you up at five."

"But Mark," I said, trying not to sound whiny. "Please..."

Mark placed his hand behind my head and grabbed a handful of my hair, pulling my face towards him. "I know how much you want to be fucked, Heather," he growled into my ear, making me shiver. "I love that all week, while you're working, before you sleep, you'll be thinking of our date next weekend." He kissed me, deeply, making me melt.

"Try not to touch yourself this week. Save yourself for me, for next weekend. Now, scoot."

Mark let go of me and sat back in his seat. He wasn't even going to walk me to my door. I was disappointed and a bit hurt, but tried my best to pull myself together as I got out of his car. I stood on the sidewalk and watched him pull away, hoping he would turn around and come back to me, to give me what I needed so badly. When his car was out of sight I sighed and went inside.

Chapter Four

SCHOOLING

The following week was probably the longest workweek I'd ever had, apart from the week after Ryan and I broke off our engagement.

Mr. Richards welcomed me back warmly, asking how the break was.

"It was lovely. You were absolutely right, I needed to get away for awhile."

"Good to hear. I hope you're ready for some work, we've got an interesting case for you to look at. The files are in your office."

The case occupied my thoughts during the day, but every night when I laid down in bed, I had to fight myself to keep from rubbing my cunt, or from giving myself any sort of relief. I didn't know why I wanted to do as Mark asked, but I couldn't stop myself from obeying him. His requests... asking me to stop talking, to remove my panties, to save my orgasms for him... I wanted so badly to please him. To please the perfect stranger who flooded my every thought.

I called Rebecca mid-week to tell her about my upcoming date with Mark. I kept some details from her, but told her that he still hadn't fucked me.

"He is having me over to his apartment this Sunday. For dinner. What do you think, Rebecca?" I asked.

"I think he probably wants to take his time. That's a good sign, you know. It means he likes you. He respects you too much to have a one night stand."

"But that's what I wanted!" I exclaimed. "I thought that I was offering something that most guys would *love*. I just wanted to get fucked and then be done with it. I'm way too busy to have a 'relationship'."

"Well, Heather, maybe you don't know what you want," Rebecca replied. "He sounds like a nice guy. If getting fucked is all you think you want, maybe you shouldn't go out with him again. You could end up hurting him."

"Somehow I don't think I could," I said truthfully. "And besides, I do like him. I'll just... I'll be honest with him. If he can deal with my schedule, maybe something resembling a relationship could work out. It wouldn't hurt to have a regular... well, it wouldn't hurt to have sex occasionally."

"I think it would do you a lot of good," she said, laughing.

I worked just a half day on Saturday, giving myself the afternoon to shop for something slightly more casual, but still sexy, to wear the next day for Mark. I avoided the expensive shop where I had been so humiliated the previous week, and instead went to a mall near my apartment.

I picked out a casual black corduroy skirt and decided to pair it with sandals and a blue blouse I already owned.

On Sunday, I spent the morning worrying about my date while I did laundry and vacuumed my apartment, hoping to distract myself. By four thirty in the afternoon I was dressed and ready to go. I sat by the front window of my apartment, watching the road and waiting for the car to show up.

At five o'clock on the dot, a black car pulled to the side of the road. It was different than the black BMW Mark had driven last week. The driver got out and stood beside the car. He glanced up in my direction, and, seeing me in the window, waved. My ride.

When I got outside I realized the driver was the waiter who had welcomed me upstairs at Dynamic. He half-smiled at me and opened the back door, gesturing for me to get inside.

"Hello again," I said, trying to be friendly.

He nodded in response.

There was a small partition between the back and front of the car, making it impossible to have any conversation with him while we made our way to Mark's apartment. I sat back in the seat, trying to calm myself down.

We drove for about thirty minutes, towards the same part of town as our first encounter at the club. We pulled into a parking complex and Mark was outside waiting for us. He greeted me warmly, kissing me lightly on my lips, and walked me to the entrance of his apartment building. The doorman let us in, using a key to open an elevator on the far end of the lobby.

"You have your own elevator?" I asked, somewhat incredulously.

"I'm just renting this apartment temporarily," he answered, ignoring my actual question.

His apartment was *gorgeous*. Clean, tastefully decorated, and very open. There was an appropriate amount of clutter in the living areas, indicating that Mark was a human rather than a workaholic maniac like myself. He led me to the kitchen where he poured himself a whiskey.

"Would you like a drink?"

"Um... sure." My head was spinning a bit. A drink? Yes, *please*.

"Whiskey? Wine?"

"Whatever... anything is fine. Whiskey is fine," I said.

"Ice? Club soda?"

"Yes please."

He set my drink on the counter next to his and looked at me. "How do you feel?" he asked.

"Fine. Why do you ask me that?"

He stepped towards me, yanked up my skirt, and quickly, almost roughly, slid a finger into my cunt. "Because," he murmured softly in my ear, "I want you to tell me how horny you are."

I gulped and gasped as he gave my pussy a few quick thrusts with his finger before pulling away from me.

"You need something, don't you Heather?"

I nodded. My face burned, flushing with both arousal and the embarrassment of being so completely obvious.

He handed me my drink, which I took a huge sip of.

"What is it you need?" he asked.

"I need to get fucked," I whispered. His eyes bore into me.

"Good," he said, stepping back and smiling. "Sit down."

I sat down at the kitchen table and watched as Mark rummaged through his refrigerator for a few seconds. He produced a plate of dolmathes – stuffed grape leaves, along with an assortment of other finger foods. My mouth watered a bit as I realized I had once again, in my nervous state, forgotten to eat.

"Enjoy," he said, sitting beside me. "I figured that we could just snack tonight. If you want more food we can order pizza later."

I smiled, appreciative that Mark was not so fancy that he was above calling for take-out.

"This is wonderful," I said sincerely. "I haven't had dolmathes in years." I bit into the pickled stuffed grape leaf and moaned. These were delicious.

"I collect and preserve my own leaves every Spring. These are made with the smaller, tender leaves, which I save for special occasions." Mark popped one into his mouth. For some reason, I loved watching him chew. *Oh*, how I wanted his mouth on my body.

We chatted amiably as we snacked on the dolmathes, hummus with pita bread, and olives. I enjoyed sipping the whiskey, feeling the alcohol spread through my system and help me relax. Now that I knew Mark a little bit, I *was* more relaxed with him.

After a small lull in the conversation, Mark leaned back and looked at me. "Take off your clothes," he said.

I looked back at him, instinctively wanting to giggle and protest. His expression was serious. My fight or flight reaction was overtaken by the never-forgotten instinct to fuck. I unzipped my skirt and shimmied out of it, letting it fall to the floor. My panties followed. I unbuttoned my blouse and pulled off my bra. When I looked up at Mark again, I felt more naked than I ever had before. He sat back in his chair, letting his eyes wander all over my body.

"Turn around," he said. "Show me."

I slowly turned around in a circle, wishing he would just cut to the chase and ravage me. Mark, however, had other plans.

"Follow me," he said, turning towards the living area. "But fold your clothes first."

Working fast, I neatly folded my skirt and blouse and set

them on the counter. I finished my drink in one gulp and followed him. I found him seated in the middle of a large leather couch. He motioned for me to come towards him, and then, firmly grabbing my hips, he sat me down on the wooden coffee table in front of the couch.

There we sat. Mark was fully clothed and I was stark naked in the middle of his living room.

"Heather, I have a proposal for you," he said.

I made a small whining noise, realizing that there would be at least a short delay between the present and Mark fucking my brains out. He pushed my legs apart and sharply slapped the inside of my right thigh.

"Ye-ow!" I squealed. "What the fuck?!"

"Heather. I have a proposal for you." He looked at me, his expression stern, and waited for my reply.

"Well, what is your proposal?" I asked, rubbing my thigh.

"I would like you to be my slave."

Just like that. A simple sentence, changing everything. I looked at him, waiting for him to smile, laugh, or in any way show me that he was joking around.

"I... no... I, I gotta go," I stammered, standing up. *Get dressed, leave, fast,* was all I could think. Before I could take three steps, Mark grabbed me, and plopped me right back down on the table in front of him.

"Heather, listen to me, and listen to my proposal. If, by the end of tonight, you want to say no, I will drive you home or call you a cab and send you on your way, with my blessings. But," he paused, "Heather, I know you need this. You may not know it yet, but this is what your body wants. What your mind wants. You want to be controlled. Don't feel threatened or unsafe. I would never cause you real harm or put you in any type of danger."

Mark stood up, and held out his hand. "Come on. Come with me."

I paused, weighing my options once again. I wondered if I was so truly sex-deprived that I could even consider whatever perversions he was proposing. I felt my rationality fighting against my curiosity.

Mark sighed impatiently. "Heather, where is your phone?"

"In the kitchen. In my purse. By my clothes."

"Go get it. Send your friend... Rebecca, right? Send her a text with my address, and a message that you're fine but that this is where you are. Then, come back here."

That would work. That would make me feel less crazy and stupid for being here, with a relative stranger, who wanted me to be his 'slave'. I got up to go get my phone. Before I could leave the room, Mark grabbed my arm and turned me towards him.

"When you return, you will listen to me with an open mind. When I tell you to do something, especially something as simple as taking my hand, you *will do it*. Understand?" His tone was grave and my pussy tingled a bit as he held my arm tightly and stared down at me.

"OK." I scampered to the kitchen and, my hands shaking slightly, I sent off a text message to Rebecca. Faster than I could believe, I got a message back: "Have fun."

I returned to the living room and Mark was sitting back down on the couch. I looked at him expectantly.

"Phone?" He held out his hand. I handed it to him and he slid it into his pocket. "Now, my dear, you are confused. Hesitant. I understand that. But you're also safe. And you *are* mine, at least for the next few hours."

I swallowed hard and stared at my feet.

"I want your obedience. So far, I haven't gotten that. Not even with simple commands. Even when you did obey me last week, you did so with such obvious hesitation."

He's lecturing me, I realized. *What the hell.*

"So," Mark continued, "this is a preview of what will happen to you if you fail to obey me, even once, for the rest of the evening." He reached up and firmly grasped my upper arm, pulling me over his lap.

"Oomph" I grunted, surprised. I struggled to get back to my feet, but Mark held me down easily, locking my legs under his right leg and holding my hands behind my back.

"This, Heather, is what I'm talking about. I'm not going to punish you right now. Consider this a warning. Just relax."

"How do you think this is at all relaxing for me?" I said, trying to keep my voice level to retain just a shred of dignity. "I am naked, over your la- .. OW!"

Mark laid a firm slap on my ass. Then another.

"Mark, ow! Ow! What are you do - OW!"

"Shut. Up," he said, smacking me after each word. "Your spanking stops when you can keep still and quiet for five spanks in a row."

I sucked in my breath and willed myself to be quiet. I counted silently. Each spank was harder than the last. *One... two... three... four... five...*

"Good girl," Mark said. He rubbed my ass softly which was a nice change. I realized that I was in no position to fight anymore. He had me for tonight. Mark was so much stronger than me, I had no chance of fighting him. If he was going to throw me over his lap and spank me if I hesitated... well, I'd be in for a *long* night. I relaxed over his lap and started to enjoy the sensation of his hand rubbing the sting out of my bottom.

"Now," he said as he pulled me off his lap, standing me on my feet. He stood up beside me and extended his hand. "Come with me."

I took his hand and he led me into the long corridor of his apartment. At the end of the hallway, Mark fished a key out of his pocket and unlocked a door. He flipped on the light and I looked at what appeared to be a basic office area. A large desk took up the corner of the room. There were two daybeds on both adjacent walls, backed with big, comfy looking pillows. Behind the desk was a huge chest, and a full bookcase.

"Your office?" I asked.

"Sort of," he said. "Go sit over there." He pointed to one of the day beds, and I took a seat and watched him rummage around the room for various objects.

"Slavery," Mark began, "means different things to different people. Do you know much about BDSM?"

"No." I knew that the letters BDSM meant Bondage, Discipline, Sadism and Masochism from some friends in college, but not much more.

"Well, what *do* you know about BDSM? What comes to your mind when you think about it?"

"Um... whips. Chains. Goth people. I don't know." My head was spinning, and I realized that the room was very brightly lit. I was still naked, and was being asked about a topic that I was in no way comfortable discussing. I slid further back on the daybed and pulled my knees to my chest, covering my breasts.

Mark smiled. He sat down next to me holding a manilla folder and a few stacks of papers. "Sit in front of me."

I scooted over to sit in front of him. He put his legs on either side of my body and pulled me close. His cock pressed against my butt, hard, through his pants. He fondled my breast with one hand while flipping open the folder with his other hand.

"Look through these photos," he said, handing me a small stack of 8 by 10 snapshots.

The first was a woman, tied up and kneeling. Her legs were spread wide, and the way her arms were tied behind her made her breasts thrust out. A ball-gag was crammed in her mouth, and her light blonde hair was falling out of the loose ponytail behind her head. To her left, a man, in black pants, held a long rod. The photo was composed in a way that the man's face was not visible.

The next photo was another woman, on all fours. Something was stuck in her butt, making it look like she had a long, furry tail. I giggled and quickly moved on.

The third photo was a masked-man in the center of the scene sitting in a straight-backed chair with a naked woman draped over his lap. Her face was looking at the camera; her expression making it quite obvious that she had been spanked – hard.

Finally, a picture that I found myself just staring at. A bright room was lit by sun shining in through a large window. It was normal scene, with a couch, fireplace, and end tables. Above the fireplace was a beautiful abstract painting with soft colors that matched the room perfectly. The shelves were lined with books, magazines, and nick-knacks. On a large easy chair sat a man reading behind an open newspaper. At his feet, curled up, sleeping peacefully: a woman, naked save for a collar around her neck.

Everything about the fourth photograph looked so *normal*. No weird outfits, strange toys, or anything out of the ordinary. Except that naked woman. It was intriguing, to say the least.

"What do you think?" Mark asked, pulling me out of my trance. He slid his fingers down my body, over the patch of hair on my cunt and felt my pussy. "You're very wet," he whispered.

I squirmed. "I don't know what I think. It's so... *weird*. But the last photo looks... kind of normal."

"Those are friends of mine. They have a nice relationship."

"She is his slave?" I asked tentatively.

"Yes. Has been for years."

"And that's what she wants?"

"Yes. In fact, I'm pretty sure she was the one who suggested it to him."

"But... *why would she do that?*"

"For her, being his makes her happy. She doesn't want control, or the hassle that comes with control. She likes pleasing him; his pleasure makes her happy. And, he is naturally dominant. Leading the relationship, and leading her, is what feels right for him. Equal roles wouldn't make either of them happy or fulfilled.

"Think about it, Heather," Mark continued, "Haven't you been in a relationship, even platonic, where one person naturally makes most of the decisions? For instance, take Rebecca. Think about your friendship. Who, would you say, is the naturally dominant half of your relationship with her?"

I thought for a minute. She did usually make the decisions about where to go dancing, where to eat, what we should wear. The other night, it was Rebecca who picked out the club, and Rebecca who decided when it was time to go. "I guess it would be her. Rebecca. But it isn't like she tells me what to do all the time. I'm not a pushover. It isn't like... *that,*" I said, looking down at the photo.

"Of course not. But my point is that, in all relationships, there is usually a dynamic of power, of dominance, and of submission. In some relationships, the dynamic changes over the course of the friendship. Even in the BDSM world, some people switch from being dominant to submissive, either with different partners or even within the same partnership. Exploring these ideas: dominance, submission, and slavery, is one way to have a deeply meaningful and passionate relationship. It is more honest when brought into the open. For me, it is the only way. I have no interest in an equal relationship with you, Heather."

"Well, great." I rolled my eyes and sat up a bit. Relationship? He pulled me back towards him, hugging me to his chest.

"And you, Heather, are curious about all this. You're holding yourself back." He fingered my cunt playfully and nibbled my ear. I moaned softly. "You don't realize this, but you are deeply submissive. I could tell when I first saw you at the club, and I can see it in your eyes when you look at me." His fingers began to rub my clit and his other hand massaged my breast. I relaxed into his embrace, enjoying the sensations.

He continued, whispering in my ear, "You came here wanting sex. I know that's what you think you need. But what you really need is to be put in your place. To kneel, to serve. To put your life in the hands of your Master." His fingers were moving faster, and I moaned a little louder, tilting my pelvis to give him better access to my pussy.

Then, he stopped and pulled his hand away. I gasped – I needed him to continue. "Please..." I whispered.

"No," he answered. "We have more to discuss."

Over the next two hours, Mark taught me about BDSM. I couldn't believe much of what he told me. I had never heard such things before. I knew about people wearing leather, but this was deeper than fashion. He told me about the club we met at, how half of the upper room was for 'play'. On some nights, the whole club was open to kinky people – Masters, slaves, 'switches'. He explained different types of relationships; how some people just have some power-play in the bedroom, and how others are in their roles all the time – '24/7'. We looked at more photos together.

I leaned against him and sighed. I had no idea what to do. It wasn't like I could ask a friend what to do, or get advice from anyone in my life. I thought about Rebecca, but this would be far too wild for her to understand.

"You work tomorrow, correct?" Mark asked.

"Yeah."

"Can you get there a little late?"

"Sure. I'll just call them in the morning," I said.

"Good. You'll sleep here tonight."

I looked at the clock on his desk – it was nearly midnight. I would have stayed awake if he would just fuck me. What good was this role playing if I couldn't get fucked?

Mark led me back down the hallway and showed me into my room for the night. I was slightly disappointed that it appeared I'd be sleeping in his guestroom, not with him, but was so tired and overwhelmed that it didn't really matter.

"I don't have clothes. Pajamas," I said, hoping to be lent a shirt or sweats or *something*.

"The blankets are warm. If you need anything, I'm two doors down." Mark turned me towards him and gave me a kiss. "Sleep tight, beautiful."

And he was gone.

I woke feeling very well-rested. Judging from the amount of sun flooding through the windows in the guest bedroom, I guessed it was well past eight. I stretched out under the blankets. I hadn't noticed last night that this mattress was *so* much more comfortable then mine.

In my sleepy state I considered dozing off again, but then my brain spun through the events of the previous evening. There was no way I was going back to sleep.

I saw my phone on my nightstand. Did he give it back to me last night? Or did he come into the room after I'd fallen asleep? I made a quick call to work to tell Mr. Richards' secretary that I would be coming in late today.

The guestroom had a private bathroom, equipped with lots of fluffy towels, soaps, and a bathrobe. I hopped into the shower. The warm water comforted me a bit as I thought about what I would say to Mark. I poured copious amounts of soap into my hand and covered my body with suds. I let myself get aroused by the thought of Mark taking me, kissing me, spanking me...

But I couldn't. *I couldn't say yes.* There was my career, my life, and my sense of normalcy. I just couldn't agree to be someone's *slave.* Rinsing off, I stepped out of the shower and covered up my body with the robe. I would have to tell him no.

No.

I found Mark sitting at the bar over the kitchen counter, sipping coffee and going through papers. His briefcase was open beside him and he was deep in thought. He wasn't wearing a shirt, just flannel pants. The shirtless look was a good one for him. I watched him for awhile, admiring his body. He looked so relaxed.

"Good morning," I said, making him jump a bit at the sound of my voice.

"Hey, sunshine! Good morning to you, too." He hopped up and pecked me on the cheek. "You must have slept well." He grabbed an empty cup that was sitting next to a carafe and poured me coffee. "Sugar?" he asked.

"Black." I sat down on the stool beside his. "What do you *do,* anyway?" I glanced at the papers he was sorting through, not making out what any of the numbers or information meant. Or any of the words, for that matter. "Is that in Portuguese?"

"I invest," he said. "And yes, it is Portuguese. So..." he trailed off.

"So."

"Hmm..." he studied me, and pulled me back up to my feet. He wrapped his legs around my body, held me tight, and kissed me.

And I *melted*. I moaned through the kiss, aroused by everything that had happened even though I knew I would have to turn him away. His hands felt for the belt on my robe and untied it. He pulled the robe off, his hands groping me, my breasts, my ass, rubbing my body. His fingers found my cunt; wet, eager.

He broke away from our kiss and his teeth found my neck, biting gently and growling softly. "*Mine*," he said.

"Mark..." I began, trying to pull away from his embrace, to push myself back into reality. "This can't happen."

"It will happen." He grabbed my hair and pulled me over to the dining table while I squealed helplessly. He pushed my upper body onto the table and held me down. "Stop struggling."

I stopped. Breathless.

"Beg me to fuck you," he said.

"No Mark, I can't," I whispered, my voice throaty.

SMACK. He slapped my ass, *hard.*

"Ouch!" I cried.

"Beg me to fuck you. Beg me to take you as my slave."

"Mark I can't... I don't know..."

SMACK.

"Ouch! Fuck, Mark, ow! I can't do this!"

"You can. You need this." He leaned over and whispered gruffly in my ear, "Remember last night, when we talked about safewords? Yours is 'butterfly'. Say it and I'll stop, and you'll go home. Say it, and you'll never need to see me again. Understand?"

"Yes," I gasped.

SMACK.

"Owwwww Mark! Please! Please no more." I was suddenly confused, conflicted. I could end this whole scenario, the whole confusing prospect of a relationship, with *one little word.* Why wasn't I saying it?

SMACK. SMACK. SMACK. Hard spanks were raining down on my ass. I cried out. My vision became clouded with tears.

"Tell me what you want. Beg me. Now." Mark's voice said to me, firm and strong and he continued to smack my butt and watch me squeal.

"Say.." *SMACK* "..it.." *SMACK* "..NOW.." *SMACK.*

"Ow oh god, fuck me Mark, please. Please fuck me. Please take me. Take me as your slave," I cried out loudly, amazed by the words that spilled out of my mouth.

Mark stood behind me and rammed his cock into my pussy, not going slow, not easing in.

"Ugh," I grunted under him, spreading my legs wide.

He thrust into me without restraint, taking me like I had never experienced from anyone before. His thighs slammed into my sore ass, making me moan with every stroke.

"This.. is... not... for... your... pleasure..." he grunted.

I heard my voice whispering, "Fuck me, please, fuck me, take me as yours."

Mark sped up and finished, slamming into me one last time and groaning loudly as he came. He pulled out of me and it was over as quickly as it had begun. I held my place over the table, breathing heavily. He pulled me up and kissed me gently.

"Good girl." Mark smiled at me. I was confused, but oddly

comforted.

"When can we meet again?" he asked.

I didn't want to leave him. I wanted to stay, I wanted him to help me with my confusion. But I shook my feelings aside. I reminded myself what I knew to be true: *Work first, Heather.*

I ran through my week in my head before responding. "I could be available Saturday afternoon."

"Mmm, good. I look forward to it." He kissed me softly, with tenderness, like a feather grazing my cheek. "I will pick you up at work. Two o'clock sharp; can you be ready by then?"

"Yes," I whispered, melting with the sensation of his touch.

Mark called me a cab and I was out of his apartment before I could even finish my cup of coffee. I had finally gotten what I wanted. He fucked me.

But what really happened?

Chapter Five
THE FASHIONISTA

I re-played Monday morning over and over in my head throughout the week. Since Mark's restriction on making myself cum no longer applied, I brought myself to orgasm nearly every single night before falling asleep. At work, I was slightly distracted and more than once had to consciously pull myself out of a daydream at my desk.

My office-mate, Erik, who I'd always found a bit too forward, wasn't above pestering me when he noticed my inattentive behavior at a meeting on Thursday.

"What's with you, Heather?" he asked me as we were making our way back to our office after the meeting.

"Nothing," I said, my tone slightly defensive. "It's just, that meeting really wasn't covering any of the cases I'm working on at the moment. Kind of pointless, you know?"

"Yeees," he said, drawing out the vowel in a teasing way. "But you've been kind of distracted all week. I work ten feet away from you, you know. I read people for a living. You -" he paused as we entered our office. He grabbed my arm to make me look at him directly. "You went on a date, didn't you?"

I shook him off of me and put the notebook and folders I was carrying on my desk.

"No," I responded slowly, thinking. Did I really want anyone from work knowing that I was potentially seeing someone? That my mind wasn't fully on the office?

Erik sighed. "Look, Heather, you can trust me. I know you work hard here; that's why Mr. Richards gave you some extra vacation time. You're a valuable employee. I wasn't asking in order to criticize you. I'm just curious, that's all. You've been a little distracted this week, sure, but that just makes you seem more *human*. Hell, Heather, prior to this change I kind of thought you were a work-zombie."

I looked up at him, saw his broad smile, and realized he really didn't mean any harm. He was attractive; the tall, dark, and handsome type. I had a small crush on him when I first started working with the firm.

My crush ended the day we became office-mates. While charming, for sure, Erik wasn't brilliant. But he was kindhearted.

"Thanks Erik. Yeah, I did go on a date. We're going out again. Saturday afternoon."

"Good! See? Not so scary to share a little information with the person who you probably spend the most time with, proximity-wise, in the *entire world*."

I giggled, then quickly covered my mouth. I wasn't used to banter in the office. Erik just grinned at me and took his place at his desk. He appeared to immediately forget about our conversation as he furrowed his eyebrows at his computer screen and clicked away at the keyboard.

I sat down at my desk and chewed on the end of my pen,

thinking about how next Saturday might go. I hadn't really allowed myself to consider what I had agreed to last weekend.

'*Slave*'. What did that really mean? Was it just constant role-play? Or was I really submissive? I doubted that I really wanted Mark to always be telling me what to do. But, on the other hand, when he had expressed his dominance during our first dates, I had felt a bit more at ease.

I made it through Thursday, then Friday at work. On Saturday morning as I was getting ready to leave my apartment, Mark called.

"Hello, there," he said when I picked up the phone. "All ready for work?"

"Yeah," I responded. I was glad he had called. I wasn't sure if I needed to have any special clothing for our date this afternoon. "Well, mostly I'm ready. Just packing up some clothes for this afternoon. Casual?"

"No need to pack anything at all," he replied, sounding jovial. "Heather, do you have a long overcoat?"

"Um... yeah," I said, glancing up at my coat. I wore it regularly, whenever there was even a slight risk of rain or chilly weather.

"Does it go down to your knees?"

"Almost," I said.

"Good. I'll be outside of your office at 2:00pm sharp. Please be there to meet me on time. Wearing the coat. And nothing else."

I sharply sucked in a breath of air, surprised by his command. "But, it will be obvious, Mark. I always wear pants to work. People will know."

"So wear a skirt today."

"But Mark..."

"Heather, this is a simple request. I will be *very* disappointed if you cannot even accomplish the most simple of tasks." Mark's tone turned from jovial to stern with ease. I sighed.

"OK," I agreed.

"Good. Until this afternoon, then."

I hung up and walked over to my closet, feeling a bit uneasy. Other women wore skirts to work, but my normal attire was pantsuits. Digging through my clothes, I found a knee-length skirt I'd worn a few times before, and paired it with a blouse and jacket. When I looked in the mirror I was relieved. I still looked quite professional.

I wore the coat over my clothes and was happy to see that it went just below my skirt. No-one would be the wiser this afternoon when I met Mark.

At the office, I began to pack up my things around 1:30pm. I had been thrilled to watch Erik leave around noon; I'd be able to strip myself down in the comfort of my own office rather than in the bathroom.

I locked the office door and looked over to the full length mirror that hung on the wall beside Erik's desk. *Showtime, Heather*, I thought to myself, psyching myself up.

I pulled off my blouse and skirt, folding each item carefully and setting them on my desk. My panties and bra came off next, leaving me naked for the first time ever at work.

With the coat on, Mark was right, no one would know that I was naked underneath. But *I would know*. Why was I doing this? If Mark considered this a simple task, what more would he ask me to do?

The clock read one fifty. I put the clothes into a plastic bag and gathered my briefcase and purse. Walking the long hallway out of the office proved easier than I had imagined; none of the temps, interns, or receptionists worked on weekends. The lawyers were at their desks, hardly paying any attention to the rest of the office.

Outside it was a beautiful, sunny day. I spotted Mark's car across the parking lot, and waved to let him know I was there. The driver's side window opened, and I could vaguely make out that he was on his phone. He waved, then motioned me to come to him.

The office parking lot was huge since we shared the building with a few other businesses. I grumbled to myself as I made my way to his car, my humiliation of being naked under my coat extended. I wanted to be *inside* the car. Hidden. I quickened my pace.

"Hello, my dear," Mark said as I approached. He turned away from me and I heard him murmur something into his phone before he hung up.

"Hi," I replied.

"Go on, get in," he said.

I put my belongings in the backseat before climbing in to the passenger's side. Mark turned towards me when I got in, grinning.

"So, you're naked under there, huh?" he asked. I ignored that his tone slightly reminded me of a teenage boy first getting his girlfriend to get naked. Instead, I nodded.

"Good," he said. "Unbutton the coat. Show me."

I cringed at his words, and looked around the parking lot. It was nearly empty, and we were far from any of the buildings. I unbuttoned the coat slowly, and taking one last glance around to check for my privacy, I pulled it open.

"Mmm," he said, letting his hands roam over my breasts, then down to my pussy. "You're wet again."

I blushed, inhaling softly as one of his hands brushed against my clit.

"I like taking things slow with you. It keeps your arousal so high, doesn't it? Keep the coat unbuttoned. You can cover yourself up though, while we drive."

I thankfully covered myself, and buckled in.

"Tell me about your week," he said.

There wasn't a lot to tell, but I recounted my relatively boring week for Mark as he drove. I told him about Erik knowing that I had been on a date, and Mark smiled.

"What about you?" I asked. "What did you do this week?"

"Me? Well," he reached over and squeezed my thigh. "I had a very good week. In my line of work, some things can go very poorly. Or they can go very well. This week, things went very, very well."

I considered asking him for details, but I looked around and realized that we were very close to my apartment. With a sinking feeling I watched as we took the exact turns that would land us near the store that I had bought my green dress.

"Mark... where are we going?" I asked, worried.

"I noticed the dress you wore to Haven was designed by a friend of mine. It looked good on you. I want to see what else she might have that you could wear. And I think..." he said as he pulled into the parking lot, "that she sells a lot of her line here. What do you think?" He turned to me.

"I can't go in there like this," I whispered. I couldn't face Jasmine and Rose again without clothing; they would think I was completely insane.

Mark obviously didn't care that I was mortified. Again, he parked in one of the furthest spots in order to maximize the time I'd need to spend outside wearing just my coat.

"Get out, let's go," he said. He came over to my side of the car and opened my door for me. I stepped out, reluctantly, clutching my coat over my body.

"Let your arms fall to your sides, Heather," Mark said,

gently pulling my hands off of the coat.

"Mark I can't! The coat is still open – someone might see me," I said, protesting. I felt slightly panicked.

"Do. It." His voice was strong and stern. I obeyed, dropping my arms to my sides.

"Good girl," Mark said. "Now, follow me."

As I walked and the breeze brushed me, the coat fell open, exposing me to anyone who cared to look. I was torn between walking fast to get out of being naked in the middle of a parking lot, or walking slowly to avoid getting to the store. I kept up with Mark, looking around frantically, hoping not to be seen. Two young guys were leaving a fast food place nearby and I saw them point and laugh at me. I blushed. This was *horrible*.

To my surprise, rather than enter the shop at the main entrance, Mark used a key and opened an unmarked door to the side of the store. The entrance hallway was dark, for which I was immediately thankful.

"Wait here," Mark said. I obeyed as he went inside to find Rose or Jasmine or whoever was working that he wanted to speak with. In less than thirty seconds he popped back into the hallway.

"No one here minds if you're naked. Take off that coat, and come on in."

Fuck! I pulled off the coat and followed him meekly into the main store. I watched Rose and Jasmine both share a knowing glance before looking back to me. Out of the corner of my eye I saw two women who were shopping. They both looked at me briefly, and, uninterested, went back to discussing the clothes they looking at.

"Back so soon, Heather?" said Jasmine, with a condescending tone. I just stood there, willing the floor to open up and engulf me.

Mark smacked me on the ass and said to me sternly, "You will answer people when they speak to you."

Ugh of all the bad luck, I thought to myself. I couldn't believe that I was 'slave' to a guy who just happened to know everyone at a store that I loved and had just shopped at. I snapped myself out of my self-pity and looked straight at Jasmine.

"Obviously, I'm here," I said.

"Well, aren't you snide?" she snapped at me, looking to Mark, who was smiling. "Mark, what are the rules with her?"

"No penetration. You can touch her all you want. These rules may change later; Heather and I haven't completely discussed our arrangement yet," Mark said.

Rose stepped in, taking my hand and leading me across the store. "Mark says he wants to pick out a few outfits for you designed by Rachel. Why don't you step into the dressing room and Jasmine will be in shortly with some selections. Mark?" she turned to get his attention. "Sir, would you like to help Jasmine look for clothing, or join Heather and I in the dressing room?"

"I'll join you both in a few minutes," Mark said, turning towards Jasmine.

I entered the dressing room with Rose, hoping that she wouldn't continue to embarrass me by bringing up the obvious fact that I walked into her store completely naked. She looked at me and smiled. Then, she did something that I will forever be grateful for: she walked over to the corner of the room, stood on her tip-toes, and opened up a cabinet. From the cabinet Rose produced a bottle of tequila.

"I think that Mark might be more than just a few minutes. In any case, while we wait, why don't we enjoy a drink?"

I nodded appreciatively and sat down on the couch with Rose, no longer caring if my naked skin touched their precious fabric. She didn't seem to mind either. Rose took a swig right from the bottle.

She said, "Arg!" like a pirate and handed me the tequila. I took a swig too.

"Ech!" I said, not used to drinking hard liquor straight. It washed through me and I took another gulp before passing the bottle off to Rose.

"So, does Mark come here a lot?" I asked.

"Not so much anymore. Since his last girl," she replied.

"Do you know him well?"

"No." She tipped the bottle back to take a sip. "But, I know he's a good guy, Heather."

I was oddly reassured by Rose's statement. Rose was, for the moment, the only mutual acquaintance that Mark and I had 'Acquaintance' was a bit strong of word to describe our non-existent relationship, but Rose, at the very least, was friendly towards me.

"Does he know Rachel, the designer, well? He recognized her dress on me, which is apparently why we're here."

"Mark has supported Rachel's work since the beginning of her career. She wouldn't have gotten as far as to make that dress if it weren't for him. I think, when he first saw her work, he knew she had talent."

"Huh," I said.

"Listen..." said Rose, her tone becoming serious. "I don't know what Mark has planned for you today. But just know he'll take care of you. You'll be OK."

A knot formed in my stomach as I wondered why Rose felt the need to tell me this. She passed me the bottle, and I took another swig, hoping to calm my senses.

"That's enough now," she said. "I need to stay out of trouble, too." She returned the bottle to the upper cabinet and handed me a glass of water. As if on cue, Mark joined us in the dressing room, Jasmine following just behind him.

My jaw dropped as I took in the sight of Jasmine: she had changed into a tight black corset that pushed her breasts up, her nipples totally exposed. She wore a miniskirt that barely covered her cunt. Mark was carrying piles of clothing. In Jasmine's hands were a long flogger, a paddle, rope, and a riding crop. I instinctively covered my chest and my pussy with my hands.

"Jasmine will be helping you try on some outfits, Heather," said Mark, ignoring my obvious distress. "Rose, can you schedule Heather an appointment at Claire's?"

"Of course, sir," said Rose, dismissing herself from the room. I felt immediately alone without Rose there as a companion.

I watched as Jasmine put down the flogger, the paddle and the rope. She came over to the couch and stood above me.

"Come on, bitch, get up!" she said. She raised the riding crop above her head and brought it down forcefully on my thigh. I shot off the couch and stood at attention, waiting for Jasmine's next command. I looked to Mark for help, but he was busying himself sorting through the clothing.

Over the next hour Jasmine forced me try on a huge array of shockingly slutty and revealing outfits. Anytime I didn't zip up fast enough, or I didn't undress quickly, I received a quick series of bites from her crop. I stopped paying attention to how I looked in each piece of clothing as it promptly became clear that my opinion was far from relevant. When Jasmine and Mark liked a certain skirt or brassiere they made me bend over, spread my legs, squat, and perform a series of moves to make sure it pleased them from all angles. I was mortified, but didn't have much time to consider my emotions as I worked fast to avoid the pain of the dreaded riding crop.

Rose returned and asked if she should help.

"I want the uniforms," demanded Jasmine, and Rose hurried out of the dressing room. She soon returned with an armful of outfits. The first was a school girl uniform, which Jasmine threw at me to try on while she sorted through the rest.

"You can't be serious," I said to Mark.

"Watch yourself," he replied sternly.

I slipped on the plaid skirt. It was cut to sit low on my hips, and the total length couldn't have been more than seven inches. The outfit came with a white cotton thong; surprisingly the most tasteful panties I had tried on yet. The blouse was white, low-cut and translucent. I pulled on the knee-length white stockings and slipped my feet into the brown, flat Mary Janes. Jasmine tied my hair into two high pigtails on either side of my head with red ribbon. She turned me towards a mirror, and all three of us took in the reflection. Jasmine and Mark stood on either side of me, and I in the center, gaping.

I looked like a school-girl pornstar. A weird combination of innocent and slutty, prude and whore. Mark smiled at me in the mirror.

"Jasmine, I think the schoolgirl needs a paddling. Can you make her ass bright red for me? I want to see how that short little skirt looks on a punished girl like Heather," Mark said.

"It'll be my pleasure," Jasmine replied, and turned to smile coyly at me in the mirror. "Bend over the couch, whore."

I trembled with fear. The language and actions of Jasmine and Mark were so new to me, I could barely process what was happening. I was both offended and aroused. Being spanked by Mark's hand was probably nothing compared to the pain of a wooden paddle yielded by Jasmine, who just seemed cranky and mean. I slowly made my way to the back of the couch and bent my torso over it, resting my hands on the seat. Jasmine came up behind me and hoisted me up so my ass was facing the ceiling, my head unceremoniously smashing into the seat of the couch. She flipped up the little fabric that was left covering my butt and yanked the thong down to my knees. I groaned as I felt the lack of any panties and tried not to imagine what I must look like, bent over the couch with my naked ass in the air. Even my asshole was probably exposed.

"How many spanks, Mark?" asked Jasmine.

"Let's start with ten," he replied. "Heather, you will ask Jasmine to spank you. After the ten spanks, we will see if you need any more. At the end of your punishment you will thank Jasmine for taking the time to redden your tight little ass."

I was grateful that I could somewhat hide my face in the seat of the couch as I sensed Jasmine behind me, preparing to paddle my butt. Slowly, I croaked, "Jasmine... will you... please... spank me please?"

"What's that, slut?" she responded, resting the paddle on my butt.

Bitch, I thought, and tried again. "Jasmine, please, will you spank me?"

"Spank you *where?*" she asked.

I swallowed hard. "Will you spank my bottom, please, Jasmine?"

She giggled. "Why yes, Heather, I'll spank your *bottom*." I felt the absence of the paddle for just a split second, and then,

CRACK!

I jolted up, crying out as the pain shot through my ass. I grabbed my butt and hopped up and down, squealing in anguish. Jasmine stood back and watched me, smiling.

"She hasn't had much experience with punishment yet, has she Mark?" Jasmine asked, turning to Mark, who was also watching my display of pain with amusement.

"No, not yet. Heather, get back into position. Don't lose

control like that, you'll embarrass yourself."

I looked down at the ground, ashamed. Slowly I draped myself back over the couch, back into position.

Mark directed his attention to Jasmine and said, "We will give her another chance and start from the beginning. If she looses her position again, we will add more spanks. Three spanks for every time she moves out of place."

"Sounds good to me," said Jasmine. "Heather, we're starting over. Don't you need to ask me something?"

"Erm... yes... Jasmine, will you please spank my ass with your paddle?"

CRACK! CRACK! CRACK! Jasmine gave me three quick, unbelievably hard smacks in a row.

"Yeowwww!" I cried out, clutching the couch seat with my hands, willing myself to stay put. I threw my face into the cushions to muffle my cries of agony. Jasmine's hands began to rub my ass roughly. Even though her hands felt a bit cruel, I welcomed the touch as it helped ease the stinging pain just a tiny bit.

CRACK! CRACK! She delivered two more smacks to my quivering butt. I began to cry into the cushion. I couldn't believe the amount of pain coursing through my body.

CRACK! A sharp, quick stroke just below my ass, where my legs were clutched together, sent a wave of pain directly to my pussy. I couldn't hold still. My hands flung back to grab my ass and protect myself from further onslaught.

Just as quickly as I committed the transgression I realized my sin and placed my hands back in front of me, leaving my ass bare and vulnerable to Jasmine's next blows.

"What do you think, Mark? She realized she fucked up. Should we let it go?" Jasmine asked. I immediately felt grateful – she was taking my side!

"No," said Mark, and my stomach turned. "She had four left. Now, seven. She must learn to obey."

My cries became sobs as I waited for the next spanks. Jasmine rubbed my ass, gently this time, and leaned over to whisper to me, "Hey. You'll be OK. Breathe."

CRACK! CRACK! CRACK! Three spanks in a row, delivered so quickly that I had no time to process any individual stroke or prepare for the next.

"Eeeooowww!" I exclaimed. I was sure that my cries could be heard by any customers in the store, and possibly by anyone outside in the parking lot. With all my might I clutched onto the cushions and willed myself to stay put.

CRACK! CRACK!

"Gawwwd Jasmine, please!" I plead, hoping she would take pity on me and stop paddling so hard.

"Two more spanks, Heather," said Mark. "They will be the hardest yet. *Stay. Still.*"

I braced myself, tears running down my cheeks.

CRACK!

CRACK!

"Owwww eeee" I cried out. *Done.* The tenseness of waiting for every stroke left my body and I collapsed into the couch, sobbing helplessly. Jasmine and Mark's hands explored my ass cheeks, feeling the radiating warmth from the strict, hard paddling.

"Do you think she's had enough?" Jasmine asked.

"For now," Mark replied. "Heather, stand up and show us that slutty school-girl outfit now."

I stood up and turned to face them, and Mark gestured towards the mirror. I gawked at my reflection. My eyes and face were red, tears running down my cheeks, and the pigtails were now lopsided, my hair messy. The thong was around my ankles.

Mark turned me around, lifted the skirt, and we all looked at my ass in the mirror: a deep red where the paddle had placed its marks. I wondered if I would have bruises.

"You look beautiful," said Jasmine. I looked at her, surprised at the sudden compliment.

"What do you say, Heather?" prodded Mark.

"Erm, thank you Jasmine," I said.

"Thank her for paddling you," he said, smacking the front of my thigh sharply with his hand.

"Thank you Jasmine for paddling me," I said politely.

"Heather," said Mark, "You'll be returning to this store at least once a month to refresh your outfits and buy something new that will please me. When I am not here, you will report directly to Jasmine. Any disobedience will be met with punishment, first from Jasmine, and then from me later on. You will address her as 'Miss Jasmine'. Understood?"

"Yes," I replied meekly.

"Good. Jasmine, please ring me up for these items," Mark said, gesturing to a pile of clothing. He selected a tight black one-piece dress and handed it to me. "Put that on."

I pulled off the school girl outfit and shimmied into the super-tight dress. It was basically a long tube, sitting just above my breasts and going to just below my ass. Every curve of my body was obvious through the thin fabric.

Jasmine walked over to me and pinched my nipples, making them even more erect and poke out through the dress. "She really is pretty, Mark," she said. I blushed from the attention.

"Yes, she is. Jasmine, what do you think, these boots or heels?"

"The boots," said Jasmine without taking her gaze off me. She untied my hair and combed it out with her hands. Then she scrunched it up until she was satisfied; my natural small amount of waves accentuated by the treatment.

I pulled on the boots they had selected. It took me awhile to lace them up. They nearly came up to my knees and had very high heels. Looking at my reflection, I could hardly believe it was me I saw in the mirror.

"When will she come back?" Jasmine asked Mark, handing him the credit slip to sign.

"In a few weeks. I'll call ahead." He handed her the slip of paper and slid the receipt into his wallet. "Thanks Jasmine, you helped a lot," he said. He leaned over and kissed her, deeply. I felt a twinge of jealousy as I watched them, and felt extremely awkward. I looked down at my feet.

"OK, slave-girl," Mark said, smiling at me. "Let's go."

Chapter Six
THE BARE TRUTH

In the parking lot I asked Mark where we were going next.

"Claire's," he answered, without offering further explanation.

Not far from the shop, we drove into a residential neighborhood. Mark pulled into a driveway outside of a beautiful bungalow. Outside, a woman was weeding her garden. When she saw us she stood up and waved, smiling. I was relieved. She seemed friendly, and for some reason the neighborhood setting made me very comfortable.

We got out of the car and Mark introduced me to Claire, who held my hand and walked me inside. Mark followed, shutting the front door behind him.

"So, what would you like done?" Claire asked Mark.

"She should be completely bare, please. I'd like to watch this time."

I looked back and forth from Claire to Mark, my ease of

mind immediately replaced by anxiety.

"What?" I asked.

"You're getting waxed, hun," Claire responded cheerfully. "You can leave your clothes right here beside the door. Then, come on back!"

"Leave the boots on, Heather," said Mark.

I looked at Mark warily. I had never been waxed before, but at least it was in the realm of something I would have considered doing, before... all *this*.

"What did you think of Jasmine?" Mark asked, watching me as I shimmied out of the dress.

"She's... she's kind of mean," I said truthfully.

"She's actually quite nice, once you get to know her. I enjoyed watching her spank you."

I blushed and looked away.

"You're confused," he said. "It's natural. But hey, Claire is really nice, and you'll like being waxed. Have you ever had a completely smooth cunt before?"

"No. I normally just keep it how it is."

Mark slipped his fingers between my legs and rubbed my pussy, pulling me close to him.

"You're very wet," he whispered. "Claire will be amused."

My face turned red at the thought of yet another woman seeing my cunt today and noticing my inappropriate level of arousal. I shook off the feeling of dread, took a deep breath, and tried to be brave.

Mark led me down the hall into a small room filled with salon equipment. In the center of the room was a padded table fit with stirrups, much like a gynecologist's office. Claire was busy preparing the wax. She called over her shoulder for me to have a seat on the table. Mark helped me up and placed my booted feet in the stirrups. I desperately wanted to close my legs, to hide my wet pussy. But he made that impossible. Using a strap on each side of the table he secured my ankles to the stirrups. Then he adjusted the stirrups, pulling them as far apart as possible. I groaned from both the humiliation and because my legs were stretched to the most uncomfortable limit.

"We'll have to work on your flexibility," Mark said as he took a seat beside me.

"Thanks for your empathy," I replied sarcastically. He responded by giving me a sharp slap on my breast. I bit my lip so as not to cry out, and inwardly cursed myself for responding to him with attitude.

"I'm all set," Claire said. She stood beside the table and peered at my pussy. "Hmm... she's so wet. We need to dry her off a bit before I can begin. Will you hand me a few paper towels, Mark?"

"Of course." Mark retrieved a handful of towels from near the sink and handed them to Claire, who blotted up my juices gently. I covered my face with my hands, utterly humiliated for what seemed like the millionth time today.

"Don't worry honey," said Claire, noticing my shame. "This won't last long."

She tossed aside the towels and began applying wax to the hair above my cunt and along my pussy lips. Using several pieces of cloth, she covered the wax, pressing firmly to be sure all three layers: cunt hair, wax, and cloth, were well attached.

I took a deep breath, knowing what was coming.

"Mark, do you want to pull them off?" Claire asked. My eyes grew wide and I looked at Mark, who looked amused.

"Not yet."

Claire pulled off the strips, one by one, as I grimaced, gasped, and grabbed the sides of the table in an effort not to cry out in pain.

"OK," she said. I looked up, teary-eyed. *That wasn't so bad.*

"Time to turn over," she said.

Oh... no....

Mark un-did the straps and I pulled my legs together. He helped me turn over and told me to place each knee in the padded U-shaped knee-rests that I hadn't noticed were on either side of the table. Then, using more conveniently placed straps, he secured my knees in place.

"Head down on the pillow," he said.

I buried in my head in the pillow and tried to ignore the fact that my ass and pussy were spread wide open in front of both Claire and Mark. I wondered what Claire thought of my red punished ass. I felt wax being applied around my anus, and more strips placed. Claire took her time pressing the strips down as Mark and she discussed mundane subjects like business and the weather. Mark opted to pull the strips off this time and did so quickly, four strips in a row. I cried out into the pillow.

"It's OK hun, it's over now," Claire said soothingly. She began to apply a cream to my pussy lips and around my asshole. It was nice to be touched in a gentle way after the tortures of today. Too soon, Mark untied my legs and sent me to get dressed.

Mark and Claire both joined me a few minutes later. Mark bent me over, kicked my legs apart, and spent some time inspecting my cunt and my ass in front of Claire.

"You always do such good work, Claire," he said appreciatively. "And hey, look how wet she is again. She must like having a nice bare cunt."

"Should I make another appointment for a month from now?" she asked.

"Yes, please. She'll probably come alone next time."

"All right darlings. See you when I see you, Mark. Heather,

see you soon."

We pulled out of her driveway and I found myself anxiously awaiting a cue of where we would be going next. I hoped we would go to my apartment. Or his. Or anywhere *private*.

"Here," Mark said, pulling a bottle of water out of a box in the back seat. "Drink."

I took the water gratefully and drank nearly half of the bottle immediately.

"Are you hungry?" he asked.

"I could eat."

"We'll go out, then. It will give us a chance to discuss our arrangement. Sound good?"

"OK," I said, disappointed we'd be going to a public place.

"Play with your pussy until we get to the restaurant. You may cum when I turn off the engine."

Too tired and worn down to even consider hesitating, I leaned back in the seat and played with my cunt. It felt different, *good*-different, to have no hair between my fingers and my pussy. I slowly began rubbing my clit, closing my eyes, not thinking about anything in particular. It felt like the car was going fast. The heat from my spanked ass combined with all the sensations of being touched all afternoon, violated in ways I had never dreamed... I soon brought myself to the brink of orgasm.

"How much longer?" I asked urgently, wanting to cum *now*.

"A few more minutes."

I pulled my fingers away from my clit in frustration.

"Don't stop touching yourself, slave. Just don't let yourself cum yet."

I lightly touched my cunt as I was told, rubbing very gently. Mark reached his hand down, placed it on top of mine and made my hand rub harder. Squirming in the seat, I was so close to cumming but knew I had to wait.

"Please," I pleaded, "please stop."

"Stop?" he answered playfully. "Doesn't it feel good?"

"Yes... but... I'm so close," I said, struggling to pull myself together. Mark pulled his hand away and I breathed a sigh of relief.

I lazily continued playing with my clit for a few more minutes until we pulled into the parking lot of the restaurant. Then I rubbed myself hard, harder, faster, until he finally turned the car off and my whole body erupted in an explosive orgasm. Mark's hand clamped over my mouth as I cried out in pleasure, muffling my sounds from being heard by anyone inside the restaurant.

"Ooooohhh..." I said as I finished.

Mark smiled at me. He pulled a briefcase from the backseat and handed me a few tissues. "Wipe your cunt juices up."

Inside, we chose a table in the far corner of the restaurant. I had been here once before, a family-run Indian place with excellent food. He had good taste. I excused myself to use the bathroom, and marveled at how even peeing felt so much different after being waxed.

Back at the table, Mark looked at me with a serious expression.

"All right, Heather, let's have a little chat."

I looked at the table, trying to avoid his strong gaze. He reached over and put his hand under my chin, tilting my head up to meet his eyes.

"Sometimes," he said, "I'll require that you avoid eye contact with me. But for right now, I want your attention. Understood?"

"Yes," I whispered.

"So. Last week you begged me to take you as my slave. Do you remember that?"

I shifted uncomfortably in my seat as my mind recalled last Sunday morning, bent naked over his dining room table. I *did* beg him... but somehow it didn't really feel like that's how it all played out. But I knew what he wanted me to say, so I responded: "Yes."

"Good. Now, you must have some questions about what that means."

"Yeah... I mean... how would it work... between you and me?" I asked hesitantly. Then all the questions that had been popping up in my brain throughout the week spilled out. "Would I have to quit my job? I can't quit my job. My job takes so much time... and what would it be like, anyway? All the pictures you showed me last week were so different. Would you just tie me up all the time? Make me be naked and kneel?"

Mark laughed. I must have looked offended, because he quickly said, "Hey, no, those are all valid questions. It's just funny."

"Why?" I demanded indignantly.

"Because... I can't really explain exactly how a relationship between us would be. It could be that we play the game that you are my slave for a few months, but the chemistry never really works, you never submit, and we end our contract. Or, it could be that things develop and you find out more about yourself than you ever thought possible."

"But, what about day-to-day?"

"Well, you have a job. We'd work around that. I know you're passionate about your career. So, we need to set up some boundaries. I will, beyond those boundaries, control you and own you to your very core. But if you decide you never want to be told that you can't work, I respect that." Mark paused, thoughtful. "I've owned a few slaves. Most just for fun. Every relationship was very different. Beyond my relationships, *every* master-slave agreement is a bit different. Some slaves don't want to retain any control at all. I would like that, from a slave, eventually. But I would never start out with that, *especially* with someone as inexperienced as you. I have my boundaries too; the agreement we make must grant me several rights as your owner. But I am human, and an understanding person.

"On a day by day level, you will do as you are told. I will play with you, show you new things. Sometimes, when we are together, it will seem as though it is just a normal relationship. We'll cook together, watch movies, go on walks. But you lose your right to set the course of events the way you want it. If I want a blow job in the middle of a movie, you'll give me one – happily. Some days I'll demand you work without panties, or that you wear a see-through blouse to go shopping. If you make a stupid decision, I will correct you. If you screw up, I will punish you. I may decide to give you pain just because it pleases me.

"And, you will find yourself experiencing an enormous sense of relief. I can see this in you, Heather. You need to give up control. You need to be told what to do."

Mark paused, waiting for my reaction. I didn't really know what to say. I was opening up my mind to the idea maybe I was one of those freaks.

"Can we..." I began, slowly. *Was I really going to say this?* "Can we just... can I just... try it? To see if I like it?"

"You won't like it all the time," Mark responded.

"Yeah but... what if I hate it? What if it makes me miserable?"

"Well, Heather, you're a lawyer. What do you think you'd do if you don't like it?"

"I guess we'd just break up?"

Mark smiled. "Yup. It's that easy. This isn't *actual* slavery. Some people, very few, do enter contracts where there are legal ramifications for ending the relationship. And there are some BDSM communities where relationships tend to be on the questionable side of 'consensual'. We will make a contract that is just between us; not legal. It will include my expectations of you and your personal limits. I will have rules for you that you'll need to follow. You will learn how to please me with your obedience, and your servitude."

I sat silently, thinking over what he was saying. It was a lot to consider, and there was still a lot I didn't understand.

"I think your head is full," Mark commented, smiling slightly. Our food arrived and we ate mostly in silence. We had both ordered the day's special, a large plate of chicken biryani. I couldn't finish even half of the huge portion of food, and found myself playing with the rice and peas on the plate, trying to make some sense of the situation I was in.

"Heather, I know you're confused. Just tell me this: From having spent some time with me, getting to know me, do you trust me? More or less?"

"Yeah. I mean, I think so. More or less."

Mark smiled. "Good. When you can say that you trust me completely, I'll know that you're mine. You work on trusting me, and I'll make sure that I am trust-able. Sound like a good plan?"

"OK," I agreed. I liked it that he at least occasionally attempted to put things in simpler terms for me. Trusting someone seemed completely different then being a slave to them. I wondered what I was agreeing to.

"Wonderful. Listen, Heather, I have a meeting that I can't miss. I'm going to call my driver to pick you up here and take you home."

"What?" I asked, surprised.

"What was unclear?" he asked. His tone was almost businesslike.

"Nothing," I said, looking down.

"Good." Mark made the phone call. The car would pick me up in minutes. "Heather, what do you normally wear to your office?"

"It's business attire. Occasionally business-casual," I responded, not getting very specific.

"Yes, but what do *you* wear?"

"Suits. Pants and a jacket."

"And do other women at the office wear strictly pants, or do they wear skirts?" he asked.

"Both."

"How come you don't wear skirts?"

"I don't know. I feel like pants might be more... professional."

Mark raised his eyebrows. "I want you to wear skirts. You have beautiful legs – it's a shame that you're hiding them."

"But Mark, I seriously *never* wear skirts. Today was the first day in like... forever," I said.

He looked over at me, his eyes sharp. Then he spoke, slowly and deliberately, "Heather, you have two assignments for this week. One is to buy some skirts that are appropriate for work, and start wearing them. At least twice next week. The *other*, perhaps more *important* assignment," Mark said, emphasizing his words, "is to consider our arrangement very carefully. We haven't discussed the finer details of your service to me yet; we will save that for our next meeting. But you must understand that I do not take your service lightly. Protesting like you just did is unacceptable. I'm not the sort of Master who wants a bratty child. I expect you will make your share of mistakes as I train you, but when I say I want you to do something, Heather, guess what happens?"

"I do what you say," I whispered.

"Correct. In the future, you'll learn to anticipate what I want so I won't need to tell you what to do. You'll just know. Slowly you will learn to please me."

Mark stood up and gathered his coat. "Come, get your things from my car."

We didn't say much as I transferred my purse, briefcase, and work clothes from his personal car to the car that had picked me up a week ago. Mark kept the purchases from Second Skin with him.

"We will meet again next Sunday. We'll meet at the convenience store, in the parking lot, on the corner of your street at five o'clock. Does that work with your schedule?" he asked, stepping towards me. He grabbed a handful of my hair and forcefully turned my face to look at his.

"Yes," I replied.

"What is that store called?"

"It's Ralph's. Everyone just calls it that, anyway, since the owner, Ralph, is always there. I don't know if it has a name actually," I said, surprised I didn't know the answer to that question.

"Very good. I want you to wear the exact same outfit you are wearing now, nothing more. With *very* heavy makeup. When I see you, you should look like a whore. Understand?"

"Yes," I said. I didn't protest, even though I knew I couldn't wear the skimpy black tube dress and the big black boots in broad daylight by my apartment.

He pulled me even closer and kissed me, hard. I moaned beneath him and enjoyed being taken by his mouth. His strength, and yes, his dominance... for some reason it just instantly made me aroused.

"If you aren't there, I will assume you have changed your mind. This is your opportunity to back away without even saying a word. If you are there, I will assume you have thought very hard about what being a slave means, and that you are ready to begin your service. Do you understand me, Heather?"

"Yes, Mark."

"Good."

With that, he was gone. I got into the car he had called for. I couldn't even see the driver through the tinted windows and wondered if it was the same young man as before.

On my way home I sat back in the comfy seat of the car and imagined my next meeting with Mark. I knew I wouldn't change my mind; I was so aroused thinking about what he would make me do I could barely wait to get home and make myself cum. I wondered when he would make me kneel like I had seen in the photos, or when he would have me suck his cock.

Mark always ended things when he wanted. I wondered if the meeting he spoke about tonight was real; it was nearly eight o'clock. Who makes meetings so late? And for what?

I contemplated whether I should talk with Rebecca about Mark. I quickly pushed that thought from my head when I realized I'd have to explain so much to her and still probably come off sounding insane. She'd surely try to convince me that this is all a bad idea.

I pulled my overcoat on as I noticed that we were close to my apartment so I could hide my skimpy outfit from any of my neighbors who happened to be out. I was glad I did, because the building adjacent from mine was having a large barbeque. What would my neighbors have thought if they had seen me dressed the way I was? What if Mark ever made me wear something so revealing in public, where I might see someone I know?

Do you trust me?

Mark had asked me that, and I wondered if I ever could. Could I trust him? Or was my career too much to risk?

Chapter Seven
THOUGHTFUL DAZE

At home, I made myself some peppermint tea and drew water for a bath. I lit candles and poured about half a bottle of bubbles into the tub, along with some sea salt and lemon essential oil. Inhaling the soft smell of the oil, I moved the water around with my hands, encouraging the bubbles to grow. As I undressed, I looked at my butt in the mirror. I traced my hand along the marks. It didn't hurt much anymore, but there was a small bruise on my left cheek. I felt a little embarrassed, thinking about what happened with Jasmine in the store. And how Mark allowed it to happen... how he *encouraged* it to happen.

I turned around to face the mirror and examined myself, fresh from the waxing. Completely bare, the lips of my pussy were so obvious. Before my pubic hair served as sort of a shield, but now... I felt *so naked*. I touched my cunt lightly, letting my fingers get used to the new feeling of my skin.

The bath was amazing. It was a welcome relief and

opportunity to relax at the end of a fairly intense day. I caressed my body gently: my torso, breasts, then legs and feet, as I washed myself. Considering how tired I was from the day, and how much information I'd been given to process, I began to understand why Mark was taking things so slow with me and not fucking me. Though I wanted so badly to have him inside of me again.

I let my hand wander down to my pussy, parting the folds and pausing at my clit. Would Mark ever touch me softly here? Would his fingers be gentle, or forever forceful to reiterate his dominance?

When I collapsed into bed, I enjoyed the feeling of my skin hitting the sheets. I snuggled all of the covers around me and fell asleep, imagining him holding me close.

On Sunday morning I woke early. I spent the morning at my apartment, doing a little bit of work to prepare for a meeting I had with Mr. Richards on Monday morning. I considered his role with me. Was he dominant? Beyond supervising me and others at the office, did he fall into the dominant role outside of work?

I wondered about Erik, who at times seemed so goofy and somewhat immature. I wondered if I was dominant with him.

Mark was right. Nearly all relationships have some sort of power balance. I thought about my parents. My dad was the patriarch, and in his Mormon household he was definitely in charge. I hadn't told Mark yet, but my family was polygamist. Closeted, to avoid excommunication from the Mormon church. My mother married very young, and was his third wife. She had me when she was only 17. Dad was dominant with her, but not in a pleasant way. I shuddered thinking about her. I hadn't spoken with her since I called home to tell her that Ryan and I wouldn't be married. And that I had passed the bar and become a lawyer. She had sounded so disappointed about the wedding, and barely listened when I told her the good news. She had never had the opportunity for a career; Father wouldn't have his wives work, even though his managerial job at a supermarket could barely feed his four wives and thirteen children. I pushed my mom from my brain. I couldn't compare her situation and mine. It just wasn't the same.

In the afternoon I decided to go shopping, to buy the skirts Mark requested. I was slightly annoyed that he wanted me to change my normal outfit for work, but couldn't really come up with a good excuse for why I thought it was inappropriate.

I bumped into Rebecca at the mall. I was surprised to see her.

"I've got a client near here," she explained. "Want to chat a bit as you shop? I'm just taking a long lunch. My client is kind of driving me insane."

"Sure," I agreed. "Who's your client?"

"I'm doing some logo and graphic work for the sports shop down the road. But the guy who is assigned to work with me is totally unprepared, and he keeps hitting on me. I might cancel my contract with them. Luckily, I've got enough work right now that I don't need any one client. God, just after college I was so desperate for work. I much prefer the options that I have now."

"Yeah, that's great. Options are good," I agreed. I admired her for doing independent contracting. Most people didn't have the initiative to start their own business, but I knew Rebecca was making much more money than she would have if she had just joined a design firm.

"What are you shopping for? Anything in particular, or are you just killing time too?" she asked.

"Skirts," I said, somewhat ruefully. "For work."

"The pantsuits not working out for you?" she asked, smiling.

"I just thought I'd change things up a bit."

"Come on, let's go in here," Rebecca said, leading me into a department store on one edge of the mall. "So how are things with that guy? Mark, right?"

"They're good. Slow, but still good. I think I really like him," I said truthfully.

"Had sex yet?"

"Just once. And... it was quick."

"Bummer. When do you see him again?"

"Next weekend."

"How about this?" Rebecca said, holding up a knee-length skirt. It was blue, cut straight, and looked modest enough. I was glad she was here, she was much better at this than I was.

"Sure, I'll try it on."

"Hang on, let's pick out a bunch to try on at once." Rebecca made her way across the floor of the store, piling up skirts and jackets in her arms. "OK," she said, grabbing my hand. "To the dressing room."

On our way she managed to find a few dresses for herself to try on. "I can't help myself," she explained. "I love shopping."

I was happy to see that this dressing room offered more privacy than Second Skin. There were three separate stalls with tall doors. I heard a couple of ladies chatting to each other through the walls between their dressing rooms.

"There's just one open. Wanna share? They're big here, anyway," asked Rebecca.

"Sure," I said. She'd seen me changing countless times in college. And, today I'd managed to pull on a thong *before* going shopping.

Rebecca stripped quickly, nearly before I had the door

closed behind us. She pulled on a pretty purple summer dress and spun around to look in the mirror before pulling it off.

"You're fast," I said.

"I know what I want," she said, shrugging.

I pulled off my jeans and grabbed one of the skirts off it's hanger.

"Uh... Heather?" said Rebecca.

"What?"

"Did Mark... um... *spank* you?"

I spun around, realizing that even though the pain was gone from my butt, the marks still showed from my paddling yesterday. I dropped the skirt and covered my ass with my hands. *What could I say?* There was nearly no excuse that would hide the fact that I'd been spanked. I didn't fall down onto a paddle a dozen times. I looked at Rebecca who was standing there, in her bra and panties, staring at me. Waiting for a response.

"No... I... um..." I stammered. I reached for my jeans. I had to leave.

"Hey," she said, grabbing the jeans out of my hands. "Don't worry. I'm not here to judge. Hell, I've had my share of kinky sex, Heather." She bent down and grabbed the skirt I'd dropped. "Try this on."

I pulled on the skirt without saying a word. I felt uncomfortable and didn't know what I could say. I turned towards the mirror and wished I had worn a blouse instead of a t-shirt. The skirt looked nice, and came to just above my knees. It fit me snugly, but wasn't so tight that I'd feel weird wearing it at the office. If I'd worn a blouse I could get a better appreciation of how the entire outfit would look.

Rebecca read my mind. "I'm gonna go grab a different top for you to wear while you try these on," she said, pulling on another dress. She left me alone.

I took off the skirt and looked at my butt to see how bad it looked. There were just a few marks of the outline of the paddle. Just a few, but it was quite obvious what had happened. I quickly pulled on the next skirt before Rebecca returned.

She handed me a blouse she'd found and I put it on. Much better; I actually looked pretty good.

"Heather, are you still embarrassed?" she asked bluntly. "Don't be, OK?"

"Well it's kind of hard not to be, Rebecca," I said, frustrated. How could I explain to her what I was feeling?

"You'll get over it," she said. "Remember how open I was about sex in college? I haven't changed much. You, however, clearly have. Which is good. You were kind of a prude."

I glared at her. She laughed.

"Listen, I just want to ask you..." she said, pausing slightly. "I want to ask you... it's all consensual, right? I mean, it's one thing to have some kinky fun, but quite another to be beaten without consent. Was this something you wanted?"

I looked down at the floor, holding back tears. I didn't want to admit anything to Rebecca. But if I didn't admit it, she'd think Mark was abusing me.

"It's all consensual," I whispered. I was sure my face was beet red. My previous delight in having Rebecca help me shop had been replaced by the urge to get out of this conversation.

"Good," she said brightly. "Seriously, don't worry about it. I've been spanked before, too. I've even spanked guys before. It can be totally erotic."

I smiled. "Thanks," I said. It was nice of her to admit that.

I tried on the rest of the skirts. They all fit about the same. I picked out five of them: two blue, one gray, and two black.

Rebecca didn't buy anything. She walked me out to my car.

"Are you going back to your client?" I asked.

"Yep," she said, sighing.

"Good luck."

"Thanks. It was good to see you today, Heather," she said. She leaned over and hugged me.

"You too. Thanks for your help," I said.

"Anytime."

On my way home I started to cry. I wasn't sure why; Rebecca had been very understanding and had done her best to ease my embarrassment. I wasn't even sad. Perhaps it was partly tears of relief. Rebecca knew now that I was at least a little bit kinky, and she didn't seem especially surprised or astounded by that. Maybe the whole slave thing wasn't so abnormal. At the very least, kinky play in the bedroom wasn't totally uncommon.

My meeting with Mr. Richards on Monday went very well. He was pleased with my work since I'd returned from break. I was happy for the rest of the day, and stayed at work until nearly eight in the evening. I'd been given two new cases: one which would be long term, representing and advising the owners and board of directors at a new private country club on the north side of town. I spent the day going through their employee records, checking their accounts and looking at the previous lawyer's notes.

With two new cases, my week flew by. I decided to spread out wearing the skirts that Mark required. I wore a blue one on Wednesday, and a black on on Saturday. Saturday, I decided, would be a day I always wore skirts. The office was always half-empty, so I'd be less obvious.

I did some work at home on Sunday morning before getting ready for my date with Mark. I didn't want to think about the fact that he wanted me to dress like a whore and walk down my own street. Around three o'clock, two hours before I'd meet him at Ralph's convenience store, I pulled on the dress and the boots and looked at myself in the mirror.

Sadly, even without the heavy makeup on, I looked like a prostitute. There was no hiding the fact that the intent of this dress was to show off my body. My nipples poked out so obviously, and as I spun around I realized people would even be able to make out the crack in my ass as I walked.

I'd have to disguise myself, I realized. I sprayed down my hair with water, then used handfuls of gel to scrunch it up into messy curls around my head. I rummaged around the shelf in my closet and found a black fedora hat and large, black sunglasses. I did my makeup. I found a hardly ever used stick of bright red lipstick. With the red lipstick, black eyeliner, and black mascara I barely looked like myself. With the addition of the black sunglasses and the hat, I doubted anyone would know it was me walking down this residential street in a whore's costume.

Satisfied, I confidently left my apartment and made my way down the street to meet Mark.

Chapter Eight
A DIRTY CHILL

The walk went quickly. Ralph's was just a block from my apartment. All of my work to disguise myself was for nothing; hardly anyone was outside.

Mark was dressed very casually in old blue jeans and a black t-shirt. Instead of his usual BMW, he had a brown, dented Honda. He kissed me when I arrived, then stood back to look at me.

"Didn't I tell you to wear the dress and nothing more?" he asked.

"I'm not wearing anything else," I said.

"Take off the sunglasses and the hat."

I took them off sheepishly, knowing I hadn't done as he had asked.

"Wait here," he said. He went into Ralph's and I waited impatiently. It was still very light outside and I was worried that I would see someone I knew.

Mark returned. "Follow me," he said. He led us around to the back of the store and unlocked the men's bathroom door. He pushed me inside and locked the door behind us.

"Bend over and put your hands on the sink, Heather."

I looked at him, then at the sink, then back to him. "Really?" I asked. The sink didn't appear to be very clean.

Without a word, Mark pushed me forcefully down to the sink. I used my hands to catch myself and he covered them with his. I felt his whole body around me, his strength and power so obvious. His hands were so much bigger than mine, holding me down.

"If you move these fucking hands before I'm done, you will be a very sorry little slave," he growled softly into my ear. I shuddered under him. I was scared.

"Did you think that I wanted you to wear a little disguise along with your outfit, Heather?" he asked, standing up and positioning himself behind me.

"No," I admitted.

"Did you think I wouldn't notice that you disobeyed?"

"I... I didn't know. I didn't know if you were serious," I said. I looked down at the sink and saw rings of mineral deposits. I decided I did not like men's bathrooms.

"Look back at me, Heather," he said. I looked at him and was relieved to see he had a small smile on his face. "You can rest assured, my dear, for any future commands that I give you, that I am *always* very serious."

He reached to his back pocket and produced a wooden spoon. "This," he said, "is something I usually carry when I'm going out with a slave or submissive girl. In public, it is very difficult to discretely give a naughty girl a proper punishment. But I can use this quite effectively without producing a lot of noise. As long as you keep quiet, Heather, your neighborhood shopkeeper won't be the wiser. You may face forward now."

I looked forward, a bit annoyed. I didn't want to be punished. It seemed so unfair that he would spank me for a simple misunderstanding.

Mark pulled my dress up over my ass, bunching it up at my waist. He wasted no time and used the spoon to pepper my butt with a series of spanks.

I bit my lip to keep myself from crying out. It was worse then his hand, and maybe even worse then the paddle Jasmine used to spank me. It *stung.* I clutched the sides of the sink as hard as I could, not knowing if I would be able to keep myself from using my hands to block the blows. Before long I was hopping from foot to foot, moving my ass around to try to avoid his spanks.

He stopped and I breathed a sigh of relief. His hands grazed my skin softly. "Do you think you've been punished enough, Heather?" he asked.

"Yes," I said quickly. *Definitely.*

"I disagree, but I prefer a change in venue. Wash your hands."

I washed my hands thoroughly. Mark pulled my dress down and led me back out to the parking lot.

"Get in. I'll return the bathroom key to Ralph," he said, unlocking the door to the car.

We drove for over a half hour. I realized he was taking us to one of the sketchy parts of town. I couldn't remember the last time I'd been to this area. He pulled into street parking and gestured to a restaurant across the road. It was a diner that desperately needed new siding. On the glass door entrance was a neon 'open' sign.

"Do you think a lot of your colleagues go to restaurants like this?"

"Um, *no*," I said.

"Or friends?"

"Nope."

"Or estranged Mormon relatives?" he said, looking at me and smiling.

"More likely scenario, but no. I don't think so."

"Good. Let's go."

"Like this? *Here?*" I asked nervously, looking down at my outfit. My dress barely covered my tits and my ass, and my boots and makeup just made the outfit over the top. In this part of town, I'd be assumed to be an *actual* prostitute wearing this kind of thing.

"Ah. Your hesitation reminds me that you still deserve a little more punishment. And I love embarrassing you. It's so easy. Come on, follow me. I have an idea."

I reluctantly followed Mark as he quickly walked across the street and into the restaurant. It was crowded, to my disappointment, and I felt the eyes of the customers on me as we entered. Mark signaled a waitress and asked to speak to the manager.

Seconds later, a man around 50 years old with a bit of a gut sauntered up to us.

"What do you want?" he grumbled, glaring at Mark and eying me with lust. He spoke with a bit of an accent that could only be described as 'rural'. I stepped behind Mark a little bit more, trying to hide from the man's gaze.

"Hello, sir," Mark began, reaching out to shake the man's hand. "Listen, I have an odd question for you. Do you have an office where we can speak privately?"

The man looked Mark up and down and asked, "Is you a cop?"

"No, sir."

"Fine, then. I'm Wayne. I don't got no personal office. You want private... we could talk in the refrigerator. It's a walk-in fridge, just got 'er installed last week."

"That would be *perfect*," said Mark. We followed Wayne back into the kitchen, which was surprisingly clean. He opened the large, steel door of the fridge and shouted out to the cooks, "HEY – WE'S GOT A PRIVATE DISCUSSION TO HAVE. STAY OUTTA HERE FOR A FEW MINUTES."

The three cooks murmured and nodded, not paying much attention to their boss. We all entered the refrigerator, and Wayne shut the door behind us and turned on the light. My nipples immediately hardened from the cold and I shivered in my skimpy dress. The light was florescent and bright. I wished Wayne had an office. A dimply lit office would befit him well.

"Do you wanna sit down on something? There's buckets under that shelf," he said.

"No, I don't think that's necessary," replied Mark.

"So what do you want?" Wayne asked, his voice slightly irritable. He was staring directly at me though speaking to Mark.

"Well, I've got a bit of a problem," Mark began. "This young lady is on a date with me. She's been a bit naughty. I want to give her a spanking, but I'm just too far from home to spank her in private. I know this is a really strange request, but would you mind if we spank her here?"

My jaw dropped open. I couldn't believe these words were flowing so easily out of Mark's mouth.

"Well I'll be goddamned," said Wayne. I looked at him, wondering if he would kick us out immediately. "You sure you ain't a cop?" he asked.

"I'm not a cop," said Mark.

"And her neither?" he asked, leering at me.

"She's a waitress."

"Yeah, figures," said Wayne. "I got half a mind to spank some of the waitresses here, spillin' every damned thing and takin' thirty minute cigarette breaks. Like they're queens or somethin', right?"

"That's exactly right," said Mark.

"Well, you wanna spank her in this here 'frigerator, well you can go right ahead. Only thing is I get to watch."

My stomach turned over and I looked at Mark, desperately wanting him to take me away from this terrible situation. He looked back at me and smiled slyly.

"Actually," Mark said, "if you don't mind, I think it would do her good to get a spanking from you."

Wayne looked at Mark, then at me, and back to Mark. A broad smile formed across his face. "Well I'll be goddamned," he said again. "This day sure is turnin' around. I had my best cook quit this mornin', and the wife's all angry at me about somethin' stupid or other. If it wouldn't suit me to spank your pretty little girlfriend, I dunno what would. Goddamn."

"All right then. Do you mind doing it here?" Mark asked.

"I don't mind one tiny lil' bit," said Wayne.

"Very good. Darling, please take your dress off and bend over. You can rest your hands on your knees."

In spite of the cool temperature of the refrigerator I could feel my cheeks burning with shame. I pulled my dress off and handed it to Mark. Then I turned towards the walls behind us and bent over. My mind was spinning with the humiliation of being so exposed to this *stranger*. The only comfort I felt was that I knew I'd never see this man again.

Wayne let out a long, low whistle. "Boy, does your girl have a nice ass."

"She does... but she definitely needs it reddened on occasion. It helps to keep her in line," Mark explained. "Have you spanked a girl before, Wayne?"

"Well not just like this, that's for sure. I's smacked my wife good and hard on the ass once in awhile, but only when I'm screwin' her," he said.

"OK. Go on and give this naughty girl a few spanks," Mark said. I cringed, dreading this man touching me more than the pain of the spanking to come.

Two astonishingly light spanks fell on my ass, followed by a quick grope of both of my ass and then two more light spanks.

"Here," said Mark. I looked up to see him holding his hand cupped a little for Wayne, demonstrating. "Try it like this."

SMACK!

"Ow!" I cried as Mark spanked me hard.

Wayne let out another low whistle. "Well I'll be damned," he said.

"Just give her a few like that, and then rub her butt for awhile. Then a few more, and so on," Mark said helpfully. I shot a glare back at him and he grinned at me.

Wayne was a quick student and did just as Mark said, alternating firm smacks on my ass with copious amounts of rubbing and groping. I was cold and ashamed and wanted nothing more than for this punishment to be over. The heat of the spanking only relieved the cold feeling on my ass. I shivered from both the pain and the chill and I couldn't tell the difference between the two sensations.

"I think that's pretty good, Wayne," Mark finally said. I breathed deeply with a rush of relief. "Stand up and thank him, darling."

I stood up and turned around, debating whether I should cover my tits or my bare cunt from Wayne's creepy eyes. I tried to cover both, using my left hand and arm to conceal my breasts and my right hand to hide my pussy. I looked up at Mark and saw his eyebrows furrowing. He shook his head and I sighed, placing my hands at my sides. He wanted to show me off to this man.

"Thank you, Wayne, for spanking me," I said.

"You sure are welcome, girl," Wayne replied. "Hell, I'll spank you *anytime.*"

"Here's your dress, put it on now," said Mark.

As fast as I could, I put on the dress and pulled it as far down over my butt as I could.

"We're going to grab a bite to eat here, Wayne. Anything on your menu that you recommend we try?" asked Mark.

Wayne opened the door and I nearly ran out to the kitchen. I was *cold.* All three of the people working in the kitchen looked up at us when we left the walk-in refrigerator. Had they heard anything? Had they heard *everything?*

I barely listened as Wayne droned on and on about the food. He led us back to a corner booth in the front of the restaurant and handed us both laminated menus. There were windows all around us, brightly lighting our table.

"Well it was sure nice meetin' you both. What did you say your names are?"

"I'm Steven," said Mark quickly. "And this is Kate."

"All right. You two enjoy your meal. Ya'lls welcome back, anytime." Wayne paused before leaving us, taking a few inappropriate seconds to look at me. I shrunk down into the booth.

Chapter Nine
NEGOTIATION

When Wayne left us alone, Mark pulled out his car keys and slid them across the table in my direction. "Go to the car. In the backseat is a knapsack. Bring it here, please," he said. "If you hold yourself like a proud little slut instead of someone who obviously wants to cover herself up, I won't have Wayne give you another spanking before we go."

I swallowed and stood up slowly. I didn't know if I could hide the fact that I was mortified to be dressed like this in public. Mark stood up with me and put his hands on my shoulders. He kissed my forehead and smiled.

"Let your shoulders back. Relax. Swing your hips. Every single man will be watching you with desire as you walk, and some of the women too. Pretend you're a model on a runway. You're hot, Heather, and that's nothing to be ashamed of."

I closed my eyes and took a deep breath. I could do that. I knew I'd never see these people again in my life. On the off chance that I did see them again, they wouldn't recognize me. I could barely recognize myself.

I walked out to the car, concentrating on letting my hips swing from side to side. My stride was long and confident. When I got outside I glanced back towards our booth and could see Mark watching me from the window. He waved.

I retrieved the bag and threw it over one shoulder and sauntered back to the restaurant. A lot of eyes were on me as I made my way back to the booth. I concentrated my gaze on Mark, willing myself to ignore the unwanted attention.

"Good girl," he said as I sat down. He had ordered a pitcher of water and two cups of coffee. He opened the bag and produced a notebook, a printed sheet of paper, and two pens. Handing me the notebook, he said, with a business-like tone, "Make a list of your boundaries. Your limits."

"I... I don't know what I need to include. Like, I don't want you to hurt me... I don't want you to kill me..."

"Err on the side of including too much. Then we'll talk it over." He pulled out a book and began to read, leaving me to make my list on my own.

I had never really had to consider what I didn't want done to me. I sometimes wished *more* was done to me before. With Ryan and my previous boyfriends, there was always mutual respect and consent with everything. Ryan and I didn't have the most amazingly interesting sex life, but we did try things that were new to both of us. And we always talked about it before doing it. When Ryan asked me about anal sex, I balked at the idea forever, until finally giving in once as a birthday present to him. He would never have just... raped my asshole. But I wondered if my previous relationships would have been better if there was an element of surprise.

My rational brain went at full force as I thought about how

absurd this afternoon had been. Dressing like a whore in front of my neighbors, being spanked in a gross bathroom, and then later by a gross man. Mark glanced at me and saw my wrinkled forehead staring at the closed notebook in front of me.

"Don't think so much, Heather. Just open the notebook and write."

I sighed and did as he said.

1. I don't want to quit my job. Work comes first.

2. I don't want my co-workers or friends to know.

3. I don't want to be killed. Or damaged permanently. Or tattooed or pierced.

4. I don't want plastic surgery.

5. No sex with animals

6. Nothing involving children.

"OK," I said, and slid the list over to him. He briefly glanced at it, then handed it back to me. He unfolded a piece of paper with a printed list.

"Listen to this list, and add anything you may have missed or not known enough to consider," he said.

He read the list. I started to feel a little light-headed. Cattle-prods? Catheterization? *DIAPERS*?

"Jesus," I muttered as I continued to add more items to my list. Mark chuckled at my reactions as he explained certain sexual activities I'd never heard of. I shuddered when he told me about waist-reduction: methodical placement of tight corsets in order to permanently make someone's waist very small.

I added these limits:

7. No catheters

8. No golden showers

9. No cattle prods
10. No diapers
11. No waist-reduction
12. No knife play
13. No severe pain
14. Nothing to do with feces EVER
15. No water torture
16. No breath play
17. No animal roles
18. No public collar

I looked at my limits and checked the printed sheet twice. Some things were unfamiliar, others irrelevant. Mark took a look at my complete list and nodded.

"Some of these, Heather, I would like you to put under your 'soft' limits. Meaning that we have an understanding that you are afraid of trying some things, but that we can work on your limits. Others should be 'hard' limits – things that you know you will never, ever want to do or have done to you.

"So let's take a look at your list, shall we?" he asked, not really looking for an answer.

"Number one. Work comes first," Mark began reading my list out loud. "Yes, I know from the little time we have spent together that you have a very busy schedule. Which actually suits me fine, since I work a lot too, though my hours are a bit more flexible. But one concern I have is that you will use work as an excuse to avoid progression as we begin our journey as Master and slave. So, my dear, I have a stipulation to the first 'limit'. You'll allocate at least ten hours a week for me. I *hope* we can manage to schedule more time together, but for the beginning that is the minimum I require. Every Monday afternoon, you will send me a list of at least ten hours that week that you will definitely be available. The hours must be between nine in the morning and midnight. Sleeping together doesn't count. If, for whatever reason, I can't rearrange my schedule to fit within your needs, some weeks may pass where we end up under ten hours. Does this work for you?"

I thought for a bit. Ten hours would be a stretch, for sure. But a lot of my co-workers managed to have relationships. Some of them even had *children*.

"What if I can't manage ten hours one week?" I asked.

"Things happen," he said. "If it bothers me, I may punish you. If you do it often, I'll definitely punish you. If you deliberately avoid seeing me, we will terminate our relationship."

"OK," I agreed. "Ten hours a week. I'll e-mail you the hours every Monday."

"Very good," he said. "Number two. You don't want your co-workers or friends to know about the roles we have in our relationship. That's fine with me, except I do encourage you to be open with at least some of your friends. Drop hints. You'll feel better if you have people you can talk to and be open with. I imagine someone like Rebecca wouldn't judge you too harshly."

"Do you think she knows about that club Dynamic... and what happens there, sometimes?" I asked.

"You could ask her that," he replied. "Number three, you don't want to be killed, and no permanent damage. That's reasonable.

"Number four, no plastic surgery. Also reasonable.

"Numbers five and six, no kids or animals. Those are part of my hard limits too.

"Number seven: no catheters. Heather, this is an example of what I think you should consider a soft limit. Would you be opposed to being catheterized for an emergency medical need?"

"Well, no, but that's just... gross to do it for, um, play," I replied.

"I'm not saying I have a huge catheter fetish. I haven't ever played with them before, and it really hadn't occurred to me to do so before you added this to your list. Part of what I expect of you is that you open your mind up to new experiences, and you let me use your body in ways that please me. I will introduce your body and brain to experiences that shake up your world a little bit. I may push you on some of your soft limits as we grow to know each other better. In the future we will discuss this list again, and you may have gained enough trust in me to remove some of these limits from your list completely."

"OK," was all I could think of to say.

"So I will mark this as a soft limit?" he asked.

"OK."

"Good girl. Numbers eight, nine, and ten should be soft limits as well. Cattle prods, golden showers, and diapers."

"Diapers? *Really?*"

"Again, by suggesting you open your mind to things doesn't mean that these things are my huge fantasy either. I don't think wearing a diaper would hurt you. You're just afraid of the taboo."

"OK," I agreed. "Soft limits."

"Number eleven, waist-reduction. I think that is covered by number three, permanent damage. Number twelve will go under soft limits."

"What is it?"

"Knife play. Do you know what knife play is?"

"No. Would you throw knives at me, like in the circus?"

Mark chuckled. "No. Knife play is just the threat, the danger, the thought that I *could* do something harmful."

"Oh," I said.

"Soft limit."

"OK."

"Good. Number thirteen will not be a limit of yours. You will receive pain from me."

"But it.. it says *severe* pain." I said.

"It does. But you do not know enough about yourself to place that restriction on me. Plus, you have your safeword. One of my goals as your Master is to make sure you *never* need to say that word. So I will do my best to make sure I don't push you past your limits. Did you even consider saying your safeword with Jasmine at Second Skin?"

"No... it didn't really occur to me."

"Well *never* forget that it is an option. You're allowed to end any scene that is happening." Mark paused, thoughtful. "It will deeply sadden me if you ever use your safeword. But it won't be an automatic end to the relationship, or make me mad at you. We'll discuss it if it happens. If you use it during punishment, we will more than likely start the punishment over at a later date. Using your safeword isn't a way to get out of anything that is happening to you. It is a way for you to tell me that you are past your mental or physical limit."

"Well then why are we even discussing *these*?" I gestured towards my list.

"Because, Heather, I want to push you, to help you grow. But I don't want to make you safeword for something that could easily be avoided. Since I know me peeing on you would be too much for you right now, I don't see how it would do either of us any good to have me make the mistake of pushing you past what you're able to take."

"Have you... has anyone ever used their safeword with you?"

"Once. My first slave. I tied her up in a way that made her arm go numb, but I... I was young, and I didn't believe her when she told me how her arm felt. I was flogging her. She said her word. I untied her immediately, and we talked about it. The safeword helped protect both of us. It was okay. It's okay to say your word. When you need to. What is your safeword?"

"Butterfly."

"Good. Do you understand that severe physical pain is not one of your limits?"

"I guess."

"Yes or no."

"Yes, I understand."

"Fine. Moving on. Number fourteen, no feces play. That's fine with me. Numbers fifteen and sixteen are soft limits – water torture and breath play. Are you agreed?"

"No!"

"Water phobia?" he asked.

"No.. well... no, the breath thing. I have to breathe. I can get... I can get a little claustrophobic."

Mark smiled at me. "Don't worry. Breath play will stay a hard limit for now. We'll talk about your phobias and other issues soon. Number seventeen, no animal roles? Couldn't you imagine dressing up as a little kitty for me? Curled up at my feet, or beside me on the couch?"

I stared at him blankly.

"Well?" he asked.

"Would I have to wear a tail... in my butt?"

"I don't know," he laughed.

"Fine. Not a limit."

"Good. Onto your last limit: no public collars." Mark put the list down. "Heather, if I collar you, you will wear the collar with pride. On my part, I will make sure that any collar you wear in public is discreet. Do we have a deal?"

"OK."

"Good girl. Let's order some food."

Mark ordered us both hamburgers which were surprisingly good, and we chatted amiably. At times I had to remind myself that, while the conversation certainly seemed normal, the circumstances were not. In spite of the situation, my outfit, and my bruised and sore backside, I found myself laughing at his jokes and speaking with him seriously about topics relating to current events. He didn't mind if I disagreed with him on political issues or even, to some extent, moral issues. But every once in awhile during lunch, he slid his hand under my dress, reminding me that I was his to touch whenever he pleased.

"All right, Heather," Mark said, pushing his plate to the side and leaning in towards me. "We still have some things to discuss before I take you home today. You say you're a little bit claustrophobic. If I tied you up and trapped you in a small cage for a few hours, would that frighten you beyond what you're comfortable with?"

I coughed, nearly choking on a french fry as he so swiftly turned the topic of conversation into a situation that was bizarre and unreal to me.

"That would freak me out," I responded.

"Freak you out, as in you would feel unpleasant? Or freak you out to an abnormal level of anxiety?"

"I would *completely and utterly* freak out." I said this slowly to be sure he understood.

"And what if I was standing right next to the cage, and it wasn't locked. Would that freak you out?" he asked, adding, "Completely and utterly?"

"No. It would... I would not enjoy it. But it wouldn't kill me."

"OK. Good girl," he said. "Well, this week I want you to spend some of your free time, when you have any, looking through BDSM information on the internet. Try to read a variety of stories and watch different videos. I want you to imagine yourself in various situations, and I need you to tell me if you have any other anxieties or issues that we should discuss. Understand?"

"Yes."

"Furthermore, you will read about every item on the printed list of potential limits and contemplate whether or not you really want to engage in some of that behavior. You will put a star by anything that turns you on, and an 'x' by anything that scares you. Understand?"

"Yeah."

"Good. Now, onto some basic rules regarding our interactions. Whenever it is appropriate, you will address me as Sir or Master. That means when I ask you a question or give you a command, you should respond with 'Yes Sir', or 'No Sir.'

"And, when we are chatting amiably and I ask you for your views on a topic like, oh, I don't know, mangoes, you can use your judgment about how you address me."

"Mangoes?" I asked.

"You'll understand what I mean soon. For example, when we were chatting about the education funding being passed next week, and I asked your opinion, it isn't entirely critical that you follow up your opinion by addressing me as Sir. I want your respect. I *demand* your respect. But I'm also human, and so are you. Not many Master/slave relationships exist without the understanding that there will be inevitable, and actually very enjoyable, interactions as peer to peer. You'll get into the groove of understanding when and how you should address me formally. For certain, when we are around other people in the scene, you will always address me as Sir or Master. When we are around your vanilla friends, you will not."

"OK," I said, feeling a little unsure.

"This is a situation where you can say, 'Yes, sir.'"

I blushed. "Yes, sir," I said softly.

The waiter came to take our plates away, and I shifted uncomfortably in my seat. My ass still hurt, and the bench was wooden with zero cushioning. Mark noticed my movements.

"How do you feel?" he asked.

"My bottom hurts."

"And your pussy?"

"It.. it is wet..."

Mark reached over and pinched my nipple, *hard*, though the dress. He looked at me with his piercing green eyes, and asked again, "How does your pussy feel, little slave?"

"It's wet, *Sir*, ye-ow!" He gave my nipple a sharp tweak and sat back, folded his arms across his chest and stared at me.

"You, my sweet," he began, "will learn very quickly how to please me. Reach down and rub your cunt."

I flushed with embarrassment, glanced around the restaurant, and timidly moved my hand down, under my dress, and rubbed my cunt. Hot, smooth, and *very* wet, my fingers found a rhythm and before long I was, in spite of myself, very close to cumming.

"That's enough," Mark said. I stopped immediately and looked at him expectantly.

What now? I thought.

"Time to go," he announced, reading my mind. He pulled out his wallet to pay for lunch.

"Hey, Mark... erm... sir... I can pay for some things." I had *no idea* what sort of etiquette was expected in this kind of situation.

Mark smiled at me appreciatively.

"Thanks, Heather. I rather like not thinking about who will pay for what, and, since I'm doing OK with money, I don't mind paying while we're together. I do like that you're able to support yourself financially. Your strength and your career are both very attractive qualities to me." He folded some cash and placed it under the bill.

Outside, Mark held my hand on the way to the car.

"Time to take you home," he said. "I have some surprises for you when we get there. Do you need to get anything done for work tomorrow, or can you just relax?"

"I can relax."

Mark smiled. "Good."

He parked across the street from my place and we walked to my apartment, carrying two duffel bags. A few neighbors were out walking their dogs or jogging – I hoped they didn't notice me and my tramp like outfit.

Inside, Mark asked me to show him my bedroom. I let him in, thankful I had taken some time to straighten up before leaving. He pulled a small bag out of his coat pocket and produced five items: a large dildo, a notebook, a butt plug, a small tube of lubricant, and padded cuffs.

"Have you ever had anything up your ass?" he asked.

"Just Ryan. Once, for his birthday."

"Hmm," he said. "Strip."

Trying my hardest not to let my hesitation show through, I took off my clothes, hands shaking. I really didn't want anything going up... *there*. Naked, I stood before him and waited.

Mark got up and dumped the contents of the bags onto my bed. It was some of the clothing he'd bought for me at Second Skin.

"Put these clothes away," he said.

"Yes, sir," I replied and pulled empty hangers out of my closet. I sorted through the pile of shirts, skirts, bras and panties. As I worked, Mark opened every drawer in my room, flipped through notebooks, and looked through anything out on my shelves.

"What's this?" he said with a grin as he pulled my one and only vibrator out from where it was buried, under piles of neatly folded blouses in the bottom drawer of my dresser. I rolled my eyes at him and he tossed it on the bed next to the other objects.

When I had finished, he surveyed my work and pulled out a few items. Three pairs of panties, four bras, and a pair of four inch heels.

"All right, my dear. Tomorrow you go to work. I assume you work through Saturday?"

"Yes, sir. Sometimes Sundays as well."

"Fine. You will wear each of these panties for exactly one day, and each of these bras for one day. On the other days, you will not wear panties or a bra. On one day, you will wear these heels. You will record all of this in this notebook," he said as he held up the notebook, "which you will have with you at all times when you are not with me. Understood?"

"Yes, sir," I said softly. Inside I was frantically thinking through how I would manage to dress for my office without a bra, and what my co-workers would think of the tall 'fuck-me' high heels.

"When you are not with me, you will sleep wearing these," he said, holding up the cuffs. "They're Velcro, and easy to put on yourself and remove. Try it now."

I struggled for just a minute with the straps before managing to cuff my hands together.

"Good. Now remove them, and come bend over my lap," said Mark as he sat down on the edge of my bed. I awkwardly put myself across his lap. He separated my ass cheeks and I tensed up.

"No..." I whined softly, without thinking.

SMACK! SMACK! SMACK! He spanked me three times, *hard*, and I bit my lip to not cry out.

"I'm sorry, sir," I apologized.

"You will relax, *right now*," he said as he spread my butt cheeks and fondled my asshole. I covered my face with my hands, blushing deeply. Even when I let Ryan fuck me there I had made sure the room was very dark so that he wouldn't spend a lot of time *looking* at it.

Reading my mind, Mark said, "You will get very used to me seeing and touching every single part of your body. Remember who's body this is now."

I heard him open the lube and felt a cold sensation as he rubbed my ass with it. Slowly, he began to penetrate me with his finger. I willed myself to relax and take big breaths, trying to open myself up for him.

"That's a good girl," Mark said as he slowly butt-fucked me with his finger. "Who's asshole is this?"

"Yours, sir."

He continued for a few minutes, allowing me to relax and get used to the intrusion.

"Reach back and spread your ass open for me, slave," he said as he pulled his finger out. I slowly reached my arms back and did as he said. Holding my ass cheeks, I spread them wide, exposing myself completely. I felt the cool tip of the butt plug at the entrance of my asshole and winced.

"This, slave, is a *small* butt plug. You will wear it three times this week: twice while you are sleeping, and once more on the same day you wear your slutty high heels to work. Each time you must wear it for a total of twelve hours without removing it. So, if you only plan to sleep for six hours, you might need to bring it to work with you and insert it before you come home to sleep." He applied pressure slowly and I wiggled beneath him, moaning softly. "If you fail to complete the twelve hours and remove it to take a shit, it does not count. If you fail to complete the task within a week, you will be punished. You will record your hours in your notebook. Understood?" With that, he applied more pressure to the plug, pushing it all the way into my ass.

"Owwww YES SIR!" I cried, kicking my legs and squirming on his lap, hoping to relieve the pain I felt in my butt. Mark lifted me off his lap and plopped me on the ground so I was on my knees in between his legs. He handed me the dildo.

"Sit on it."

I stared at him with wide eyes. My ass was so full already, and the dildo looked huge. I wrapped my hand around the shaft and my thumb could just barely touch my middle finger. Placing the dildo between my legs, I slowly lowered my pussy onto it. With the tip inside, I worked my body up and down, trying to let myself adjust to the girth. My cunt stretched painfully around the fake cock as I began to fuck it, lowering myself farther and farther onto the dildo with each thrust. Mark looked down at me with lust in his eyes.

"Close your eyes," he said.

I obeyed. His hand reached for my head and pulled me towards his crotch as I continued working the entirety of the dildo into my cunt. I felt his cock against my cheek and opened my mouth, trying to taste him. He pulled me back and slapped my face with it, not letting me take him in my mouth. I groaned. I wanted so badly to please him.

"Is the dildo inside of you?" he growled at me.

"No, sir. Not all the way yet."

"You have ten seconds to get it inside of you. Go."

I knew the dildo was only three-quarters in my pussy. Somewhat frantic, I fucked the cock harder, willing myself to open up and take more. I spread my knees apart wider. He counted, "Five... four... three... two... one..."

"Aghhhh," I cried out in pain as I forced my pussy to take the rest of the huge dildo and impaled myself onto it. I threw my face into his lap and began to cry.

"How's that feel?" Mark asked me, stroking my hair as I whimpered.

I was humiliated, my pussy stretched and my cunt so full, my asshole stuffed with a butt plug, naked and crying on the lap of the man who forced me to do all of this.

"It hurts so much, sir," I moaned. It honestly didn't hurt as much as feel incredibly uncomfortable and weird.

He grabbed my hair and pulled my head up, putting his cock near my mouth.

"Open your eyes. You're going to suck me off while you fuck yourself."

Opening my eyes, I saw his cock for the first time. I marveled at the fact that I immediately found it beautiful. It was completely erect, thick, the head like a precious mushroom. His balls bulged out from either side at its base, and his pubic hair had been carefully trimmed. I wondered if he trimmed the hair himself.

I took the head of his cock timidly into my mouth. With one hand I reached back and slowly fucked myself with the dildo. I moaned around his shaft as my pussy stretched more to accept the continued invasion. He still held tight to the handful of hair and forced my face up and down, using his hand to fuck himself with my mouth. I desperately tried to gasp for breath when I could as he slammed my face closer and closer to the base of his cock.

"Fuck yourself with the same pace as I'm fucking your mouth. Use both hands."

I fucked myself as hard as I could, trying to match the speed he was setting for me with his cock. Tears rolled down my cheeks as I grunted and moaned. I was sweating and breathing hard, my arms tired and my jaw sore. Mark's thighs gripped my shoulders as he groaned loudly and held my head firmly. His cum hit the back of my throat. He loosened his grip on my hair but kept me in place until I had swallowed his load.

Then he pushed me off his cock and I fell back onto the floor, gasping as my sore ass hit the carpet.

"Touch your pussy, Heather," he said.

I reached down and gasped. My cunt was *dripping,* the wettest I'd ever felt it. I looked up at him in amazement.

"You're very aroused, slave. You must like being treated like a slut?"

"I don't... know. I mean, *no,* I don't, but I don't know... I don't know what's wrong with me."

"You can remove the dildo."

I gratefully pulled the dildo out of my pussy.

"Come lay on the bed," he said.

I willed my legs to help me stand, and staggered up and over to the bed. I lay down beside Mark. He looked at my body. He lazily caressed my breasts, his tender touch such a change from just a moment before.

"There is *nothing* wrong with you Heather," said Mark. "You will have a lot of mixed emotions as you get to know your slutty, submissive side. But you should never feel like you are flawed. Understand?"

"Yes, sir," I replied softly.

He rubbed my pussy, teasing me, smiling as I moved my hips in an attempt to make him brush my swollen clit. He slapped my pussy lightly, making me yelp.

"Eventually," he said, "you will learn to accept what I do to you without trying to make things go your way."

He flicked my clit softly and started rubbing it, slowly. As he quickened his speed I moaned loudly, I wanted to cum *so bad*. He alternated between rubbing my clit and lightly slapping my pussy. I was writhing under him, and begged for release.

"Please Master, please let me cum, please let your slave cum!" I cried.

With that he quickened his speed, slapping and rubbing, and as I was getting close he smacked my pussy hard and said firmly, "Cum *now*, Heather."

I gripped the blanket on either side of my body and arched my back, letting out a guttural moan of ecstasy as I came hard for the second time that day. My orgasm went for nearly ten seconds as he kept rubbing my clit. Finally I collapsed onto the bed, covered in sweat, my chest heaving up and down as I caught my breath.

Mark patted my incredibly sensitive pussy lightly, making me groan. He smiled at me. "I like watching you cum."

Giving me a few minutes to recover, Mark went to the bathroom to clean up and brought back a warm, damp washcloth. He carefully wiped my swollen pussy clean. Rolling me over, he firmly grasped the butt plug and warned me to relax myself, as he pulled it out with an audible 'pop!'. He placed it and the dildo on top of the washcloth on my nightstand.

"You should keep your new toys very clean," he said.

"Yes, sir."

He put on his coat and pulled me up off the bed.

"Time for me to go, my new little slave. Will you remember your assignments for this week?"

"Yes, sir."

"Write them down in the notebook, just to be sure." He pulled me towards him and gave me a long, sensual kiss. I melted into him, not wanting him to go.

"I'll wait for your e-mail tomorrow about when we'll meet next. And," he said, "here's your phone. I added my number. Oh, and, Heather? No pantsuits this week."

He pecked my cheek and let himself out.

Chapter Ten

KITTIES PLAY

I went to sleep immediately after Mark left, both physically and mentally exhausted. The next morning as I was eating breakfast I decided to quickly jot down the assignments he had given me for this week. Suddenly I had a sinking feeling in my stomach.

I had forgotten to put on the cuffs last night before falling asleep.

Taking a deep breath, I noted the transgression in the notebook after the assignments and went to my closet to figure out what to wear. I was irritated that he wasn't allowing me to wear pantsuits. I'd thought twice a week was more than enough to wear skirts.

A quick check of the weather assured me it would be a cool day. This meant I could easily keep the jacket on all day, so it wouldn't matter at all if I wasn't wearing a bra.

I decided to go without bra and panties both, and skip the

butt plug for today. I carefully tucked the notebook into my purse and drove to work. The tight skirt pressed up against my shaved pussy, and thinking about being naked under my outfit had me wet by the time I walked into my office.

I delved into the new case and buried myself in the paperwork until well past lunch. It was nice to forget about everything that had happened and just focus on work. Occasionally when I needed to make copies of something or use the bathroom, I was reminded that I was naked underneath my outfit. My pussy was still tender from fucking myself with the giant dildo. Sitting on my chair was a bit uncomfortable because of my spanking from Wayne and from Mark's wooden spoon. But other than occasional reminders, I cleared my head and didn't think about being a slave.

Around four in the afternoon, I remembered that I needed to email Mark about my schedule for this week. I checked my calendar and wrote him a quick message:

Hi Mark,
Here are the hours that I think will work this week. It is more than ten, so adjust as you want within them. I get to work at 9:00am on Mondays.
Wednesday 7:00pm – midnight
Sunday 2:00pm, free until Monday work.
-Heather

About five minutes after clicking "send" I received a message from him:

Good. In touch.
-M

I stayed at work that night until nearly ten o'clock. It did feel really good to get back into the groove. And my time with Mark had relieved a bit of the sexual tension that had been building inside of me since my break-up with Ryan.

Tuesday and Wednesday went smoothly at work. I ignored the butt plug that I had stored away in the drawer of my nightstand, but remembered diligently to cuff my hands before sleeping. Both nights, after cuffing myself, I made myself cum thinking about Mark and as I dozed off I imagined him holding me.

On Wednesday afternoon I got a phone call from Mark at my desk.

"Are you wearing panties?" he asked, not saying hello.

"No," I replied.

"Butt plug today?"

"No."

"Where will you be at seven?"

"Either my apartment or office – where do you want me to be?"

"I want you at your apartment. You'll answer the door naked. See you soon, slave."

I felt my pussy tingle and glanced over at Erik to see if he had been listening to my phone call. He seemed engrossed in paperwork, but said over his shoulder, "Got another date, Heather?"

Damn it.

"Yeah," I said.

"Cool." He turned back to his work.

I smiled. Erik was very laid back. I was lucky to have him as my office mate; there were a *lot* worse options among my co-workers.

I packed up my things at five, which would give me over an

hour to bathe and get ready for Mark. I took my time in the bathtub, soaking in the bath salt and lathering myself with the bubbles. I washed and dried my hair and put on a very light layer of makeup.

At a quarter to seven I was ready, pacing, waiting for Mark to arrive. He knocked, as usual, right on time. I let him in, hoping for an embrace or a kiss. Not this time.

"Kneel," he said, and I dropped to kneel at his feet.

"Crawl." He walked towards my bedroom. He was carrying a bag and I worried that it would be more toys. I hadn't attempted to use the butt plug since he put it in on Sunday and didn't think my asshole could take anything much bigger than that.

"I brought your outfit for tonight. Get dressed, we're going to go meet some of my friends." He dumped the clothes onto the bed and turned to leave the room. "You have five minutes. You can pick out your shoes."

I looked at the clothes in disbelief. I had tried them on in the store and just sort of rejected the idea that he might have me wear them. The shirt was a tight spandex tank top with holes where my nipples poked out. He paired the shirt with shorts that were so tight they clung to my pussy and would show my 'camel-toe' to anyone who even as much as glanced in my direction. Furthermore, they were *so* short. The bottom of my ass cheeks poked out – a week ago I would have considered them panties rather than shorts.

I pulled on the clothes with great reluctance. I couldn't even bring myself to look in the mirror; instead, I focused on finding shoes. Mark obviously wanted me to look like a slut, so even though I really wanted to pull on a pair of sneakers I knew I should find something that would please him. I settled for the heels he assigned me to wear at work this week. I may as well get comfortable wearing them.

When I showed Mark my outfit and the shoes, he looked me up and down and I could see approval in his eyes. He motioned for me to turn around, so I spun for him, playfully glancing over my shoulder like a model would. Grinning, he pulled me towards him and finally kissed me and embraced me in a big bear hug.

"I missed you," he whispered, holding me.

"Me too." I nuzzled my head into his shoulder.

He kissed the top of my head and announced that it was time to go. Just as we got to the front door, he stopped suddenly, turned around, and looked at me with concern.

"We can't go yet!" he said with urgency.

"Why not?" I was worried something was wrong with my outfit, or the apartment or perhaps my kitchen was burning down.

"You took too long getting ready, slave. Time to redden your ass a bit before we go see my friends."

"What? How long did I take?" I thought I had been quick getting ready. I hadn't dawdled much except to pick out shoes.

"Five minutes and thirty-five seconds. You must be spanked for this." Mark grinned at me as he pulled me over to the couch. I half-protested and half-giggled on the way, understanding this was for fun more than for punishment. He sat down on the couch, yanked down my shorts, and pulled me over his lap.

"I'm glad to see you weren't tempted to wear panties," he said with approval, giving each of my ass cheeks a light spank. "That, my dear, would have earned you an *actual* punishment. For now, you've earned thirty-five spanks for your lateness. Count each one."

Spank!

"One," I giggled. Compared to previous spankings, this was easy. I counted as he spanked me and wiggled around on his lap.

Spank! Spank! Spank! Spank! Spank! Spank! Spank! Spank! SPANK!

"Ooof, ten!" I said. Mark swatted me hard on the tenth spank, and I reached my hand back unconsciously to protect my bottom.

"Hand down," he said. "Even though I'm not *really* punishing you, Heather, I still like watching you squeal in pain. Part of the privilege of a master is to play with their slaves when they want. Plus, I want you to go meet my friends having obviously been spanked. You can stop counting now. Just concentrate on holding your position. If you can, let yourself go and just accept that you are being spanked. The pain will subside then, and you'll enjoy this."

I put my hands in front of me and took a deep breath. Just when I thought this would be easy...

SPANK! SPANK! SPANK! ...

Mark began spanking me earnestly. Rather than focusing on my bottom, he spanked my upper thighs where the red skin would be very obvious under my shorts. I tried my best to accept the pain but it was no use. His spanks were sharp, and hurt so much more on my thighs than they had before on my ass.

SPANK! SPANK! SPANK! ...

"Ohhh god Mark, erm Master, please..." I pleaded softly, trying my best to take the spanking without much complaining.

SPANK!

"That's thirty, Heather. Five more. Go get me something to spank you with. Get back here in thirty seconds. Go!"

I jumped up and ran around blindly, not sure exactly what he wanted me to find. I'm sure there are a myriad of objects suitable for spanking a young woman, but I hadn't the slightest clue about household things. I finally spotted a wooden cutting board in my kitchen that hung on a hook on the wall. It was thick wood, and had a handle. I grabbed it and ran back to Mark.

"Here," I said, shoving the board into his hands. He started laughing.

"WHAT are you laughing at?!" I demanded irritably.

"Well, it's just that... that's going to hurt a bit, my dear. Go on, bend over. I'll demonstrate."

I tentatively bent over, grabbing my knees with my hands.

THWACK!

"FUCK!" I shouted, leaping up and grabbing my ass with both hands. "Oww! OW!"

Mark stood back to watch me hop around the room.

"Someday, slave, I'll need to punish you with something like this. It is inevitable with a long term relationship. Even if I don't *need* to punish you, I'll do it anyway. To help you grow. But you aren't ready for a lot of pain from this board. It is an inch thick and made of hardwood. Even if I spanked you *lightly* it would still pack a punch. And, I very rarely spank lightly. But anyway, bend over, four more to go."

My jaw dropped as I looked at him as though he were insane. He laughed.

"Don't worry. I'll really try to spank lightly. But these four are all landing on your thighs. It will still hurt."

I bent over and braced myself, slightly trembling with anticipation. I bit my lip, determined not to cry out.

"Thwack! Thwack! Thwack! Thwack!"

Four times he brought the board down on my thighs. They burned with stinging pain, and I felt the pain shoot up to my pussy. Mark helped me stand up and handed me my shorts. I must have looked miserable because he reassured me that I could simply go naked instead of wearing any clothing. I decided quickly to pull the shorts on over my reddened ass and thighs, and we finally made our way out to meet his friends.

After less than five minutes of driving, we pulled into a driveway.

"Wait, Mark. This is my neighborhood!"

"I know," he smiled.

"But I can't be dressed like this... not in front of my *neighbors*."

Mark smiled at me reassuringly. He reached over to rub my leg, running his hands over my pussy.

"Trust me, Heather. You can be dressed like this in front of these people," he said. "Heather, tonight you will do your best to behave. You're going to be pushed, as always, and some things that happen will make you uncomfortable. But you must have trust in me that everything will be all right. If you're a good girl, you'll probably make some friends. Please..." he paused, thinking. "Please obey me tonight. I know you aren't used to this yet, but I don't want to punish you harshly so soon. You are so willful, so I have a fear that you might embarrass me. Obey me, and we will both have a good night. Disobey me, and you'll be punished in ways you won't enjoy. Understand?"

I took in a deep breath. All the playful talk and demeanor leading up to now had not prepared me for such a serious speech. If I hadn't been punished hard yet, but still had bruises that lasted a full two days, what the hell would an actual punishment bring? My stomach was queasy with fear.

"Yes, Sir," I whispered.

Mark nodded, and got out of the car. He took my hand, leading me to the front door. He purposely walked briskly so I'd have to jog to keep up. At the door, he gave my bottom a firm squeeze and kissed my forehead.

"Knock," he said.

I knocked three times, praying that whoever was behind the door had earlier experienced some sort of emergency and would not be there to answer. No such luck.

A young, thin Asian woman opened the door. I stepped back in surprise when I saw her. She was completely naked aside from her long black thigh-high stockings and high heels on her feet. She had a red ball gag in her mouth. Her short black hair fell to just below her chin. Her breasts were small, with tiny dark nipples. I looked at her eyes and gasped.

I knew her.

Michelle. From the office. From my law firm. I grabbed Mark, looking at him anxiously and hoping he would see my fear. My actual, huge fear of being discovered by my workmates or friends. He held me tight.

"Michelle," began Mark. "Please extend a nice greeting to my slave, Heather."

"Wwebscosm, Heasthers," said Michelle through the gag. She held the door open and gestured us inside.

Once inside, I looked at her again and saw something in her eyes. *Understanding.* She knew. Michelle was, like me, a young and successful lawyer trying to make a career for herself at a very competitive firm. Apparently, like me, she was also a slave and pervert. I felt so many things all at once and worried for a brief moment that I might need to use my safeword. I looked anxiously at Mark for some sort of help or advice.

"I brought you here to meet Michelle. You could use a friend you can talk to," he said to me softly as we followed Michelle into the house. "Do not worry about being exposed at work. Michelle has been serving her master for nearly a year and has managed to keep her work life separate from her slave life. I'm sure she has advice for you."

We were shown into the living room where Michelle

promptly knelt on the floor by a handsome man. He set down a book he was reading to greet us.

"You must be Heather," he said, standing and extending a hand to me. "I'm Master Stephen."

I shook his hand. Besides Michelle being gagged and naked, and my ridiculously obscene outfit, it was like meeting in any normal social setting.

"Michelle," said Stephen, unclasping the gag and gently opening her mouth to pull out the red ball, "why don't you and Heather work on some dinner for us."

"Yes Master," Michelle responded. She rubbed her cheeks and flexed her jaw a bit. Smiling up at me, she held out her hands. I helped her to her feet and followed her to the kitchen.

"So," Michelle said, pulling on an apron and passing one to me. "This is weird, huh?"

"More than weird. This is insane. I would have never guessed. I just had no idea," I said.

"Stephen told me this morning. Watching you at work today, I did notice a little difference in your demeanor. You seem more relaxed. Before you were kinda..." she trailed off.

"Kinda what?"

"Well you just didn't seem very... *approachable*. I don't know exactly. But anyway, I was happy to hear that I'm not the only slave at the office. It can be kind of lonely. Today, I knew you hadn't been told yet, so I couldn't say anything to you. But I had such a hard day. It would have been nice to have someone I could talk to."

I tried to think if I had even noticed Michelle today. We had barely spoken to each other before, so beyond nodding to her in the hallway, she hadn't left much of an impression on me. I looked at her, and realized I was actually seeing her for pretty much the first time.

She set a cutting board in front of me and passed me a few bell peppers. For a few minutes we just worked silently, chopping vegetables and thinking. I wondered if Michelle could actually be a friend; someone I could relate to and who might understand me. It wouldn't kill me to have a co-worker to eat lunch with once in a while. So far everyone in the office fit into three categories: Helper-bees (interns), people I needed to impress (the partners and my boss), and background scenery (people like Michelle). It wasn't as if I had tons of time for new friends or acquaintances, but friendly conversation would be a welcome change.

"So," Michelle said, breaking my train of thought. "I'm just gonna make a stir-fry. Can you go ask Stephen if we'll be joining them for food?"

I nodded and started for the other room.

"Hey," she called, looking at me over her shoulder. "Make sure you address him as Sir, OK? Oh and ask if we can open some wine!"

Stephen and Mark were sitting across from one another, hunched over a game of chess. Mark smiled at me when I cleared my throat.

"Michelle wants to know if we'll be joining you, sir," I said to Stephen.

"Yes. Tonight will be mostly relaxed," Stephen said, barely looking up from the game. He made a move and Mark cursed under his breath.

"And she wants to know if we can open a bottle of wine, sir."

"Fine. Bring us a glass before you serve yourselves."

I served them the wine and Mark paused, looking up from the game to see my outfit. The apron provided much appreciated coverage. Appreciated by me. It was lost on Mark.

"Take off your clothes if you're going to be wearing that apron. You're way too *covered*." He reached behind the apron and yanked down my shorts, making me suck in my breath as I was reminded of the 'playful' spanking he had given me earlier. He turned me around so my ass was facing Stephen.

"Shirt off," he said.

I removed the apron and pulled off the shirt. Mark reached up and gave each of my nipples a firm tweak before dismissing me with a nod. I scurried back to the kitchen, pulling my apron back on.

Michelle grinned at my new state.

"It's fun, isn't is?" she mused. "You never know what to expect."

She was busy at the stove. I poured her some wine, not feeling a bit useful. My cooking skills were very, very limited. Occasionally I boiled eggs for breakfast or opened a can of soup. Michelle moved around the kitchen with ease, dancing around me as I got in the way. She hummed happily as she minced a clove of garlic, cleaned lettuce, and generally displayed a much higher level of productivity in the domestic goddess realm than I.

"Wanna make a salad dressing?" she asked.

"Um... Michelle... I don't know how to cook," I admitted. I chose not to show my surprise that one would actually *make* a salad dressing. I had a year-old bottle of ranch sitting in my refrigerator at home and had never in my life considered making dressing.

Michelle laughed and handed me a block of cheese and a jar of olives. "Here, slice this to put out for the guys. Stephen will be hungry faster than this rice can cook for dinner."

I sat down at the counter to get out of her way, and arranged slices of cheese and olives on a platter she slid over to me.

"So," I began, "why was today so rough for you?"

Michelle sighed and took a sip of wine. "It was just... Stephen makes sure that he stays mostly out of my life at work. If he orders me to masturbate in the restroom, or wear silly panties, or anything like that, I can't really concentrate on my cases. But today... well, my team finished up a huge case last week. So he knew I could afford to be a bit... out of my element. He told me about you, which was actually really exciting. I was thrilled to find out you're in this lifestyle. But then he gave me a really hard task to do..." she paused, looking a bit pained. She looked at me, and then looked down at the floor.

"What? What did he make you do?"I asked. She looked so embarrassed. I was leaning forward, eager to hear the rest of the story.

"He rigged my panties to hold a vibrator that was set to go off at random intervals throughout the day. And he... he made me... OK, this might freak you out a little," she said, which made me even *more* interested to hear the story.

"He said that every time it went off and started to vibrate, I had to think of... licking your pussy," she said, continuing to concentrate her gaze on the floor. "So *all* day, I was so turned on, with the vibrator and thinking about you, but I wasn't allowed to talk to you about it or even hint at anything or approach you. I couldn't concentrate on anything at all. I finally called Stephen at noon to ask if I could leave work early. I was so flushed and so worried that someone would be able to tell I was aroused or smell my sex. And then he made it even worse. He told me to go to the bathroom, switch the setting on the vibrator to medium and constant, and that I could leave work only if the battery ran out."

"Oh my god," I said, completely in awe and horrified for her. It impressed me how she was able to talk so easily about such personal things. "What happened then?"

"Well, I did as he said. The battery didn't run out until four thirty! I tried to sit at my desk and concentrate... and I wasn't allowed to cum, which made it worse but maybe better since if I had started cumming, I don't know what would have happened. I finally locked myself in the private bathroom and just sat there, making myself calm down, until I finally felt the vibrator weaken. That was around three, and I was able to get some more work done as it kept vibrating on for another hour and a half. When I got home I accidentally cursed about it, which is why I was wearing the gag when you arrived."

"That's *horrible*," I said with sympathy. I stood up and hugged her, and she hugged me back gratefully.

"I didn't know if I should tell you. Does it make you feel weird that I was thinking about you when the vibrator turned on?"

"Well, yeah. A little. But you don't think... they wouldn't make us do that, do you?"

She looked at me, surprised. "Of course," she said frankly. "What did you expect?"

My throat went dry. I hadn't even thought of the possibility that Mark would want me to be with a woman. I had always considered myself totally heterosexual; *men* turned me on, not women.

"More wine?" Michelle tipped the bottle towards my glass.

"Please." I sat down and tried to calm my nerves.

"Hey," she said, looking at me carefully. "It's not that big of a deal. Trust me. I don't know what their plan is tonight. I think they just wanted to introduce us... well, not *introduce* us, but, you know what I mean..."

She checked the pot of rice on the stove and lowered the flame.

Mark and Stephen joined us, done with their game of chess. As predicted, they were hungry. Michelle set the platter of appetizers I'd arranged onto the dining room table and they both smiled in appreciation.

"Take those aprons off while you wait, girls," said Mark.

We slipped out of the aprons and stood close together, waiting for further instruction. Both of the men ignored us and took seats at the table, sipping wine and snacking. They chatted easily; they were both in very good moods. It was obvious that Mark and Stephen had been friends for a long time. I wondered how they had met – if they had known they were Masters before they knew each other, or if they discovered it during their friendship.

"Use one hand to rub your pussy, Heather," said Mark casually. I did as he said and closed my eyes. Somehow by keeping my eyes closed, it felt as though I was beyond where they could see me. Perhaps a fallacy, but it was somewhat comforting. I heard movement and quickly peeked, noticing that Mark and Stephen both rearranged their chairs so that they could have a good view of both Michelle and I.

"Michelle, did you tell Heather about your day?" asked Stephen.

"Yes, Master," she said softly.

"Was Heather surprised?"

"Yes, Master."

"Did you tell her how badly you want to eat her?"

"No, Master."

"Tell her," he said. "Heather, why don't you open your eyes and join our conversation?"

I opened my eyes reluctantly and tried to avert my gaze away from anyone in particular. I settled on staring at a picture of a mountain scene hanging on the wall as I slowly rubbed my cunt.

"Heather," Michelle began, speaking quietly and deliberately. "I didn't say this, but it is true. I really do want to lick your pussy. I want to make you tremble. I want to eat you until you cum."

My throat was dry again and I shook a bit, feeling so vulnerable and anxious. Neither Stephen nor Mark cared to cut through the silence that was making me more and more uneasy. I glanced at them. They were both calm and relaxed, just watching us.

Michelle broke the silence. "Master, may I check on dinner?"

"Yes, slave."

"May Heather join me?"

"No."

My heart sunk. I wanted to get out of this situation, to be *anywhere* else but right here, in front of Stephen and Mark, naked and touching myself.

"She's beautiful, Mark," commented Stephen. "So obviously innocent. So transparent."

"She is," said Mark. "She has a lot to learn. A bit willful. But she wants to be good. In her heart she's an obedient slave. We just need to work on training her mind."

Stephen looked directly at me while he spoke to Mark. "Michelle will be so disappointed if she doesn't get to lick her cunt tonight."

I looked at Mark, pleading with him with my eyes, frantic for help. Mark smiled at me. Reassuring.

"We have plenty of time to have them play. I have lots of ideas for the fun we can have with both of them. It's been awhile since I've had a new slut to share with you," said Mark.

"It has."

Michelle came back, holding a tray full of food. Stephen hopped up to help her set out the dishes on the table, and Mark got up and stood in front of me.

"You can stop rubbing your cunt," he whispered, reaching down to feel how wet I was. He caressed my body, pausing to rub my nipples until they stood straight. He ran a hand up my back and grabbed a handful of hair at the nape of my neck, tilting my head back until I was looking right at him.

"You're a good girl," he said softly, kissing me tenderly. At that moment I felt so cared for and safe. I just wanted to crawl into his arms, to be held by him. He released his grip on me and announced, "Shall we wash up and open another bottle?"

We sat down to eat, once again moving strangely yet fluidly from sexual undertones into normal conversation. Michelle and I chatted amiably about work, co-workers, and the partners at the firm. It was the first time I'd ever had a conversation about work with anyone who I actually worked with. I found out that she had a crush on Erik when she first got the job with our firm, and I giggled, admitting that I had felt the same until sharing an office with him.

When our plates were empty, Michelle asked politely to be excused to clean up. Stephen nodded, and I joined her.

"Come downstairs when you're done. We'll give Heather a tour to show her just a little of what the future holds."

"What's downstairs?" I asked tentatively once the men were out of earshot.

"Toys and games," she said. "Some fun stuff, some... not so fun stuff."

I placed myself at the sink and began scrubbing dishes – cleaning was something I could actually help with.

"Does Stephen... does he ever punish you?" I asked.

"Only if I really fuck up," she responded. "Why – have you

already been punished?"

The concern in her voice was obvious. "No, no," I said quickly. "Well yes. I've been spanked and punished. But not for anything very bad. I don't know. I don't want to be punished for anything bad."

"Some people make a distinction between being 'disciplined' and 'punished'. I doubt you've really been punished yet. You'd know. I was punished for the first time about a month into our relationship," Michelle said. "It was one of the most awful experiences of my entire life. It wasn't so much the pain or the degradation... but it was how disappointed Stephen was. When we play, when he beats me or humiliates me, it's different. But during the punishment, his eyes were filled with sadness. It wasn't fun or sexual.

"Stephen differentiates punishment from day-to-day corrections. If I do something wrong, and it's an honest mistake, he might give me a little spanking or scold me, or make me do something demeaning like write lines or stand in the corner. Or, depending on how he's feeling, he'll just gloss over it. But to be *really* punished, it has to be for blatant disobedience. And the consequences are horrible."

"What did you do to be punished?" I asked with interest. "And what did he do to you?"

"He asked me to do something that was outside of my comfort zone. And... I don't know. I don't really want to talk about it much."

"Oh, gosh, I'm sorry Michelle. I was just asking because this is so new to me. But I understand it isn't my business." I wiped down the sink and counters with a dishtowel and lay it out to dry.

"I know, and I'll tell you eventually. Just try to be good. That is my advice. If you are good, you'll mostly have a nice time." She grinned at me. "And sometimes, you'll have an *amazing* time. Let's go downstairs!"

She eagerly led me to the basement. My mouth dropped when we entered the room. The basement had been converted, not surprisingly, into some kind of sex room. I had imagined this, but I had not expected it to be so beautiful. Long, steel candle holders lined the edges of the room, the candles providing enough light to see quite well. Strings of reddish light went along the tops of the walls, making selected areas even more well lit. I didn't recognize much of the furniture, nor the toys, although a few things I had seen before when Mark had shown me pictures and described certain scenes and supplies.

I looked up at the ceiling and saw about 20 hooks placed along the beams. Along one edge of the room were several chests, all fitted with a thick padlock. Stephen and Mark had one chest open and were rummaging through it, speaking quietly. Michelle grabbed my hand and walked me over to near the chest, where we waited patiently behind them.

"Michelle, tie her to the cross please. Facing out," Stephen said without looking back.

Michelle looked at me, her eyes obviously excited. She led me to the St. Andrews cross that was positioned in one corner of the room. Mark had mentioned this particular piece when he talked to me about bondage and furniture. He said it was perfect for rendering a slave helpless, spread, and exposed.

Too confused and bewildered to protest, I let Michelle secure me tightly to the cross. She tied my arms first, then my legs and ankles. I looked at her for support or advice. She just shrugged.

"I have no idea what their plan is, hun," she whispered, checking each binding to be sure I was set in place.

"Trust me. I'm stuck," I said to her, a bit sarcastically.

"Be good," she said, giving me a quick kiss on both of my cheeks. She knelt a few feet away from me and was quiet, watching the men and waiting with me.

I could hear my heart beating as I turned my gaze to Mark and saw him holding a bath brush in one hand and a flogger in the other. He walked slowly towards us, taking in the image in front of him. I saw his arousal, both in his eyes and by the growing swell in his pants.

Mark held the flogger up in front of me for me to see it well under the soft blue light by the cross. The handle was long and black. Over a dozen long, thin strands extended from the handle. The strands were well over a foot long. I couldn't tell what sort of material it was made of, but the way Mark swung the flogger about made me think it wasn't leather. I hoped it was something soft, like cotton.

"Heather, you'll be interested to know that Michelle has been learning how to use the flogger," Mark said, smiling down at Michelle. "One has to take great care when flogging, spanking, or abusing a slave in any way. It is important to learn how to flog properly so any unwanted injury is avoided. Isn't that right, Michelle?"

"Yes, sir," Michelle whispered hoarsely, her eyes full of lust.

"Would you like to practice a little bit on Heather tonight?" he asked her.

"Yes, sir."

"Get up."

Michelle stood up and Mark handed her the flogger. I began to sweat with fear and excitement. I felt the familiar tingle of arousal building in my pussy and flushed with shame, realizing that this was turning me on.

"May I have permission to touch and flog your slave, sir?" Michelle asked.

"Yes you may, Michelle. The only requirement is that once you start, you will not stop for ten full minutes. Stephen wants you to build up your arm muscle stamina, and as you probably remember, your last attempt for ten minutes was very poor. Stephen, if I recall correctly she only made it through seven minutes without tiring?"

Stephen was still busy rummaging through the chest on the other side of the room. "Yep. She might need some motivation."

Mark turned to Michelle. "Face Heather, ass towards me."

Michelle turned and bent a little at her waist, presenting her butt to Mark.

He gave her a solid SMACK on the ass with the brush. I jumped as much as I could under the restraints and cringed, my heart going out to her. Amazingly, Michelle didn't move a muscle, and only gasped softly in pain.

"Thank you, sir," she said.

"You're welcome. You'll only earn swats with this brush if you slow or stop your flogging."

"Yes, sir, thank you for motivating me," she said politely.

"You may begin when you're ready."

Michelle turned to face me and gave me a quick smile. Instead of starting immediately, she used her hands and gently touched my body. First, my face, her fingers ran along my jaw and down to my neck. I trembled. She lightly massaged my left breast, then my right, pausing to flick my rock-hard nipples. Her fingers drew circles around my naval and slowly made their way down to my pussy. As her nail grazed my clit I involuntarily let out a small moan.

"You're dripping wet," she said, loud enough for Mark and Stephen to hear. She pulled her hand away and I unconsciously tilted my pelvis towards her, hoping for more of her touch. She stepped back and I took a deep breath.

Whooosh — snap!

The sound of the flogger running through the air and hitting my skin registered in my mind a full second before I felt the stinging pain. I bit my lip as Michelle laid into me with the flogger, strike after strike without pause. I wanted to beg her to stop, to give me a break, but I knew if she faltered she would receive much worse from Mark. She moved around me as she aimed the strikes at different parts of my body: my breasts, my stomach and thighs. Occasionally one of the tails swung around and hit close to my pussy, or my nipples, causing me to cry out.

Mark watched Michelle studiously and offered advice.

"Switch hands if you need a break, you need to work on your left hand control anyway. Don't worry about marking her, someone much stronger than you would need to use that flogger to leave any marks. Make sure you don't forget to apply some strokes directly to her breasts."

On that comment, I blurted out a loud, "Nooooo!"

Whoosh — snap!

She aimed well and I cried out loudly in pain as all of the flogger tails landed on my tits.

"Five minutes left," said Mark.

Michelle was sweating and I could tell she was beginning to tire. My body was acclimating to the sensation of being flogged and I felt myself relaxing. Occasionally I cried out when she landed a particularly hard swing or aimed for my breasts, but to my amazement my body began moving into her strokes.

I was enjoying this.

I looked at Mark, who was watching the scene carefully. Stephen joined him.

"She's getting tired," he said.

"Which one?" asked Mark, smiling.

"Mine. Yours is just getting wet."

I cringed, well aware of how obvious my excitement was. Mark landed a quick swat to Michelle's ass with the brush and she cried out, quickening her pace.

"Thank you, sir," she said, and followed up by giving my thigh a hard swat.

"Owwww *shit* Michelle!" I cried, glaring at her for taking her spank out on me.

"Hmm... I like that," said Mark, spanking Michelle again.

Michelle began flogging me with renewed vigor, aiming for my sensitive parts and giving me sets of consecutive swats on the same area of my body. I closed my eyes and absorbed the pain, hearing occasional smacks as Mark continued to motivate her with the brush.

"One minute," he announced.

My body was writhing in pleasure from the pain.

"Please, Michelle... harder," I heard myself begin to beg. "Please... please... please..."

I continued to beg softly until Mark announced that the ten minutes were complete. Michelle dropped the flogger and threw herself to her knees.

"Please Sirs, may I eat her?"

"We'll let her decide," Mark replied. He stepped towards me and rubbed my aching pussy.

"Slave, do you want to cum?" he asked me.

"Yes sir yes, please sir, yes," I managed to choke out, so full of arousal I could barely speak. I pushed my pussy into his hands as I felt him begin to pull away.

"Beg her to eat you, to make you cum. Or you will not cum at all tonight," said Mark.

A flight of emotions raged through my mind. I couldn't beg her... but I *had* to cum. I felt cunt juices dripping down my legs as I writhed on the cross, so full of need.

"Heather, please let me," said Michelle, crawling over to me and reaching up to graze my inner thighs with the tips of her fingers. The moment her hands touched my skin I couldn't hold back any longer.

"Ohh fuck! God yes, please eat me Michelle, please! I need to cum so badly, I want to cum, please," I rambled, begging her to touch me, begging her to eat my dripping pussy.

I felt her tongue on my legs. Starting at my knees, she kissed, nibbled, and licked her way up my inner thighs. I heard myself as if from a distance continuing to beg her, pleading with her to eat me. She took her time, slowly teasing me, making me groan. If my arms weren't secured to the cross I would have shoved her head into my pussy in order to get some release. I was at her mercy.

"Please, Michelle. Please lick my pussy, please lick my clit."

"Mmm," she moaned in reply, blowing on my hot cunt and making me shiver. "Sweet Heather, let's see if your pussy is as sweet as you."

She licked my pussy lips up and down as I struggled, trying to move myself enough to make her tongue touch my engorged clit. She nibbled on my pussy, lightly at first, then with pressure enough to make me gasp. Her fingers played with my pussy hole, teasingly entering just a bit, and pulling out.

"God, Michelle, PLEASE!" I cried out. "This is torture!"

She slammed into me with more than just one finger and fucked me with her hand.

"Yesss!" I responded loudly.

Her tongue made its way to my clit and flicked it. Relief was coming and I cried out in bliss as she fucked me hard and ate my cunt in earnest. My entire body tensed and shook as I finally came, screaming out in pure, raw pleasure.

Michelle continued lapping at my cunt gently and fucking

me until my body relaxed against the bindings of the cross. I looked down at her. She sat back on her heels, her hair tousled and her face wet with my juices.

"She's fun," Michelle said, licking her lips. "Thank you Mark, sir, for allowing me to make your slave cum."

"You're welcome, Michelle. You're a good girl."

Mark slowly released the binds that held me to the cross. When he freed each arm, he massaged it gently, easing out any kinks left from the tension of the flogging and orgasm. He held me as he untied my legs, making sure I could support myself before letting me go.

"Thank Michelle, slave," he said.

I looked at her, still kneeling on the floor, her face happy and content. I could see my shiny pussy juices on her face. Her hair was a mess. Her big brown eyes looked beautiful.

"Thank you Michelle," I said sincerely. I wondered what Mark wanted me to say. "Thank you for flogging me and for... for making me cum like that."

"You're very welcome," she said cheerfully.

Mark said goodnight to Stephen and led me upstairs. As we left the basement we could hear the sounds of sex, and I was relieved that Michelle would be given pleasure. I didn't know if I could ever do what she did, but I would have felt guilty to be the only one to receive so much satisfaction.

Instead of having me get dressed, Mark just wrapped me in his jacket and folded the clothes under his arm.

On the quick ride to my apartment we were silent. He kept his hand on my thigh as he drove, and I closed my eyes, tired. At home, he took his coat from me and told me to brush my teeth and put on pajamas. I looked at myself in the mirror as I got ready for bed. I wore an oversized blue nightshirt. My eyes, though clearly tired, looked different than normal. Post-orgasm bliss perhaps. Happy.

In my bedroom, Mark sat on my bed, his pants off and his cock hard. I dropped to my knees and took him in my mouth, greedily sucking as well as I could, wanting to give him even a small amount of reciprocation for the pleasure he gave me tonight. He groaned with appreciation.

"You were so hot tonight," he said. "Such a good girl."

I picked up my pace, using one hand to grip the base of his cock firmly and the other gently massaging his balls.

"That's a good girl, fuck my cock with your mouth. God, I'm so close Heather.... faster, slave, faster."

I moaned around his cock, the vibration from my mouth sending him over the edge.

"Ohhhh, yes Heather," he said as he came. "Don't you dare swallow my cum. Hold it in your mouth."

He pulled himself out enough so his cum would shoot into my mouth, but not down my throat. I forced myself not to swallow and tried not to gag as his warm seed filled my mouth. He pulled my head off his cock and I felt a drop of cum slide down off my lips. I clamped my mouth shut, waiting for instruction.

"Get into bed," he said. I crawled under the covers as he opened my nightstand drawer and pulled out the cuffs. He cuffed my hands together, and used a tissue to wipe the lost drops of his semen off my face.

He pulled on his pants and put on his shoes. Fishing around in his coat pocket, he produced a small egg timer. He set it on my nightstand, facing away from the bed.

"When the timer goes off, you may swallow and sleep." He leaned to me and kissed my forehead. "I'm proud of you, slave. I look forward to Sunday."

I heard him let himself out and listened as the timer ticked loudly. Breathing only out of my nose, I held the cum in my mouth, trying to stay very still so as not to swallow inadvertently. I wished I could see the face of the timer. Was it set for five minutes? An hour? I spun to look back to check my clock and realized sadly that he had turned it around as well.

After what felt like an incredibly long time, but was probably around ten minutes, with great relief I heard the timer's happy 'ding!' I swallowed the warm mouthful of cum and fell fast asleep, the taste of Mark lingering in my mouth.

Chapter Eleven
OFFICE PAIN

Thursday morning I woke up to the sound of my alarm. I'd slept in, since I usually woke up at least an hour earlier. I took a long, hot shower while thinking through the events of last night. I wondered if Michelle would say anything at work. I wondered if it would be awkward or weird.

A quick review of the tasks Mark had given me for the week made me realize I should make a plan to be sure to leave myself enough time for the dreaded butt plug. Because I had waited until now, I would need to wear the plug for nearly 24 hours straight, only taking it out briefly to use the bathroom. If, for some reason I couldn't control my bowels and screwed up one of the shifts, I might not be able to complete the task. My stomach felt a bit queasy.

I decided to wear the plug at work tomorrow, Friday. Tonight I would wear it to sleep. I shoved it into my purse, figuring that I'd need to have it in by 7:00pm in order to have it in for a full twelve hours before taking a bathroom break and wearing it at the office. I wasn't sure if I'd be able to get out of the office that early, though I would certainly try. I couldn't even bring myself to imagine trying to insert the butt plug at the office.

It briefly occurred to me that although I'd been given this ridiculous set of humiliating chores to complete, the making of the to-do list and checking things off fit in well with my personality. My office desk always had a neat list of things I needed to get done, and I loved crossing off the items. In college, my friends made fun of me for my somewhat manic list-making behavior, and loved watching me add an item to my list just to be able to cross it right off.

I skipped wearing a bra and panties and put on a thick sweater over my blouse to hide my breasts, and I quickly prepared for work. Curious about seeing Michelle, and a bit worried, I made it to the office by nine and set up for the day at my desk.

Erik was already there.

"You look nice today, Heather," he said. "You've been dressing different this week."

Gee, thanks for pointing that out, I thought to myself.

"Thanks Erik," I said politely.

Michelle poked her head into our office around ten in the morning.

"Hi Heather," she said in a sing-song voice. "And Erik. Hey Heather, want to go to the new cafe across the street for lunch with me today?"

I agreed, and we planned to meet at noon. Erik eyed me suspiciously once Michelle was gone.

"What is *with* you?" he asked.

I shrugged, ignoring his question, and turned back to my

work. I was pleased to discover that being without panties and a bra no longer really phased me. As long as I was covered enough that none of my co-workers could tell, it didn't bug me. I kind of liked feeling the fabric of my skirt against my bare butt. The starchy blouse material rubbed against my nipples, making them erect and excited for hours of the day.

I met Michelle at her desk. She was on the phone with Stephen and mentioned we were heading out to lunch, and then broke into a fit of laughter.

"Nooo Stephen, that's ridiculous. Uh-huh. OK." Her tone grew serious. "I'm sorry. Until tonight, love."

Michelle looked up at me as she hung up the phone. "I gotta stop at the bathroom on the way out. Stephen..." she leaned forward and lowered her voice to a whisper. "He says I gotta wear nipple clamps during lunch."

She pulled me into the private bathroom with her and produced a set of small, silver clamps from her purse. With no shame, she yanked up her shirt and bra, her breasts falling out and bouncing a bit, exposed. She began rubbing her dark nipples to excite them.

"So how do you feel, after last night?" she asked as though nothing unusual was happening.

"Good, I think. Surprisingly good."

She held the clips towards me.

"You don't mind, do you?" she said, not really asking. "Somehow it hurts less if someone else puts them on me."

I opened and closed both the clamps, testing their resistance and gauging how tight it would be for her. I wondered if it was even safe for her to wear them for a full half-hour lunch.

"They're not so tight, hun. Safe for up to about forty-five minutes," said Michelle, reading my mind.

"All right, then. Both at the same time, or one at a time?" I asked.

"One at a time. Make sure to place them back from the tip, on the aureola. Hurts less."

I tentatively held her breast in my hand and put the clamp in place. It was the first time in my life I'd touched another woman's breasts. She didn't make a peep as I clamped the second nipple. When the clamps were set, she pulled down her bra and shirt, grabbed her purse, and kissed my cheek.

"Thanks hun. That was easier than I expected. My task wasn't really just to wear the clamps to lunch; Stephen wanted to make sure you were the one to put them on. Let's go!"

I was surprised at how simple that had been for me. A week ago, if a woman had asked me to do that I would have run in the other direction. Today, it seemed semi-normal.

Conversation with Michelle was easy. She wasn't as shy about her sexuality as I was, but she sensed my timidness and steered any conversation that had to do with sex. But mostly, we chatted about other things. I realized with surprise that, even though I'd known Michelle for years, and despite the fact that we spent last night hanging out together completely naked, what I actually knew *about* her was very little.

She told me the strange story of how Stephen and her met. Two years ago, she had an occasional fuck-buddy who supplied her with on-demand sex. She was forward with him, asking for rough sex, pain, and humiliation. Eventually things got a little *too* steamy for him, but he gave her his friend's phone number. That was Stephen.

"Stephen is just very open with his group of friends," explained Michelle. "My fuck-buddy knew that Stephen could give me what I needed. I needed to be controlled. I've always felt that way. Haven't you?"

"No... I don't think so," I responded. "I guess I just never really thought about relationships like that."

Michelle flagged down the waiter and asked for our check. We both had a bit of work to do and needed to get back to our desks. While we waited for the bill, Michelle asked me if Mark was making me do anything at work, like Stephen had today for her.

I blushed. Part of me didn't want to talk about it, but I was so anxious about wearing the heels and the plug to work. Maybe Michelle would have advice.

"Well, for some days this week I haven't been allowed panties. Or a bra." I said.

"Yeah, I figured about the bra since you're wearing that bulky sweater."

"And... he's making me... tomorrow I have to... wear a plug."

"A butt plug?" Michelle offered helpfully.

"Yeah. And for two nights this week as well. So I need to wear it tonight to bed, and tomorrow. The same day I use the plug, I have to wear ridiculous high-heels as well. I'm going to look so bizarre." I was close to tears thinking about it.

"Well, first of all, no one but me will have any idea at all about the butt plug. Trust me. And, the heels... Heather, to be honest, I think you should just go with it. Dress sexy. You have a great body, and you dress like a total prude."

I shot her a glare. "I dress *professionally*," I corrected her.

"No, you don't. You dress like a prude. Don't you see what the other women in the office wear? Don't you see what *I* wear? You don't have to dress like a whore. But you should be proud of your body, and you shouldn't be afraid to wear clothes that make you look both professional *and* sexy."

I thought for a moment. She did have a point. Maybe rather than try to hide the heels or be ashamed of them, I could accept them.

"Maybe you're right," I admitted.

"Sometime we can go shopping together," she said. "For tomorrow, just do your best. Be confident."

I felt better having talked with Michelle. For one, she provided practical advice which would lessen the humiliation I was expecting by wearing the heels tomorrow. Additionally, she didn't bat an eye when I told her what Mark was making me do at the office. For her, it was completely normal.

I checked my watch often throughout the rest of the day, hoping to get out of the office by six thirty so I could get home and put the butt plug in for the night. Working fast, I got through some work I had been avoiding and filled my briefcase with a few things I could do at home. At around six, things were looking good.

And at six-fifteen, Erik walked in to our office, visibly angry.

"The fucking temps, Heather. They have no fucking clue." He slammed a stack of folders onto his desk and collapsed into his chair, frustrated.

Very, *very*, occasionally, office temps cause much more work than they actually do. This was one example. A young temp had mislabeled a few hundred folders with the wrong social security numbers. When Erik pointed out the error to her, she simply shrugged and left for the day.

Erik needed the situation corrected by the following morning.

"*Please* Heather. I know it's a pain, but can you please help me out here?" Erik pleaded. I couldn't say no.

Sighing, and glad I brought the damned butt plug with me to work, I agreed to stay and help.

"Dinner is on you," I said as way of agreement.

"And beer," Erik agreed. "I'll be back in twenty minutes."

So will I, I thought to myself. Erik left for food and alcohol, and I made my way slowly to the private bathroom.

Pulling out the plug, I realized with horror that I had zero lubricant. I searched my purse for lotion – nothing. I wondered if Michelle had lube with her, but remembered she had told me she'd be leaving around five today. Long gone.

I bent over the toilet and lifted my skirt. I felt oddly ashamed to be doing this to myself. Why was it easier if someone else did it to me?

Shaking off my emotions, I slowly parted my ass cheeks with one hand and cautiously felt for my anus with my other.

Yep, it's there, I thought. I spit on my finger and tried to stick it in, wincing a bit with discomfort. I tried wetting my finger with water from the sink. I managed to stick my pinkie into my ass, just up to the first knuckle.

I looked at the butt plug, sitting on top of my purse, and compared its size to my pinkie.

I couldn't do this.

I pulled out my phone and sent a text message to Mark to see if he was there and could talk. He called me a minute later.

"Hello slave."

"Hi... sir. Listen... I'm trying... I'm at work."

"You're at work, and trying," he said. His voice was cheerful; he was in a good mood. "What are you trying, my dear?"

"To use the plug. It's too big. I can't get it in."

"Michelle can do it," he suggested.

"She isn't here."

"Well, figure it out. I can't believe you waited this long; you should have gotten this part out of the way before *crunch time*," Mark said, his voice changing from cheery to stern. "And," he added, "this wasn't *supposed* to be comfortable. Don't you remember how it felt when I slammed it into your asshole last weekend? Don't you remember crying out in pain? Have you felt that pain yet, with your weak little attempts?"

"No, sir," I answered meekly.

"Do you have lube?"

"No, sir."

"Silly slut. You're going to keep the phone on and set it on the ground. Next to the phone, lay out a few paper towels. Set the plug on the towels. Rub some spit on your asshole, and sit your ass down on that plug. You'll be facing discipline on Sunday for failing to do this without help, and much, *much* worse if you can't get the plug inside your ass in the next five minutes. Go."

Hands shaking, I set the phone down carefully and did as he said. Towels first, then the plug. I spit in my hand as much as I could and rubbed my spit all over my asshole, cursing myself for not thinking ahead to bring lubricant. I squatted down, and reached under to position the plug directly on my anal opening. Slowly, I lowered myself onto the plug, breathing deeply and willing myself to relax. When I felt a lot of resistance, I raised my ass up and lowered it again, fucking myself and giving my hole time to adjust to the girth of the plug.

I was grunting a bit and squeaking as I felt the pain of the plug. When I was close to having the entire thing inserted, I heard a knock at the door along with a, "Hey I'm back with dinner! You OK in there?"

I fell backwards in surprise, the knock startling me out of my meditative state. Falling back caused the entire weight of my body to press on the plug and it popped inside of me. The pain along the rim of my asshole as it was pushed beyond what it was prepared for was immense. I bit my lip hard to keep from crying out.

"I'm coming, Erik, just give me a minute," I said, irritated. Had no woman in his life ever taught him *not* to interrupt people when they are in the bathroom?

Picking up the phone, I could hear Mark chuckling.

"I'm done."

"I thought you might be," he responded.

"Thank you for your help, sir," I said, trying hard to be respectful.

"You're welcome, slave." He hung up.

I straightened out my skirt and blouse and tried hard to adjust to the intrusion of the plug. Glancing at my watch, I realized I had been in the bathroom for over a half hour. No wonder Erik had come knocking.

Every step I took back to my office was forced as I tried to make sure I was walking normally. It felt like I had to use the bathroom, but not. The sensation was strange. After the initial pain of the entry had dissipated, the plug only caused minor discomfort. Whenever I moved at all I was reminded of the butt plug, and that I was wearing it for Mark. My Master.

Thankfully, Erik didn't ask me why I had taken so long. He had spread out all of the folders in stacks on the floor in between our desks and was busy going through them, one by one. He waved me down to join him. I inwardly cursed Mark for taking away my pantsuits, as sitting on the floor in my skirt proved more difficult than it should have been.

Erik handed me a bag of take-out.

"I got you red curry. Your fave. *And*," he gave a theatrical pause, "I bought us some cheap beer." He passed me a beer, looking apologetic. We always feel bad when one of our cases causes a co-worker extra work. With everyone so busy all of the time, every precious hour means a lot. But I didn't mind helping him, and knew that I could always count on him when I needed a favor.

"Thanks Erik," I said enthusiastically. I really did love red curry. "And don't worry. I don't mind doing this. I could use some brainless work right now, actually."

He nodded appreciatively, and as an afterthought commented, "Which makes you wonder, really, who the hell is hiring these temps and interns who can't even do a fucking *brainless* task. God that girl irritated me today. She should be fired and banned from any future temp work. Ever."

"Yeah, or spanked into good behavior," I commented, not thinking.

Erik laughed. "That was pretty funny. You know, you taking that week off was good for you, Miss Workaholic."

I grinned.

Erik and I spent the next hour and a half fixing the errors in the files, sipping on beer, and taking bites of Thai food. We didn't talk much, except a comment here or there, until Erik, who had downed an entire six-pack, broke the silence.

"So, who is he?"

I paused. *Who is he?* Did I really know who he was, besides my Master and a guy who 'invests'?

Yes, I supposed I did know.

"He's a really good person. Caring, intelligent. Careful." I turned to look at Erik directly. "I don't really know what to say about him. But I'm more *myself* with him. Which, evidently, is helping me be more myself at work. You've really noticed a change?"

"Of course. You smiled before, but now it's different. It's like a 'happy' smile instead of a polite smile. And you're dressing different... kind of. Except for your shirts. And you, with Michelle today. It seems like you actually are friendly with someone." He passed me another beer and a big stack of files.

"Yeah. I guess Mark is helping me remember what it is like to connect with someone. And that makes me want to connect with a few more people as well. Like, right now," I said, smiling at Erik and cracking open the beer.

"No kidding, a month ago and you'd have been cursing me under your breath."

"Hey!" I said, semi-defensively and giggling.

We got back to work and finished fixing the problem well before ten. Chatting with Erik made me forget about the butt plug, and I was actually happy the temp screwed up. It gave me a chance to connect with my office mate in a friendly way, and for that I was grateful.

The next morning, I woke up early and in a good mood. I knew today was the day of wearing the heels and the plug all day at work, but I also knew it would be OK. Talking with Michelle during lunch and the friendly banter with Erik about the change in my personality over the last few weeks filled me with confidence. At exactly seven, I slowly pulled out the butt plug, wincing a bit as the bulge once again stretched my anus more than was comfortable. I cleaned it and set it aside as I showered, made coffee, and microwaved last night's leftovers.

As I stood in front of my wardrobe I thought about what Michelle had said about my prudish choice in clothing. Since I couldn't wear long pants to hide the high-heels, I might as well enjoy looking sexy and stylish. I picked out a gray skirt that went to just above my knees and a tight, navy blouse that cut nicely along the curves of my waist and hips. Happy that I saved a bra and panties for today, I picked out a matching set. Pink and a bit lacy, the panties were a thong that would make my butt plug seem more secure, and the bra provided good support for my B-cup breasts.

I studied myself in the mirror, and unbuttoned the blouse

until just a tiny bit of cleavage was visible. Tucked in, the blouse and skirt combination looked quite smart, professional, and sexy. Glancing at my watch, I realized it was time to get the plug back in. Easier this time, and with lube, I didn't dawdle or balk at the pain and just worked with it until it popped into place.

As I strolled into the office I kept my face relaxed, my shoulders back, and tried my best to walk with total confidence. A few heads turned to watch me pass their offices or desks. I popped my head into Mr. Richards' office to see if he needed anything. The smile on his face when he saw me was classic.

"God damn it Heather. I'm so glad you took a week off," he said, his tone a bit amused. "I just left a few files on your desk. Are you working this weekend?"

"Tomorrow, of course. On Sunday I can come in the morning if you need me to. I think I'm doing pretty good with my work-load though."

"Pretty good? Your productivity has been impressive this month. Also, Erik mentioned that you helped him for a few hours last night. I fired that temp, by the way. Take Sunday off."

I was happy to hear that he was impressed with me. And I was even *more* confident that he liked the change in my appearance. When Mark first assigned me to wear skirts and heels, the only conclusion that I could think of was to try to dress myself down so I wouldn't look like I was trying to be slutty or sexy. Now, I felt *classy and sexy*.

Erik was gone most of the day for his case, and Michelle just stopped by once to check out my outfit and say hi. I worked hard, occasionally making excuses to walk to the copy machine or check in with co-workers, showing off my new look for those who hadn't noticed yet. When Erik arrived in the afternoon, he let out a low whistle.

"Lookin' good, Heather. Hot date tonight?"

"Nope. Just wanted a change," I replied.

I caught Erik glancing over in my direction several times as he went through his case files at his desk. All of the extra attention and my renewed confidence, combined with the reminder of the butt plug still stuck in my ass, was making me incredibly turned on. I focused on my work as much as I could until the clock hit six; the official hour that most of the firm agreed it was acceptable to leave for the day, even though a lot of us stayed later. I packed up my things and drove home, barely stopping myself from touching my cunt while driving.

At home, I made myself come three times, crying out loudly with each orgasm. On the third round, I noticed I had worn the plug for a full twelve hours. I lay on my stomach, arched my back and pulled out the plug as I rubbed my clit. The butt plug stretching my asshole threw me into another climax.

Collapsing onto the bed, I felt a bit devious and sent Mark a text message to say what I had just done.

A minute later, I received a message back: "Good girl. No more cumming until I see you on Sunday. 2 pm at office or home?"

I smiled, and texted back: "home. Not going to work, can see u earlier"

"Wear something pretty. I don't know when I'll arrive."

Chapter Twelve
A BINDING

Saturday went fine at work. I didn't wear panties, and didn't even think anything of it. I wore the butt plug for the last time Saturday night; each time the insertion and removal became easier.

Sunday morning I stared at my closet and contemplated what Mark had meant by 'pretty'. If we were going out, I'd want to be clothed appropriately. But if we were staying in, or if he had something planned, he would want me to wear something sexy and revealing.

I decided on a short blue skirt that flared at the bottom. Twirling around in front of the mirror, the skirt rose up and I could clearly see my ass and pussy lips. Panties would be important.

I chose a white lacy pair that covered me up, and pulled on a white tank top. The tank top was tight enough to provide support for my breasts, and was just see-through enough to show the outline of my nipples.

Minimal makeup and a pair of sandals later, I was ready to go by nine. I checked to be sure I had recorded my tasks in the notebook and plopped myself in front of the computer. Mark had requested that I do some research about BDSM, which I hadn't gotten around to doing. I didn't know how much time I had but I could try to learn at least a bit before he arrived.

The 'research' proved to be a beneficial distraction. Instead of being nervous about Mark's arrival, I became completely engrossed in reading through erotic stories, browsing photos, and watching videos. Some of the stories were arousing while others frankly grossed me out. The fictitious tales of actual slavery or non-consensual sex made me shudder. After awhile, I switched to blogs, and found a few interesting accounts of other Master/slave or Dominant/submissive relationships. I kept the list Mark had given me of limits to consider by the computer, occasionally pausing from the porn to star or mark an x by particular items.

A firm knock on the door made me jump. I realized with surprise that my hand was unconsciously rubbing my cunt, which was *very* wet. I ran to the door and called out, "Just a sec!" I hoped to run for a change of panties before answering.

"Open the door, *now*," was the firm response from the other side. Fuck.

Mark stood outside, dressed more casually than normal. Simple khakis and a linen shirt. He looked beautiful. I let him in and stood at attention, waiting for his direction.

He spun me around, taking in my body, before pulling me towards him for a kiss. He closed the door and pressed me up against it, a hand finding its way to my breast as he thrust his tongue into my mouth. It was not a tender kiss. His other hand made its way up my skirt and I squirmed underneath him, whining, knowing that he'd find my pussy sopping wet.

His hand pulled my panties aside and without warning he thrust two fingers up my slit, making me grunt around his tongue which was still invading my mouth. He stopped kissing me and grabbed the nape of my neck, forcing me to look him in the eyes while he finger fucked my pussy in earnest.

"Who's cunt is this, my little slut?" he asked, his voice husky. I felt his hard bulge on my belly.

"Y.. yours, sir," I managed to gasp, barely able to speak with him pounding me so hard.

"I love that my cunt is wet and ready for me."

He took his fingers out of my pussy and shoved them in my mouth, holding them there as I tried hard to suck them clean. Keeping a firm hold on my hair, he dragged me over to my couch and threw me over the back. My skirt flew up, revealing my panties which he promptly tugged down to my ankles. He spread my ass cheeks roughly and I felt his hard cock on my slit. I moaned under him, silently begging him not to fuck my ass this way.

"Tell me to take you however I want," he commanded, smacking my ass hard.

"Please, Master, take me how you wish, fuck me how you want," I said. With that, he slammed into my pussy and began fucking me hard as I grunted underneath him and tried not to cry out. His thighs crashed into my butt over and over.

I began to understand that he was using me, not for my pleasure but for his. Knowing this I stopped trying to wish him to go slower or ease up a little on me. Instead I encouraged him with my voice, begging him to fuck me.

"Oh Master, please fuck me, fuck your little whore," I moaned. "Fuck her so hard, slam her tight pussy."

With that he climaxed, groaning and slowing his pace.

"Good girl, slave," he said as he pulled out, leaving my cunt empty and still dripping wet. He lifted me off the couch and pushed me to the floor. "Crawl around and get your things. Your notebook and purse. Whatever else you'll need for tonight and tomorrow morning. You won't be back here before you go to work."

I obeyed and crawled around my apartment, my ass still exposed and my panties at my ankles. I gathered clothes for work, my briefcase, purse, and the notebook. Mark rummaged around my closet and put some of my clothing into an overnight bag. He added the things I had gathered as well and zipped it up.

"Get up and take those panties off, slave," he said, and I scrambled to my feet. "Give me your keys."

I handed him keyring which had keys to my car, office, and apartment. He grabbed my arm and escorted me out the door, locking it behind us. At his car, he placed the bag in his trunk and grabbed a pair of padded handcuffs from a different bag. He cuffed my hands behind my back, opened the back door, shoved me inside to the middle seat and buckled the seatbelt around my waist, tightening it until I grunted in discomfort.

"Pretty slave," he said, stepping back to look at me. He took his place in the driver's seat and didn't speak to me as we drove for nearly half an hour, closer to his side of town. I saw him look back at me occasionally and smile. Although I felt vulnerable and nervous by his roughness, I knew I was safe. I didn't ask where he was taking us and he didn't share anything with me.

He finally pulled into a nearly abandoned strip-mall. Unbuckling me, he yanked me out of the car, not bothering to be gentle. He closed the doors and turned towards a hardware store. I waited, watching him walk away.

"Follow me, Heather," said Mark, not looking back to

check that I obey.

"Mark..." I protested. I couldn't let people see me with handcuffs on. He turned around and stared at me icily.

"You need to begin to recognize that you do not have options, Heather. You do not get to choose whether or not you *want* to do this. When you get a command from me, you obey, or you are punished. Hesitation is nearly as bad as refusal."

I felt my face grow red. He was right. I ran to catch up with him.

The store was cold from the air-conditioning and I looked down to see my hard nipples under my tank top. Mark went straight to the customer service counter and pulled out my keys.

"I need one copy of each of these, please," he said to the young man behind the counter. I tried to stand casually, so it would just appear as though I was holding my hands behind my back. The man's eyes looked at me, pausing briefly as he saw my tits, and then back to Mark.

"Certainly," he said.

"We'll be back in a few minutes," said Mark. I followed him closely, not looking back to see the clerk's expression as we walked away. Mark walked with purpose until he found the section with ropes, chains, and cord. He examined the rope carefully before looking around for an attendant.

"Go find someone to measure out some of this rope for me," he said.

I was mortified. My entire face, neck, and chest felt hot as I looked around to try to find an employee. I finally spotted a middle-aged guy and asked him for help.

"Sure thing, lady," he said brightly. "Lead the way!"

Oh, god, I thought. "Oh, no sir. I get lost in stores like this. My friend is in the section with all the ropes and things, do you know where that is?"

"Um, yeah," he said, looking at me strangely, and led the way, allowing me to hide the cuffs from him. The section was just an aisle over; it would be impossible me to get lost unless I was a complete moron.

The man helped Mark measure out a few yards of rope. I stood quietly, sure to keep my back facing away from them and any other customers or employees. Mark thanked the man and I jumped in front of him, making sure his body blocked view of my back as we made our way to the front of the store.

He retrieved the keys from the young man and went to pay. I saw a few people give me funny looks, and I looked down at the floor as I waited for Mark to finish.

Before opening the car door in the parking lot, Mark pushed me against the side of the car that was facing away from the store. He pulled the rope out of the shopping bag and yanked up my skirt. I moaned out of embarrassment, hoping no one was watching us.

"Don't worry slave, it just looks like we're talking from inside the store. From the rest of the parking lot, however..."

He wrapped the rope around my waist. I winced; he had selected a very rough rope that hurt when pulled taught against my skin.

"Heather, my plan was to get the keys and leave. The rope is your addition, for your hesitation to follow me into the store. Understand?"

"Yes, Master," I whispered, ashamed. He kicked my legs apart and pulled the rope through them, winding it around the belt he had created with the first tie. He pulled it tight and I gasped in pain as the rough rope bit into my tender pussy. Giving it another yank and chuckling at my distress, he looped it back through to the front and pulled it tight again. With each tug I felt more pain and tears formed in my eyes. He continued until he ran out of rope, and tied it again at the waist.

"In you go," he said, opening the car door. He didn't shove me inside as before. Instead, he stepped back to watch me awkwardly sit and scoot into place. I winced with every movement. Sitting down pulled the rope even tighter against my cunt. One of the turns of rope was rubbing directly against my clit. The pain was immense. He buckled me in and spread my legs apart to look at his rope work.

"What's funny, Heather, is that if you are a true pain slut, this will get you wet. Your wetness will cause a bit of lubricant, easing the pain just the slightest amount. The lubricant will also make the removal less painful. If pain doesn't turn you on so much, you'll get no relief. When I remove this, it will hurt even more as your skin will stick to the rope a bit. Isn't that interesting?"

"Yes, sir," I said, a tear finally sliding down my cheek.

I don't know how long we drove. It felt like forever to me as I tried not to think about the pain of the rope. He parked the car on the side of the street.

"We're going to go have lunch at the club where we met," he said.

"But that's like, ten blocks from here," I replied, confused.

"I know."

He wanted me to have to walk.

I struggled out of the car and took a few steps, squeaking in pain as the rope rubbed against my clit and my anus. He had wound it *so* tight.

"Master, this hurts so much," I said, hoping he would feel sorry for me and drive us directly to the club.

"Yep. Hmm, look, I don't want to listen to you whine. Maybe you can walk alone. I'll meet you there."

"What?" I spun to him, scared. He turned me back around

and unclasped the cuffs, freeing my hands.

"I said, I'll meet you there. I'm going to drive. When you get there, just tell the host you're meeting Mark upstairs. They aren't open to the public this time of day, so I'll let them know you're on your way. Don't be too slow; you've put me in a bit of an impatient mood," he said, and turned back towards the car.

I watched in disbelief as he pulled away, leaving me with nearly a mile to walk. The car disappeared around the corner and I knew I was stuck.

"Fuck," I muttered under my breath. I inhaled deeply and began walking. He wouldn't leave me here if he didn't think I could handle this.

I knew I looked awkward and I ignored the looks of people who passed me. Whenever I felt the slightest bit of wind, I grabbed the edges of my skirt with both hands to be sure I wouldn't be left exposed to anyone who was watching.

After a few blocks, the pain became less intense, and though my clit and asshole were very sore, I could walk without huge discomfort. Finally, when I saw the club, I quickened my pace and with a sigh of relief I reached the front door.

The waiter was outside. He smiled at me when I hobbled to him.

"Welcome back," he said. I thought I heard the slightest hint of sarcasm.

"Thank you," I replied.

"I've been instructed to take your clothing. Except," he paused, "the rope."

I looked around to see if anyone was watching, and pulled off my tank top, my breasts bouncing as they were released from the tight fabric. He watched me intently, not offering the slightest bit of privacy. I wiggled out of my skirt, and handed him both items.

"Very well," he said. "Master Mark is upstairs. You may enter."

I rushed inside, eager to be protected by walls from any casual passerby. I awkwardly hobbled upstairs, getting amused looks from a group of workers getting ready to open the club later that night. Ignoring them, I looked around for Mark. I couldn't find him, but I saw the overnight bag sitting at one of the tables. I went to sit and wait for him.

A waitress came over and set a bottle of water on the table. I thanked her and guzzled half of it on the spot.

"He'll be back soon," she said. "He wants to know if you're hungry."

"A bit," I replied.

"Fine. You'll have lunch here, then." She smiled at me, not visibly reacting at all to the rope or my nakedness.

Mark came back a few minutes later. He moved the bag to the floor and looked through it until he found the notebook in which I'd recorded my tasks.

"So, darling," he said, "how was your walk?"

"Fine," I squeaked. I shifted uncomfortably, desperately wanting the rope off and wishing I had clothing to cover up. There were several employees milling about, all of whom were appropriately dressed. I felt embarrassed.

"Stand up," said Mark.

I stood up and he grabbed the belt of the rope binding, pulling me to him. I cried out softly as his tug increased the pressure on my cunt. He roughly moved aside enough rope to touch my pussy.

"Hmm," he said. "You're kind of wet, you horny little slave."

I looked down at the ground, staring at my feet.

"Would you like the rope removed, Heather?"

"Yes, sir," I responded quickly.

"Say, 'If it is your wish, Master,'" Mark instructed sternly.

"If it is your wish, Master."

"Good girl. Go find someone who will remove it for you. Stay where I can watch."

My heart sunk. He was humiliating me to my very core. Beyond doing things *to* me, Mark was making me be proactive with perfect strangers. I looked around the club for anyone who might be sympathetic and saw the waitress who brought me the water. She was setting out wine glasses on a several tables grouped together.

I padded over to her painfully. She looked up and smiled as I approached.

"Can I help you with something?" she asked politely.

"Um, yeah. Yes. Can you do me a really big favor?" I looked back at Mark who was watching with a smile from across the room.

She glanced over in the direction of my gaze, and then back at me. "Of course, hun. What is it?"

"Can you um... take the rope off of me?"

She looked back at Mark. This time I followed her gaze, and saw Mark give her a slight nod. Consent.

"Sure," she said. "I'm Isabelle, or Belle. You must be Heather."

I nodded. She started working on the knot to remove the rope.

"Damn it. Mark always ties a tight knot," Belle said. She grabbed a fork from the table she was setting and used the handle to loosen up the knot. As she pulled the rope through my legs, I gasped, now understanding why Mark warned that it may hurt with removal. I knew I was slightly turned on and wet; I couldn't imagine how it would feel if I were dry.

"It's all right, don't worry," she said, acknowledging my pain. "This will go pretty quick."

She worked fast, unthreading the rope from my cunt, ignoring my gasps as best she could.

"See?" she said, looking at me triumphantly and holding up the rope. "All done!"

I decided to dismiss the fact that I was the only naked person in the room, and rubbed my sore pussy, trying to ease the pain. My cunt felt raw from the time spent against the rough rope.

"Thank you, Belle," I whispered, taking the rope from her.

"No worries. You found a good one, you know," she said, going back to setting the glasses out.

"What? You mean Mark?"

"Of course. He's a dream for most subs who come here," she said, looking up at me. "You're lucky."

I went back to Mark's table, not *feeling* especially lucky. My pussy and asshole were rubbed raw by the rope. Even now that it was gone a dull pain remained. But I knew in my heart she was right. Mark was teaching me. I had messed up. I deserved the pain he gave, and that realization made my heart sink in my chest. I suddenly felt horrible for making him discipline me.

As I got to the table I saw Mark nod at a different employee, who walked away with my chair.

"Thank you for allowing her to remove the rope, Sir," I said softly, handing him the rope. "I'm sorry I hesitated to follow your command. I will do better in the future."

"Good slave," Mark said, looking up at me, his face full of pride. My heart leaped seeing his approval. "You will improve, everyday. You'll become a near-perfect slave for me. And whenever you commit a transgression, I will be there to help you correct yourself." He picked up my hand and kissed it softly.

Just then, the waiter returned with a small pillow and placed it on the ground by Mark's chair. I looked at Mark, and he nodded at me. I understood I was to kneel, and I took my place on the floor by his side.

He flipped open the notebook and read through my careful recording of my tasks for the week.

"How did it feel to have your little asshole plugged at work, slut?" he asked me.

I blushed. "It... was OK. I got used to it."

"And wearing the heels and the skirts?"

"I... I kind of liked that. I mean... it opened up my mind a little about what I can wear. My boss liked it too. And my office-mate."

"Both men, I assume?"

"Yes, sir."

"Interesting."

Belle came to our table with two plates of food. She placed one in front of Mark, along with a set of silverware, and one on the floor in front of me. With no silverware. It was a shallow bowl filled with what looked like brown rice, pieces of chicken or pork, and steamed spinach.

I looked up at her, then Mark, unsure. "Bon apetit," she said before fluttering away.

"Take this," Mark said, handing me a hair tie. He picked up his fork and began to eat his food.

I stared at the food on the floor in front of me, confused.

"You won't be speaking or doing anything until your plate is finished. If you use your hands to eat I'll whip you in front of everyone here. So, dig in, my little puppy."

I pulled my hair back, secured it behind my neck and bent down to eat. The food was bland but I was famished. I ate a bite and looked back to Mark for reassurance. He was ignoring me completely, instead concentrating on a book he had open beside his plate. I faced my bowl and tried, with some success, to forget that there were staff members doing things around us. But part of me imagined what they must be seeing: me, on all fours, crouched over a dish and eating like a dog.

I ate fast, wanting this mortifying experience to be over as soon as possible.

"Good girl," Mark commented when I sat up, the bowl clean. He pulled my hair until my face was looking up at him, and wiped my cheeks clean with a napkin. "Almost time to go. Do you need to piss before we leave?"

"Yes, sir."

Mark motioned for Belle, who scurried over to him. "Take this slave to relieve herself. Heather, follow Belle on all fours. Be quick."

He smacked my ass, hard, as I turned to crawl after Belle who was already several steps ahead of me. My knees hurt from kneeling so long, but I crawled as fast as I could to keep up. She led me through a corridor and unlocked up a door.

My jaw dropped when I saw what was considered a bathroom. A small, concrete room, dimly lit by a skylight no larger than a plate. On the ground were two holes, a few feet from each other. I looked at Belle with my mouth hanging open. She shrugged.

"Don't worry," she said. "It's clean. After you go, I'll hose you off over there," she nodded in the direction of the corner of the room, where a small hose was situated over a drain.

"You're... gonna watch?"

"Yep. Some slaves are never left alone here. Go on, he said be quick. Just squat over the hole, like you're peeing outside."

I hadn't peed outside for *years*. I tentatively positioned myself over one of the holes, with a foot on either side. I looked up at Belle, who nodded.

"Can you turn around?" I asked.

"No. Now GO!"

I forced myself to relax my pussy and let my bladder empty itself. I heard the sounds of the pee hitting the bottom of the hole far below me and squeezed my eyes shut. Darkness provided comfort and eased my shame.

Finally, done, I stood up awkwardly.

"No. Crawl," Belle reminded me. I crawled over to the corner of the room. She hastily grabbed the hose, turned the knob, and let a stream of water hit my tender pussy.

"Fuck! It's so cold!" I cried out, immediately forgetting my embarrassment as the ice-cold water hit me.

"Hold still, Heather. I have to do this for a full minute."

Goosebumps covered my body. She didn't relent; for 60 seconds she shot the stream of water directly at my cunt. Finally, I heard her turn off the hose and I breathed a sigh of relief.

"Come on!" she said, cheerily. I glared up at her and followed her out of the detestable bathroom, not even bothering to ask for a towel to dry myself. Mark was waiting at the entrance to the corridor. He looked at his watch when he saw us, and then looked at Belle sternly.

"Thank you, dear. Give my love to your mistress." Mark leaned over and kissed her cheek. Obviously dismissed, Belle disappeared.

Mark handed me my clothing and told me to stand and get dressed. I jumped to my feet and pulled on my skirt and tank top. He motioned for me to follow him, and took off towards the lower floor exit.

On the way out, the waiter opened the door for us, his eyes on the ground.

"Heather, I believe you've met young Alex a few times by

now, yes?"

"Yes, sir. Not by name, yet. Hi Alex," I said, hoping he would perceive that I was trying to be friendly.

Alex murmured a quick greeting without looking up. Mark narrowed his eyes and turned to face me directly.

"Alex," he began, "is in a year of service to this establishment. He is still a bit under-trained. Unlike you, my dear, Alex doesn't enjoy being dominated. His year commitment is a direct result of stupid actions he made a few months ago. Right now, you're going to correct him for not greeting you properly."

I looked from Mark to Alex in shock. Alex's face had turned bright red, and his eyes were still boring holes into the ground at his feet. Mark stepped towards him and gently kicked his legs apart. Alex didn't resist.

Mark looked to me and said, "Give his crotch twenty light smacks. Just like this, no harder." I watched Mark firmly, but lightly, smack the crotch of Alex's trousers. Alex visibly winced, but didn't make a sound. I was beginning to understand why Alex had displayed such resentment towards Mark: he was being tortured by him, unwillingly.

I faced Alex and whispered, "Fast or slow?"

He glanced up and I saw a hint of gratefulness in his eyes. "Fast," he said softly, reverting his eyes to the floor.

Mark watched me as I administered 20 smacks to Alex's crotch. He winced with each slap but never moved away. Incredibly, I felt him getting hard as I punished his cock. I finished and quickly stepped back away from him.

"Good girl," said Mark. "Thank her, Alex."

"Thank you Heather," he choked, sniffling slightly. He opened the door, letting us out into the sunshine. I didn't look back, hoping to spare him the further humiliation of being seen with tears.

Chapter Thirteen
THE BIG VIEW

"So," Mark said, ignoring what had just taken place and pulling out of the parking lot. "You made a mistake last week, didn't you?"

"Yes, sir." The cuffs.

"Tell me."

"I forgot the cuffs on the first night, sir. It was a mistake, I was so tired... I'm sorry, sir."

Mark was silent for a few minutes, making me anxious. "And, you did everything else you were told to do? You didn't forget anything more?"

"No, sir, I did everything. I wrote it down, I promise you."

"Well, Heather, frankly... you did better than I expected. You'll wear the cuffs for two hours before bedtime at least once next week as a reminder. But, I'm very proud of you. I know you had to overcome both emotional and physical hurdles this week. You did well."

A tear slipped out of my eye as I felt a huge sense of relief. I was amazed at how happy I was that he was proud of me. "Thank you, sir," I said sincerely. Mark smiled at me and reached over to rub my thigh.

In my contentment I realized I had no idea where we were. Gone was the city noises; we were driving towards the countryside. I looked at him quizzically, and he grinned at me. "We're going to have a picnic."

"But we just ate," I said.

"Not so much a food picnic. Wine, cheese, nature. I know a nice spot. I can't imagine that your palate was totally satisfied with the meal at the club." He winked at me. I opened my window and settled back, enjoying the drive.

Mark pulled in to a small dirt lot and parked. It had been awhile since I'd traveled outside of the city. The green grass, rolling hills, and blue skies made me a bit giddy. I spun around beside the car, enjoying the soft wind and the smell of fresh air.

He saw the brightness in my eyes, and commented, "You like quietness. Tranquility. You, my dear, are not a city-girl."

I contemplated this as he led me up a small trail towards one of the larger hills that surrounded us. On the top of the hill I held back my surprise: the view was astounding. We overlooked a valley. A river ran through the valley, and a small town was situated around it. Beyond the river and the town, we were surrounded by nothing but rolling hills and trees. Forest. It was amazing. The sky's blue color in contrast to the green of the hills and forests was stunning.

Mark slid his hand around my waist, gently pulling me down to sit on the blanket he had spread out. He pushed my shoulders back to the earth and slid his hand up my leg towards my cunt.

"Heather – you are beautiful," he breathed in my ear, making me shiver.

I didn't say anything as he began massaging my body. I was lost in his touch, his dominance. He rubbed his hands up and down my body, under my top, taking time to massage my breasts and ass. It was gentle, 'normal'. I moaned softly as his hands grazed my pussy.

"Mmm," Mark breathed into my ear. "You like naughty *and* nice."

His fingers penetrated my pussy. He pumped them in and out, playing me like an instrument. I was so horny, so ready to be fucked. The scenery made the whole situation even more incredible – outside, the wind flowing around us as he played with my body.

He was gentle, such a contrast to any previous play. Mark ran his hands all over me, pausing slightly to tweak my nipples and lightly slap my cunt. He kissed me, deeply.

I moaned with pleasure, unable to control myself. Mark pulled off my tank top and slid my skirt down to my ankles. "I prefer you naked," he whispered, his words making me quiver. "And I love how easy you are to play. I can make you wet so fast, you slutty little girl."

He kissed me once more, then sat up and opened up the basket he had brought along with him. I caught my breath and used my elbows to prop myself up and watch him. He poured me a glass of wine; a rosé, and looked down across the valley below us.

"Do you see those houses, Heather?" he asked, directing my attention towards the town.

"I see them," I said, nodding. "There are a lot of buildings... is it a town?"

"Kind of."

"Huh." I shrugged, and turned my attention back to my wine.

"It's called Rock Creek, Heather. An intentional community. It's three miles from here and fifty from the city. It's private. Closed to the public."

I looked again and noticed a thin line surrounding all of the houses. A wall. I looked back to Mark, wondering why he was telling me this.

"I own a few lots there, and two houses. One house and some lots on the far side of the river, and a house on this side. I've been a member of Rock Creek for ten years now. The community itself is over fifty years old. Seven hundred residences, and over fifteen hundred residents. Beyond the residents, there are over five thousand members; those who rent homes or apartments, and those who work for the community."

Mark paused to pull out a jar of olives from his basket. He popped one in his mouth and looked at me. "Don't you wonder why I'm telling you this?" he asked.

"Well, yeah. I figured you'd get to the point eventually." I smiled up at him.

"Good girl. Patience." Mark busied himself with setting out a plate of olives, cubes of cheese, and refilling our glasses with wine. He sat for awhile, thoughtful.

"Rock Creek is independent of city law. A team of lawyers is employed full time to protect the rights of members and residents and protect the sanctity of the community. Heather, Rock Creek is comprised exclusively of people in the BDSM lifestyle. Masters and slaves, switches, Daddys, Mommies, submissives, dominants, you name it. Nearly anything goes down there. The houses on this side of the river are reserved for those who want to have families: child-safe and family friendly. The other side of the river is far more open. Public nudity and play are common. Slaves crawl naked outside, serving their Masters. People are free to be themselves and live without fearing judgment."

My jaw must have been near the ground because Mark looked at me and burst out laughing.

"It's not the only community like this, dear," he said, continuing. "Rock Creek is one of many BDSM friendly neighborhoods throughout the world. But, it is the best one I've visited so far. Most are quite secretive, and can only be discovered via personal invitation. Most *need* to be secretive, in order to protect the residents and members. A lot of the people at Rock Creek have jobs and either commute or work remotely, like me. Some of the residents work for the community. With so many people, we have private doctors, pharmacists, teachers, gardeners... you get the point. There is a private police and detective agency to help work out problems within the community and keep things from getting public. There is a law firm." Mark paused, looking at me for my reaction. "Tell me your thoughts."

"I... I don't really have any..." I stammered. "I'm just surprised. That this can even... *exist.*"

"It is odd," he said, nodding. "It has taken a lot of time for Rock Creek to work out its... kinks, so to speak. The founders worked very hard to establish rules and regulations regarding privacy. All residents and members are put through a series of tests before they are admitted into the community. It took me several months to complete all the paperwork needed just to *visit* Rock Creek. Additionally, I spent a full six months to complete the tests, classes, and physical exams required in order to buy property within the community. It isn't easy to get in. I even needed to file a notice before telling you this.

"Rock Creek has a very interesting infrastructure. Certain houses on the border of the near side are set aside, without individual owners, but are furnished. They are for residents who want to invite their family or vanilla friends to visit. The lay-out of the neighborhoods can depend on kinks; there are some residents who are very open to everything, and others who prefer not to be exposed to certain kinks. Some people like to watch, or enjoy exhibitionism. Others want a bit of privacy."

"I thought you lived at your apartment," I said, interrupting.

"I live where I need to be," Mark said.

"Oh." I didn't know what that meant, but didn't feel like pushing for more information.

"Anyway," he said, "The family-friendly side is home to about half of the residents, but the numbers include children. On that side there are very strict rules regarding play in order to protect the young ones from seeing anything inappropriate. On the other side, almost anything goes. But it varies, from street to street.

"The home I own shares a backyard with an entire block of houses. Twenty-five homes all together surround my neighborhood. The backyard is beautiful, equipped with pools and hot tubs, outdoor bondage furniture, and what we call the 'play-pen'. My home is in a particularly *open* neighborhood. The last time I slept there I fell asleep listening to my neighbor getting whipped with a belt outside, in front of a crowd." Mark turned to me. I was still speechless, taking in this information, wondering what he expected of me.

"She was being whipped," he continued casually, "by one of our paid employees. She had been caught speeding near her house by our police department. Just a bit over the limit, but she has agreed to take public punishment for any community crimes. This is in lieu of regular speeding tickets. Normal societal law still generally applies, but the consequences are much different. Every member who commits a community crime is given a choice between punishment by the community, or punishment by the state. Most choose to be punished as the community decides."

"Have you ever been punished?" I asked.

"No, my sweet. If I was caught speeding, I'd just pay the ticket fine. I'd rather not be whipped in public. You, however, would take the beating." He paused to tickle my side, teasing me.

"Masters usually set up the rules for their slaves. If you were permitted the privilege of driving within Rock Creek, you'd certainly take the public beating over paying the fine. Part of your agreements on entering the community would be signing rights of your choices in these types of matters over to me.

"I've spoken with the law firm. They are interested in you. But, we obviously need more time together before coming to any agreements about this. If I decide to collar you, Heather..." he turned to face me, "we'll begin the procedure of getting you accepted here as a resident at Rock Creek, and interviewing with the firm. Until then, we will begin the process of basic Rock Creek membership. Membership isn't treated lightly, so the process will take some time. I'd like for you to be able to visit and understand more about the place before you make any decision at all."

"I can't," I said, protesting. This was completely crazy. I couldn't leave my job. I was at an incredible firm, I couldn't give up that opportunity. "I can't do that, Mark... erm.. Master. I can't quit my job, I can't move... this is... it is just..."

"Shh," Mark said softly. "You, slave, aren't *allowed* to come to any conclusions yet. You don't have enough information. Everything takes time. Just look at how far you've come in the last month." He brushed my hair behind my ears gently, and looked at me thoughtfully. "I brought you here to plant the idea in your head, to let you think about Rock Creek a bit and imagine what life might be like if you were to apply for residency. I feel..."

I looked up as Mark's voice trailed off, and his gaze moved towards the houses in the valley. He slowly took a sip of wine before continuing.

"Heather, I feel a connection with you. It's different than the feelings I get at the beginning of any new relationship. It's deeper than that. I don't know why, but when I first saw you at the club I felt drawn to you. I felt like you needed me, actually. You looked... lost, in a way. Certainly not helpless or anything like that, but you just looked incomplete. You're so smart and so talented. I can see so much potential in you. I've only known you a short while but I already feel like I own you. You're mine."

I sucked in a deep breath, suddenly nervous, in the spotlight.

"You're one of the only slaves I've even considered showing Rock Creek to... it's such a special place, I couldn't bare to show it to a slave I wasn't serious about. But with you, Heather, I just know it's right."

I started to say something, anything, to change the subject or protest again, but Mark put a finger on my lips, silencing me. He gently flipped me over onto my back, and I felt his cock, hard, against my thigh. Slowly, carefully, he entered me. It was so far from the rough urgency of his previous advances. I wasn't even particularly turned on, but yet the fullness of his cock in my pussy was welcome. It was comforting.

After he came, Mark lay beside me, holding my hand.

"You have questions?" he asked.

"Yes. No... maybe. I don't know, sir. I feel nervous. Weird. Does Michelle know about Rock Creek?"

"No. And, that reminds me, you need to keep the information I tell you about Rock Creek to yourself. If you slip up and tell someone who isn't authorized about the community, you'll risk getting a life-ban. Rock Creek belongs to a network of communities around the world. If you're banned from one, you're banned from all of them. Be cautious."

I nodded. It all made sense, and I was used to keeping things private due to my work at the firm. I couldn't talk about any of my cases outside the office, and even among my co-workers I kept most conversation very limited.

"Heather," Mark continued, looking at me seriously, "you know others who belong to the community as well. This is... well, it's another reason I figured I may as well bring you here now rather than wait. I asked his permission yesterday to be sure it would be OK to tell you this..."

"Tell me what?" I asked. I knew other people who were into this... *stuff*?!

"Mr. Richards, Heather."

I gasped loudly. My boss?! I couldn't believe it.

"No way, I don't believe it," I said, repeating my thoughts. "He can't be. He works too much. In the city. He couldn't live there. It's too far. He works more than me! I can't believe it."

"He heads up the law related stuff for the community. He works and lives full time in the city, and goes to Rock Creek when he wants a break. His slave, his wife, she died a few years ago. They used to live there together, and when she passed, he sort of... well, he changed. Being there can bring him a lot of pain. He's improved lately, but he still keeps his distance, both for personal and work related issues. When I spoke with him yesterday, he reminded me that he just loves his job. Kind of like what happened with you when you found Ryan was a cheat; he uses work to forget about his personal life."

I nodded. "That makes sense. I actually had just started working there as an intern when his wife passed away. He was part time before that."

"Yep. I told him about you."

"What?" I said, horrified. "You said work wouldn't be affected. You said you wouldn't ruin my working life." I was all at once confused, angry, and betrayed. My boss couldn't know about me.

"Relax," Mark chuckled. "You do realize he's just as big a freak as you? Mr. Richards has been into BDSM for years. *Much* longer than you. Hell, he's a member of Rock Creek. Think about it. Besides, Mr. Richards vouching for your character was one of the reasons I got permission to tell you about the place at all."

I glared at Mark, uncertain that I wanted to provide any inch of forgiveness for betraying me in this way.

"*Anyway*," Mark said, giving me a playful slap on the thigh, "He was interested to learn about you. He's been setting up connections with the law team there. I don't know what the future holds, but it could be that you end up working with Rock Creek."

We sat in silence for awhile as questions and thoughts flew through my head. It was all so surreal, so unbelievable.

"So how many..." I began, not sure where to start. I curled up my knees to my chest and stared ahead at the little town.

"How many...?" Mark prodded. "You can be open. Ask me anything."

"Well how many places like this are there? Private spaces like Rock Creek? I just can't believe there can be many... it seems like it would be so hard to keep things... well, to keep it private. I mean, do they have trouble with outsiders finding out? And what if someone changes their mind and wants to leave the community? Are they allowed to leave? What if someone has to move? And what about practical stuff, like crimes... big crime, like murder or something. What then? They can't just *spank* a murderer."

Mark laughed. "Heather, as you already know, relationships all have their own 'rules', per say, that each individual couple develops either in the beginning of the relationship or over time. We're still working on ours. So, if a slave decides she doesn't want to be a slave and wants to remove herself from the setting, there is a process within the courts of the community to deal with that. If a couple decides to be inactive, that's fine too. I know of at least two families that don't practice BDSM at all anymore, for different reasons. They're 'vanilla'. It's OK.

"The process for becoming a member there is quite intense. Most residents are exclusively members of this community, though there is a network of nearly a hundred communities connected with the governance of Rock Creek throughout the world.

"Because the membership process is so challenging, residents tend to be responsible and considerate. Most crimes committed are fairly minor and can be handled within the community: speeding, inadvertent vandalism or problems among neighbors, or breaking the general community rules. Larger crimes are handled internally whenever possible, and can even be put in front of the higher internal courts. Those accused must pay to travel to the courts, which can be as far as Ireland. They are reimbursed if found innocent. Honestly, I don't think this has ever happened at Rock Creek. It's just a good group of people. But there is a process, of course, and reaction to crime and problems, however minor or major, is always handled swiftly. For members who prefer the crime is handled by local government, *your* government, well, they have that option. But it is discouraged.

"Over thirty percent of the people who apply for membership at Rock Creek are not approved. The reasons vary widely; from psychological issues to family history or criminal record. A full health exam is issued, and members must schedule an annual exam with one of the community doctors. For those of us who engage in public play, a monthly STD test is expected, and the results are public within the community. Members with diseases are permitted. Members with certain diseases or who are HIV positive are permitted only with full disclosure given to the entire community. Members who sleep with non-members agree not to engage in any sexual contact with anyone in the community until an STD test is submitted to the record-holders; of both the member and the person they had sex with. Provided, of course, the relationship continues. So naturally I'll want a copy of a test from you eventually."

Mark paused to look for my reaction. "Questions so far?"

"It's a lot of... rules... or at least a lot of information," I said.

He nodded. "It is. I'll give you access to their 'public' information. You'll learn a lot about the place, slowly, with time. There's no rush. I'm hoping you'll have visitor rights within six months or so, and then you can get a feel for whether you'd want to live in a place like Rock Creek. I think, even if you decide you want a different Master... or Mistress... I think Rock Creek is the right place for you. You're dripping with submission, my slave. It's going to be beautiful to watch you discover yourself."

I took a huge swig of wine and handed him my glass for a refill. It was a lot to take, learning about this place. It made sense, when I thought about it, that people with similar interests would want to live near each other. I had a hippie friend in college who went to go live with a bunch of other hippies on a farm somewhere in Virginia... but this was different. From what Mark had told me so far, it was a very complex system. With courts, even, in different countries!

I couldn't keep myself from imagining life in a place like Rock Creek. I'd felt so much shame, initially, to let Mark do such... *inappropriate* things to me. Tying me up, spanking me... letting Michelle eat my pussy... but in a community, it would be different. Maybe I'd even feel normal.

And then Mr. Richards! I couldn't believe it! I'd known him for years, and I just couldn't imagine... I couldn't bear the thought of him saying anything at work. I wondered if Michelle knew about him. It seemed like there were so many coincidences.

A big breeze flew by, shaking me out of my thoughts, making me shiver. I had completely forgotten I was naked.

"Get dressed," Mark said. "It's getting late. Your brain has had enough food for thought today. We'll go to my apartment now."

I pulled on my skirt and tank-top and followed him down the hill to his car. It really had been wonderful to be outside, out in the country, to feel the soft fresh air against my skin.

Mark pulled my wrists behind my back and cuffed me before opening the backdoor for me. "When I want to talk with you or play with you, or have you play with yourself while I drive, you'll sit in front with me. We've chatted enough for today – I don't want to hear a word from you until we get back to my apartment."

Well that's just fine, I thought, suddenly very tired. I didn't really want more information anyway, at the moment. I watched the countryside fly by out the window, nodding off occasionally as we drove back to the city.

Chapter Fourteen
CRAWLING TO BED

Back at Mark's apartment building, the doorman grinned at us and winked at me as he opened the doors and led us to the elevator.

"Give her a little smack on the ass, if you want," Mark said casually, holding my upper arm. I looked at him in disbelief, mortified.

SMACK!

Mark turned me around to face the doorman. "Thank him, Heather."

"Thank you for smacking my ass, sir," I said quickly, hoping to avoid any repercussions from hesitation.

"You're very welcome, dear." He grinned at us, and Mark laughed and pulled me into the elevator.

"He likes pretty women," Mark said to me on our way up. "A good man. Very honest. Everyone who lives here loves him."

"Great," I said, not hiding a hint of sarcasm.

The elevator opened into his apartment and he pulled me inside roughly. "You should already know that tones of disrespect or sarcasm will *not* get you what you want. And guess what, slave? Every time you see him you'll politely ask him to smack your butt, you'll flip up any skirt you're wearing and bend over for him. Got it?" His voice was stern.

My heart sank and I looked down to the floor. "Yes, sir."

"Do you really *want* to present your ass to him every time you see him?"

"No, sir," I said meekly.

"I didn't think so. Consider that when you respond to me in the future."

He un-cuffed me and looked at me, his eyes severe. I blushed from the attention.

"I think, Heather, that we will work on your training just a little bit more today. Wait here, don't move."

Mark walked briskly down the hallway. I strained my ears to listen but couldn't hear anything but a couple of doors opening and closing. He returned after over ten minutes, his hands full. In front of my feet, he dropped a pair of heels from the store and a pair of elastic knee pads.

"Strip, and put those on," he said, his voice calm. "Then get on your hands and knees. You're going to practice crawling."

I slid out of my outfit, pulled on the heels and knee pads, and dropped to my hands and knees. I looked up at him, waiting for his next command.

"You look beautiful down there," he said, "where you belong. Now, follow me."

He turned on his heels and began to walk. I hurried after him. He was walking quickly, all over his apartment. I kept my eyes on him and occasionally he turned to check if I was with him. I tired, and my crawling pace became slower than his.

"Come on," he called, turning a quick corner to head back to the front door. "Speed up, keep up with me." He arrived at the spot where he had left some of his items. "I have a motivator for you."

Mark held in his hands a long paddle. The handle was nearly two feet long, and at the end was a thick piece of wood about the size of his large hands.

"This, slave, packs a punch. You're going to crawl around this apartment for ten minutes, as fast as you possibly can. If I think you're going too slow, I'll motivate you a bit with this paddle. If you stop, I'll rain down spanks on your ass until you start again. If you cause too many problems I'll add a butt plug to the mix."

I gulped audibly. I was already tired, and the paddle looked scary.

Mark continued. "I want you to pay attention to your posture as you crawl, my sweet. You should arch your back and wag your butt, and keep your arms as straight as you can. Try to be elegant and graceful. Later, I'll show you examples to help you improve. For now, just concentrate on jutting your ass out and wagging it at me as you crawl. Got it?"

"Yes, sir," I said softly. I dreaded ten minutes of Mark watching me crawl more than the mean looking paddle. I felt so naked and exposed and ridiculous.

"OK," he said, tapping me lightly. "Go."

SMACK!

"Yeoww!" I cried out as he struck me hard with the paddle. I crawled towards the kitchen quickly, concentrating on wagging my butt at him as I went. I took whatever turns I could, not paying any particular attention to where I was going. Every now and then I faltered and was promptly rewarded with a sharp spank on my butt.

"Two minutes done, slave, eight to go," Mark said jovially from behind me as I whimpered. My arms were sore but I kept crawling as fast as I could. When I made my way around the dining room table I considered crawling under it to hide from the wicked paddle, but just kept going, back to the foyer. Back to the living room. Down the long hallway and back again I crawled, with Mark close behind me.

His footsteps began to dictate how fast I needed to go to avoid being encouraged by the paddle. If I sensed him too close to me I renewed my efforts and sped up my crawl.

SMACK! SMACK!

Two times hard! As I rounded the corner at the end of the hallway. I cried out and stopped, grabbing my butt with both hands to protect myself. Faster than I could believe, Mark had both my wrists pinned behind my back and a series of smacks rained down on me until I shouted, "No, Master, I'll start again, I'm sorry!"

He let me go and I continued crawling, no longer thinking about how silly I looked. My only focus was on crawling, and crawling quickly, to avoid any more spanks.

"Nine minutes, slave. One to go!" Mark called from behind me.

One long minute later, he called time and I collapsed at his feet, breathing hard. He chuckled above me.

"You did a very good job, Heather. At Rock Creek there's an annual dog show. Crawling is judged, both by speed and poise, along with a number of other things. Maybe we'll enter you next year!"

I looked up at him in disbelief.

"It's true. It's a lot of fun. You'd like it, trust me. Now, stand up, take those knee pads off, and follow me."

Mark led me down the hallway and into a candle lit room. A

beautiful room. I looked around in awe. A large bed was in the center of the room with four wooden pillars around it. A green comforter with gold embroidery lay across the bed, casually, in a way that made it seem somewhat more natural. Several large, fluffy pillows made up the head of the bed, and on either side sat a wooden nightstand with thin, curvy legs. In one corner of the room were two comfortable looking chairs and a table. In another corner, a lovely dresser. Along the walls hung mirrors and paintings. Each mirror had lit candles placed in front of it, reflecting the light back into the room. He must have lit them before the crawling 'game'. I noticed a mirror that hung above the bed, from the ceiling.

"This is my bedroom," Mark said simply as he moved past me into the room. He opened a door I hadn't noticed on the side of the dresser to what I assumed was a closet. From it, he produced some lengths of rope and a piece of cloth.

He motioned me to him and gently pulled my hair up behind my back, securing it with the cloth. He ran the rope through my hair under the cloth, and pulled my hands up behind my head. He carefully tied my hands in place. More rope. He ran it around my elbows and tied them together.

"Notice, my love, that you could very easily pull your hands up, sliding the cloth off of your hair, and free yourself. Notice also that this rope on your elbows keeps your shoulders out and breasts on display. Do you see that?" He turned me towards a mirror.

"Yes, sir."

"If you free yourself before I tell you to, you'll sleep in the guestroom tonight. If you're a good girl, though, I may let you sleep in here with me."

I trembled as he ran his hands down the sides of my body. I *needed* to be good, I so wanted to sleep in his bed with him. I wanted to feel him next to me as I fell asleep and again when I woke.

Mark casually pulled off his clothes in front of me and I paused from worrying about the upcoming test in order to admire his body. The shadows from the flickering candle-light showed off his toned stomach. His muscles flexed slightly as he moved towards me. He smiled softly, watching my expression as my eyes roamed his body. His cock was semi-hard and looked so beautiful.

My heart fluttered a bit as he stepped towards me. I couldn't believe this beautiful man was standing in front of me with such obvious lust in his eyes. He came so close, almost touching me and I unconsciously leaned toward him, hoping to feel his skin against mine. His hands stroked my skin and I wished I could do the same to him. In the back of my mind I kept concentrating on keeping my hands in place, trying so hard to obey. My arms were still tired from crawling.

He massaged my breasts with one hand, using the other to pull me in close to him. Then, a kiss. I moaned into his mouth as his tongue played with mine gently. *Dancing.*

He pulled away from me and I gasped, longing for a return of his touch. I looked to him for direction, waiting to see what he wanted.

He lay back on the bed, his cock hard now and pointing to the ceiling. Faster than I thought possible he had a condom on and then leaned back, his hands behind his neck, head slightly propped up on the pillows.

"Come over here and sit on my cock, Heather. I want you to fuck me."

I hesitated only slightly before climbing onto the bed and swinging my leg over his body. With some amount of horror I realized the headboard was reflective glass meaning I could see my naked body over his.

"I kind of wish I was blindfolded, sir," I said with a small smile.

"I know you do. Now, begin." His voice was firm but friendly. I saw something in his expression that reminded me of the other men I'd slept with, how hopeful and delighted they were during our first times together. Even though Mark had fucked me before, I still felt like I hadn't made love with him yet. Perhaps he felt the same. Maybe this was like our first time.

I lowered my pussy slowly onto his cock, teasing the tip by moving my hips. When I had him inside I moved up and down, trying to keep balance without the use of my hands.

Mark reached up and twisted my nipples lightly, then tugging them he moved with me. Up, down, setting my pace.

He moved his hands to my hips, lifting me nearly off of his cock before pressing me down hard. Again, up and down, falling into the natural rhythm.

"You look so beautiful like that," he growled, using his pelvis to thrust into my pussy hard. "Come on, slave. Fuck your Master hard now. I want to see your tits move up and down as you fuck yourself on my cock."

His words as motivation, I began fucking him in earnest, closing my eyes to remove any inhibition caused by my glass reflection. I moaned loudly as I bounced and I could feel my breasts bouncing along with my rhythm.

"Look at me, slave," he said, reaching up to slap one of my tits. Then another. I cried out and looked at him. His green eyes looked nearly rabid with desire. "Fuck me harder, faster."

"Please, sir, help me fuck you," I cried, breathless. My legs were tired from the crawling; I didn't know if I could fuck him until he came.

"Mmm gladly," he groaned. "You can move your arms,

slave."

I gratefully pulled my arms out of the ponytail and over my head, my wrists still tied together. My hair fell along my shoulders. He lifted me off of his cock and pushed me onto my back, then plunged into my pussy with abandon. I cried out in pleasure as he fucked me hard, grunting with each strong thrust.

"Look up, Heather. Look at yourself getting fucked."

I took in the reflection in the ceiling mirror. I couldn't believe I was the person I saw – sweaty, hair everywhere, moaning as Mark fucked me. I watched his ass flex as he pounded me, saw my breasts, my legs spread wide...

"Ohhh god, sir, I'm so close," I cried.

"Cum, you slave. My little slave-girl," he murmured into my ear, pounding harder.

"Aaghhh!" My back arched and my legs shook as I came hard around his cock. My clenching pussy pushed into orgasm as he slammed into me a final time and grunted through his ecstasy.

He collapsed on top of me, breathing hard. I reached my still-tied hands around his head kissed him deeply.

"Mmm Heather," he said, breaking off the kiss, "that was incredible. I'm happy you kept your hands put as you sat on top of my cock, because I love the idea of having you in my bed tonight, your hot little cunt available to me when I want to cum again."

I moaned under him as he pulled his cock out of me. He untied the ropes around my wrists and elbows, freeing my limbs completely. I curled up against him; I'd never been so happy or calm. So peaceful. *His.*

He hugged me and held me as we both drifted off to sleep, peacefully *one*. Him and *his*.

Chapter Fifteen
PAIN GAMES

Months went by as Mark and I continued our weekly meetings. He always gave me tasks for the days I wouldn't be with him: wearing a blindfold at night, sending him a daily dirty text message, or using a vibrator at the office. Every Sunday night I waited with anticipation for the next week's list of rules or chores. Mark was genius at crafting up things that would make me nervous, humiliated or completely horny during the times we weren't together. Whenever we weren't physically connected, I had a constant emotional reminder that I was his slave, and he my Master.

Mostly we spent time alone together, though occasionally he let Jasmine at the store dominate me a bit while he shopped for new outfits for me. Once, Jasmine played with Rose and I both, tying us together face to face while flogging our asses. I feared her and her sadistic games, though always ended up wet and horny after a trip to the store.

One particular Saturday afternoon, I went outside after work to meet Mark. As requested, I was wearing my overcoat and nothing underneath. I stood near the office building, looking around for Mark who was usually early. After nearly 15 minutes of waiting, a dark blue SUV pulled up beside me. The passenger side window rolled down, and my heart sunk when I saw Jasmine was in the driver's seat.

"Get in," she said.

I crawled in the car beside Jasmine and pulled the door closed behind me. "Hello, Miss Jasmine," I said. I tried very hard to sound innocent and polite.

"Hello, bitch," she responded, starting to drive. Her tone was cold. "Mark's running late. He'll meet you at the store."

I felt a twinge of disappointment. I'd had a long day at work and was looking forward to being folded up in Mark's embrace, comforted by some time with him.

"Pull up that coat so your naked ass is on the seat," Jasmine said as we were stopped at the red light just outside of the office parking lot. I obeyed immediately, knowing any hesitating with Jasmine meant a painful punishment from her, and then later, Mark. I sat quietly, the skin of my ass touching the cool leather seat, waiting with dread for any further instructions.

"You know, I've had a really shitty week," said Jasmine. Her long fingernails clicked the steering wheel as she drove. Her eyes were focused on the road, her expression blank. "I was happy to hear from Mark. Poor Rose has been getting the brunt of my frustrations. I asked Mark if I can be hard on you today. You know what he said?"

Jasmine finally glanced towards me. Her eyes were angry. I sunk down in my seat, trying to avoid her glare.

"He said," she continued, "that it's been awhile since you've had a good beating. It's been awhile since you've been humiliated. Which doesn't surprise me. I think you have it too good with him, you little bitch. But you're in for a beating today. Mark said he'd love to come pick you up and find that his little slave-girl has been abused."

My stomach turned and I moaned softly. I always dreaded any time I had to spend with Jasmine. For me it was natural to be dominated by Mark. His dominance was accentuated by his masculinity and his physical power over me. With Jasmine, I had to try harder to be submissive. She was slightly shorter than me, and very feminine. While I'd grown to find some women attractive, it still didn't seem normal for me to be with women sexually. Jasmine knew how I felt, and I think she enjoyed her power over me even more because of it.

"Mark, as usual, wants you to try on some of our new clothing," Jasmine said casually. We were pulling into the parking lot of Second Skin. I so hoped the car would get a flat tire, or somehow something would happen to distract Jasmine's attention from me. "So we'll do that as fast as we can, won't we?"

"Yes, Miss Jasmine," I said.

"And what will we do after that, while we wait for Mark to pick you up?"

"Whatever you wish, Miss Jasmine."

She smiled. She pulled into the parking space reserved for her and shut off the engine. "Good. Get out and go straight to the dressing room. Take off that coat, and wait for me there."

I scampered out of the car and walked to the store quickly. I saw Rose behind the cash register. She gave me a small wave and a smile. I wished I could talk to her, to get advice on what to do to make Jasmine happy. In the dressing room, I pulled off my coat and hung it up. I saw a pile of clothing waiting on the couch and wondered if that was what I would be trying on.

I took my place in the center of the room. Mark had shown me several slave positions. Whenever I was waiting for Mark's return, I knelt on the floor, my legs spread slightly, and my hands resting, palms up, on my knees. For Jasmine, I stood, my feet shoulder width apart and my hands locked behind my neck. She liked me to wait in the center of the room, so all of the mirrors could display my reflection for her.

Jasmine did not keep me waiting long. She stormed into the dressing room. Rose followed behind her.

"Go lock the store," Jasmine sneered at Rose. "I don't want any distractions. And stay out there. I want you on your hands and fucking knees, scrubbing the floor. You still owe me two hours of cleaning today."

"Yes, mistress," said Rose. I swallowed hard, but waited obediently, keeping my position.

"Wait a minute, Rose. I want you to hear this before you leave."

Jasmine approached me and sharply tweaked both of my nipples. I winced from the sudden pain. She used one hand to steady my head and used her other hand to slap my face, five times in a row. I cried out. The invasion of my personal space always made me feel vulnerable and submissive.

"OK, slut. Today we are going to play a game. We have fifteen new outfits for you to try on. As I said, I want you to move fast so we can have some fun. So you will be timed. The outfits are sitting on that couch. You have fifteen minutes. If you need help with a zipper or buttons, you must go find Rose. If you take longer than fifteen minutes, I'll be forced to punish you. A stroke of the paddle for every second you are late. If you finish early," Jasmine paused, turning to Rose who was standing at the dressing room door, looking at the floor. "Rose will be punished. A stroke of the paddle for every second you are early."

I looked at Rose, then back to Jasmine, who was smiling.

"Rose," said Jasmine, "turn around and show Heather your ass before you leave to do your chores."

Rose turned and bent over, pulling her skirt up to her waist. I gasped. She had clearly been punished already. Her ass was bright red, and clear markings from a cane went from the top of her thighs to the middle of her butt. I clenched my ass cheeks instinctively. I couldn't believe Jasmine would even consider paddling Rose more.

"Rose, you may leave," Jasmine said.

"Yes, mistress." Rose left the dressing room, leaving me with Jasmine and the pile of clothing.

"May I have permission to ask a question, Miss Jasmine?" I said.

"Yes, slut."

"Will you be telling me how much time is on the clock as I try on the clothes?"

"No."

My mind raced. How could I make sure that I used more than fifteen minutes, but not so much more that I'd be in for a huge amount of paddling? I glanced at the pile of clothes. I had an idea.

"Are you ready?" Jasmine asked. She had a smile on her face. Her hands were on her hips, and she was tapping her left foot slowly. She reached into her pocket and pulled out a watch.

"Yes, Miss Jasmine," I said.

"Go."

I ran to the couch with the clothing and looked through it, frantically searching for something I'd need Rose's help with. I found a dress with a back that needed to be tied like a corset and sprinted out into the main room. I found Rose, on her hands and knees, next to a bucket of soapy water. I dropped to my knees beside her and held the front of the corset in place. She immediately started to tie it for me in the back.

"Rose, do you have a clock in this room?"

"Yes, of course," she said.

"You gotta time this. We *just* started."

"OK," she said. "Look." She pointed up to the wall. The clock read exactly four thirty.

"All right. I'm gonna try to finish just after four forty-five."

"Oh, sweetie. That's nice of you, but don't worry about me," Rose said, yanking the final tie on the dress. "All set, go!"

I ran back into the room to show Jasmine the dress. She nodded. I was able to untie it myself and started trying on the other outfits. With each one I quickly modeled it for Jasmine before taking it off. Most, like usual, went into the 'no' pile. When she liked one in particular, or knew Mark would like it, she nodded approval.

Finally I had just five outfits left. I decided to see how I was doing on time, and picked a dress that needed to be zipped up in the back. I ran out to find Rose.

"How many do you have left?" she asked.

"Four after this." I looked up to the clock. Four forty.

"Better hurry, sweetie."

"Fuck," I muttered out loud, running back into the dressing room. I got through the next three outfits easily, leaving just one that had a tie in the back. I ran out to the main room.

Four forty-four.

"This is perfect!" I said. I was relieved. I could avoid a huge punishment, and make sure Rose wouldn't get paddled.

"I don't think you understand Jasmine," Rose said as she tied my dress.

"What do you mean?"

"She's very sadistic, but she's not insane. This is an

opportunity for her to give you pain. If you end up with seven strokes, they'll be incredibly hard. If you end up with thirty, they'll be less hard. If I end up with any, they won't be as hard as what you'll get. But she'd still find something to punish *you* for. She will give you the amount of pain she wants to give you, regardless of anything you do."

I realized Rose might be right and looked up at the clock. Four forty-five! I ran back into the dressing room. I still preferred seven strokes to thirty.

Jasmine nodded when I came back, and I untied the dress and threw it into the 'yes' pile. I folded my hands behind my neck and stood at attention, waiting for the result.

"You took too long," she said, looking at her watch. "Seventeen seconds over."

"I'm sorry, Miss Jasmine," I said, my voice shaking.

She stood right in front of me, her face inches from mine. Her hand trailed around my nipple, flicking it softly. Then her fingers made their way down to my cunt. She checked my arousal and pinched my pussy lip, making me gasp in pain.

"I love playing with you, slutty girl. Your body and your brain want such different things," she said. She took a step back and looked at me. I held my breath, waiting for her next commands.

"Would you like a warm-up spanking, over my lap?" she asked.

I wondered what she wanted me to say. Occasionally Mark spanked me lightly, building up gradually. But Jasmine never spanked lightly. Ever. I didn't trust her and assumed she just wanted to add more to my punishment.

"No, thank you, Miss Jasmine," I said softly.

"Fine then," she said, turning away from me. "Go lie down on the coffee table. Face up."

I did as she said, letting my feet rest on the floor.

"Knees to your chest, feet in the air. Your hands should hold on to the back of your knees," she called from the other side of the dressing room.

I put myself into position, groaning inwardly at how exposed I was. It also pulled my skin taut, leaving my ass with much less natural padding. Would she really paddle me like this?

Jasmine walked over to me and crouched down beside the table.

"One disadvantage of most spankings is that I can't see my victim's face. In this position, I'll be able to watch you cry out in pain as I punish you. The danger to this position is that you might kick me. Believe me, if you kick your legs I will *beat you until Mark comes to save you.*" She emphasized the end of her sentence, making me tremble.

I took a deep breath as the wooden paddle touched my skin.

"I'm going to make this quick," said Jasmine, raising the paddle in the air. "I want to move on to the other fun."

The paddle was oval shaped, about the size of a paperback novel. I realized that not only could Jasmine see my face, I could see her. Normally when I was spanked I stared at the floor, or had my face buried in a couch cushion. In this position, I'd be able to see every stroke coming before I felt the pain.

She began, crashing the paddle down onto my ass and then raising it back high in the air before spanking me again. She aimed first at my ass, then at my upper thighs, making me scream out in pain. I clutched onto my legs with all of my strength. When I looked up at Jasmine's face, I saw her expression and cringed in fear. She looked maniacally sadistic, her eyes furrowed in concentration while she beat my ass and thighs. I squeezed my eyes shut, wanting to block out whatever current reality I could.

She rained down the seventeen spanks in rapid succession. Shortly after the paddling started, it stopped. Jasmine threw the paddle onto the couch beside the table and thrust two of her fingers into my cunt. She fucked me with her fingers for nearly a minute as I tried to accept the sudden change between pain and pleasure. I kept hold of my knees and breathed deeply, moaning loudly as she finger-fucked my pussy.

Suddenly she stopped. She pulled her fingers out of me and pushed them roughly into my mouth.

"Suck," she said. Her tone was irritable, as if I'd done something wrong by accepting the paddling without complaint.

I did as she said, and after I licked her fingers clean she grabbed my hair and pulled me off the table. I scrambled to keep up with her as she strode across the room. Near the wall at the far end of the changing room, she let go of my hair and shoved me to the ground.

"Stand up and face the wall. I need to check on Rose," Jasmine said, turning away from me. She didn't look back to make sure that I would obey; she didn't need to. I stood and put my nose to the wall, not willing to risk anything by disobeying Jasmine in any way.

Within a few minutes, I heard Jasmine come back into the room.

"All right, Heather. Time for some fun," she said. "Turn, face me."

I turned around and saw that Jasmine had Rose in tow. Rose was behind her, on all fours, naked. A leash was attached to her collar, the handle in Jasmine's hand. Letting my gaze wander over to Jasmine, I sucked in a breath of air. She was also naked, save for a strap-on attached to her. The fake dick was black and huge – bigger than Mark's cock. What was she going to do to us?

"Rose, in addition to being punished, has also had quite a

day of orgasms. Tell Heather how many times you've cum," Jasmine said.

"Eight times," replied Rose. Her poise was always so confident, not embarrassed at all to be naked in front of me or reveal personal information. She held her head high, and looked almost elegant on the floor beside Jasmine. I admired her for her grace.

"Eight times," repeated Jasmine. "Have you ever cum that many times in a day, Heather?"

"No, Miss Jasmine," I said.

"Well, Rose's little cunt is very tired, but I want to see her cum again. I want to see you licking her pussy until she cums. Doesn't that sound like fun?"

"Yes, Miss Jasmine," I said obediently, though I didn't think it sounded like much fun at all. I'd learned how to pleasure women just two months into my relationship with Mark. He and Stephen made Michelle and I practice on each other nearly every other week. I didn't mind it, but I wondered how long I'd have to lick Rose to make her cum another time.

"So, since I'm in the mood for games, we'll turn this into one," Jasmine continued. "While you're licking pussy, Heather, I'll be fucking and beating you. For the first three minutes, I'm going to fuck your pussy. For the next five, your asshole. If it takes you longer than those eight minutes to make my slave cum, I'll switch to paddling your ass some more. You'll be paddled until she cums, understand?"

I nodded. I suddenly was incredibly nervous; I'd never had to race to make someone cum. I didn't want to be fucked by Jasmine. She was so far from gentle, I feared she would hurt me when she got to fucking my ass.

Jasmine directed Rose to lay down on the pretty rug in the center of the room. Rose winced a bit as her ass came in contact with the floor. She spread her legs wide, exposing her pussy. I'd been forced to lick Jasmine's pussy once before, but hadn't experienced the taste of Rose.

Until today. Jasmine grabbed me by my hair again and shoved me down to the ground between Rose's legs.

"I want you on your elbows and your knees while you lick, bitch. Spread your knees apart some, and arch your back. I know how bad your pussy needs to be fucked. Show me."

Jasmine's tone was strong and set. I obeyed, putting myself into position, my face right by Rose's cunt. I saw with disappointment that Rose wasn't wet at all. I wasn't surprised, since she had just been doing boring chores. I felt Jasmine behind me. Her fingers massaged my pussy, and then I felt the cool tip of the fake cock start to enter me.

"OK, bitch," said Jasmine. "Time starts now."

"Oof!" I exclaimed as Jasmine thrust into me hard. She wasted no time and began fucking me roughly. I ignored the discomfort of the sudden invasion and started to lick Rose's cunt.

I had learned tips from Michelle about how to lick pussy. She'd been kind and patient with me, especially after I'd had a particularly horrible session with Jasmine. I started slowly with Rose because I knew she wasn't very aroused. I stayed away from her clit and softly licked her labia and tickled her perineum with my tongue. After just a little bit of attention, I heard her moan and saw that she was swelling with pleasure.

Bingo, I thought to myself. I knew if I started slow enough with her, I'd be able to speed up once she was sufficiently turned on and make her cum fast. Maybe I'd even avoid the ass fucking.

Jasmine spanked my butt with her hand as she rode me from behind. It was strange to be fucked by her like this. The cock attached to the strap-on filled me up completely, and started to feel good as she thrust in and out. I moved my hips with her rhythm. It wasn't much different than being fucked by a man.

"Play with your titties, Rose," said Jasmine. I glanced up and saw Rose immediately begin to twist her nipples and massage her breasts.

Jasmine pulled out of me and I moaned into Rose's cunt as I licked. I realized the three minutes must be up. Jasmine's fingers were at my asshole and I felt the cool, familiar drops of lube. I braced myself as the tip of the cock entered me.

"Rose, you should use your hands on her head," Jasmine said as she pushed the tip of the cock inside me. I stifled a cry of pain. I could never get completely used to the sensation of things entering my ass.

Rose was hot now, her pussy lips swollen and her clit engorged. I had two fingers inside of her and was concentrating my tongue on circling her clit. She put her hands on my head and pressed my mouth hard into her cunt. Jasmine had one hand on my back, pushing me down from the top as well while she entered my ass with the fake dick.

I gasped for air as Rose reduced the pressure on my head before shoving me back down. I was totally helpless, with Rose controlling my head with her hands and Jasmine impaling me from behind. I licked her as hard as I could, using my lips and my tongue to sop up her juices and make her cum.

"Guess what, Heather?" asked Jasmine as she gave one final thrust to enter my ass completely. When her hips crashed against my thighs I knew she was totally inside of me.

"Whafst?" I asked, my voice muffled as my face was pressed down into Rose.

"I made a deal with Rose before we began this little game. If she can hold off for ten minutes, she gets a reward. So it's you versus Rose here, make no mistake. She'll hold off if she can."

I groaned. Jasmine fucked my asshole hard, not holding back at all. I renewed my effort to make Rose cum, but realized that it would be a really difficult task. Rose had years of training. She once confided in me that Jasmine got off on controlling her orgasms and making her cum on command.

Rather than try to beat the impossible clock, I tried to enjoy getting fucked and licking Rose's pussy. I didn't mind anal sex after the initial entrance, and I also didn't mind licking cunt. I could either resist the inevitable, or at least try to have fun. The only bad part would be the two minute paddling.

When Jasmine pulled the cock out of my ass, I licked Rose in earnest. Two minutes more.

"This," said Jasmine, "will be very fun to watch."

She rested the horrible paddle against my ass, then raised it up and brought it down hard. My cries were muffled by Rose's pussy as she continued the onslaught.

I struggled to hold myself in position, to keep my ass on display for Jasmine to beat. Thankfully, while her spanks were firm and painful, she paddled slowly.

"Thirty seconds until ten minutes, slaves," she said. I shoved two fingers into Rose and heard her grunt in response. She still had her hands on my head and pressed me firmly into her cunt. I flicked my tongue against her clit and felt her hips tilt. She was close.

Jasmine began paddling me fast and I responded by licking as fast as I could.

"Please Mistress, spank her harder," Rose cried out, thrusting her pelvis up and using her hands and hips to control where I licked.

Jasmine complied and I tried not to cry out in pain. The harder Jasmine spanked, the more earnestly I lapped at Rose's cunt. She was so close. Her hips bucked slightly, and her legs clamped around me tight. Her pussy tightened around my hand. She shuddered and cried out, cumming for nearly ten seconds as Jasmine continued spanking me hard.

The paddling stopped and Jasmine caressed my ass, her hand occasionally grazing my pussy. My face was sticky with Rose's juices. I rested my head on her thigh and kept my hand in her cunt. She breathed deeply, in post-orgasmic bliss.

"Good girls," said Jasmine. "That was just over ten minutes. You both did very well."

She left us, letting us rest. I scooted up next to Rose. We lay close to each other, in silence. I let my hand rest on hers.

Rose turned her head to face me. "You're good at that, Heather."

"Thanks," I said, smiling. A year ago I would have never guessed I could be good at licking pussy.

She rolled on to her side and put her hand on my cunt. "You're wet," she said.

I nodded. I bucked slightly at her touch and moaned.

"It was really fucking hot," said Rose, "watching you get fucked while you licked me." She put a finger inside of me and I parted my thighs slightly. Were we allowed to do this? Her hand alternated between entering my pussy and flicking my clit. I was sweating slightly, and couldn't remember a time when I was more aroused. I wanted to cum so badly.

"Ah-hem!" Rose and I both looked up, startled. Jasmine stood above us, and Mark stood just behind her. They were both grinning. I blushed and closed my legs tight.

"Time to go, Heather," said Mark. He held the coat out for me and led me out of the store. I waved goodbye to Rose as we left the dressing room. She smiled back, now in Jasmine's arms.

In the car on the way to Mark's apartment, I shifted

uncomfortably. I was insanely horny. He knew it and when we got to his place he took his time before ravaging me. We stayed up nearly half the night, fucking and playing until we slept, exhausted.

I could now tell Miss Jasmine that I'd cum more than eight times in one single day.

Chapter Sixteen

OVER AND OVER AGAIN

Besides Jasmine and Rose, Mark liked to schedule play dates with Stephen and Michelle. They were mainly fun sexy house dinners that ended with Michelle and I having mind blowing orgasms at each other's hands, or by each other's tongues. Lately, Michelle had been teaching me how to give proper massages. She had taken a few classes for fun in college and could give amazing massages, both erotic and vanilla. After a few half-hour sessions with her, working on my technique, I could confidently give Mark a relaxing massage whenever he felt tense.

Even though it was fun to play with others, what I really loved most was my time alone with Mark. We were growing very close. I thought of him often when we were apart and counted down the days or hours until we could be together again.

We spent most of our nights together in, at his apartment. Sometimes I felt like his prized doll, when he dressed me up to be sexy for him or kept me naked. It was comforting, in an odd way, to not have to concern myself with how I should dress. I never had the option of choosing what we would eat, drink, or do. Practically, this gave me less to think about. When I was at work, I could concentrate on working. I didn't have to think about making dinner reservations or anything of the sort. Mark grew to know my tastes for food, for films, and for other recreational things we would do. If he cared, he'd take my preferences into consideration when he planned our evenings together.

Every weekend he taught me a new slave position. I could kneel, stand, or present myself to him in a variety of ways, all which had their own name.

He also taught me how to cook simple meals for him, how to please him orally, and how to dance for him. When I forgot a slave position or burned food, or did anything that displeased him, Mark punished me.

His punishments I dreaded, but afterward I always felt at ease. Forgiven. He spanked me regularly and made me realize that I actually like a fair amount of pain and humiliation. For punishments, he usually chose to make me do something I'd really dislike.

"You have an active mind and spirit," Mark said to me one evening after I burned myself by picking up a hot cast iron pan without an oven mitt. I dropped the pan when I felt the pain, spilling dinner all over the floor.

He lectured me. "You need to learn how to focus, even on the most simple tasks. With everything we do, we must train our minds to be aware of what we are doing. While you're cooking you're thinking about work. Or sex. Or anything other than food."

Mark ordered us some take-out to make up for my mistake. After dinner, he sat me down naked in a hard wooden chair and put a pad of paper and pen in front of me.

"Heather, write this down: 'I will pay attention to all of the tasks that I do, because I know it will please my Master to do everything correctly, with precision and without mistakes.'"

I obeyed quickly, writing down the sentence. I looked up at him for his approval. He nodded, and stroked my hair with his hand gently.

"You'll write that again, one hundred times. When you're done, come find me."

I clenched the pen in my hand and without thinking, pounded my fist on the desk. I hated tedious work. Challenges made me succeed, not stupid, repetitive tasks.

Mark raised his eyebrows at my reaction.

"This is what I'm talking about, Heather. If I'd asked you to do something complicated, you would do so happily. But with a simple thing like making dinner, you fail. Work with your brain, slave. Try to improve. And, your childlike reaction to my request earned you another fifty lines. Any mistakes, miscounting, or sloppy handwriting will earn you more lines."

It took me nearly two hours to write out the sentence 150 times for Mark. My hand and wrist ached after only a half hour; I hadn't handwritten much since I'd learned how to type.

After I finished, I found Mark in the living room, sipping a drink and reading a magazine. I took my place by his feet and handed him the papers, yearning for his forgiveness. He was right, as always. Most of the mistakes I made, both with him and at work, happened when I did simple, brainless work.

Mark nodded at my lines and pulled me up to his lap, hugging me close. I sank into him happily. The feeling of being forgiven I likened to the feeling of being accepted. With Ryan, or close friends, after a fight or problem I'd always wonder if they truly forgave me. Some friends held grudges, others did not.

With Mark I didn't need to second guess anything, or wonder where I stood with him.

He was honest with me. He corrected me when I did something wrong, punished me, then went on with things. And on the one time that he made an error – being an hour late to pick me up – his sincere apology was all I needed to offer my forgiveness.

On New Years Eve, Mark made us reservations at Haven, where we'd had our first date. I was thrilled. In the back of my mind I wondered if Mark would finally collar me.

We got ready to go at his apartment. We showered together, and covered each other with suds. He pressed me against the wall of the shower as he used the soft bath sponge to wash me. With his body so close to mine, I hoped he would fuck me right there.

"I want you wet for me tonight. Just like the last time we were at Haven. Remember how wet your pussy was that night?" he asked me, pulling my head back and forcing me to look up at him.

"Yes, sir," I said, squirming a bit as I remembered how horny I had been.

He stepped away from me and quickly rinsed off.

"Finish up," he said, stepping out of the tub. "Your dress is on the bed."

I enjoyed the warmth of the water for just a few minutes more. Though very tempted, I resisted rubbing my clit.

I wrung out my hair a bit after I turned off the water. Mark made a rule that I was never allowed a towel after a shower or a bath. Whether in my apartment or his, I was always naked after showering, letting the air dry my skin. I disliked this rule, and always turned the heat on high in my own apartment before I bathed. At Mark's, my skin got goosebumps and my nipples hardened nearly instantly. The one time I complained of being cold, Mark made me do jumping jacks to warm up until I dried off.

In his bedroom, I eagerly looked to the bed to see what he would have me wear that night. I smiled as I saw what he picked out: the burgundy dress from Second Skin that I'd turned down since the price was so high. I was delighted that he bought it for me. Jasmine and Rose knew how much I loved that dress; perhaps they suggested it.

While I waited for my skin to dry I put on makeup and dried my hair. Mark would want it up tonight. I pulled it into a loose bun, keeping some tendrils loose to frame my face.

Finally dry, I pulled on the dress and the black high-heels and met Mark in the living room.

"Jasmine said you look hot in that dress," he said, standing to kiss me. "She was definitely correct. Too bad you won't be wearing it for long."

"Wha-?" I began, then stopped myself. I thought we were going to Haven. Perhaps Mark had changed the plans.

He didn't say another word as he picked up both our coats and turned to leave. Downstairs, the doorman grinned when he saw us and I inwardly groaned. I'd gotten used to flipping up my skirts for him, but this was a really nice dress. Somehow the humiliation seemed more intense as I struggled to pull the dress up for him.

"Please spank my ass, sir," I said obediently. I'd lost count of how many times this man had seen my naked butt.

The doorman put his hand on my ass, giving each cheek a squeeze before he firmly spanked me. Normally he just patted me lightly.

"Ouch!" I gasped. "Thank you, sir."

I hastily put the dress into place and scurried out to meet Mark, who was already halfway to his car. He opened the passenger door for me and knelt down beside me when I got in.

"Are you going to be a good girl tonight, slave?" he asked.

"Yes, sir," I said. "Of course."

"Good."

He was silent on the way to the restaurant. My mind flew through the possibilities of things that he might have planned. I knew it was a waste of energy to even try to guess what was in store for me since Mark never failed to surprise me. But I couldn't help it. I fidgeted nervously in my seat, but was happy to see him taking the right turns that eventually led us to Haven.

Inside, Mark asked to speak with Chef James, his childhood best friend. Chef James came to greet us warmly. He was a short, stout man with a smiley face.

"Come on back, Mark," he said after we shook hands.

We followed him towards the kitchen, but rather than entering the large, black swinging doors Chef James unlocked a door to the right. The door was marked private, and I assumed it was a utility closet. He swung it open and stepped aside. There was a dark curtain blocking view of the room.

"I've got a great menu planned for you both tonight," he said. "Please enjoy."

"Thank you," said Mark as he grabbed my hand. He pushed the curtain aside and pulled me into the room. I heard the door close behind us.

Inside, a single table was set in the middle of the room. The table had two long candles lit on either side of a shallow vase of roses. The room was softly lit, and definitely *not* a utility closet. We had our own private dining room.

"There's even a private bathroom," Mark said. "Pretty nice, huh?"

"It's beautiful," I said.

"A beautiful spot to celebrate the beginning of a new year," he agreed. He slid his hands up the sides of my body, then over my breasts and my ass. "I wonder how many times you'll cum before midnight."

I let out a soft moan as he lifted up my dress and felt my soaking wet pussy. He flicked my clit a few times before letting me go from his embrace.

"Take off the dress," he said. "Use the bathroom if you want. I'll be right back. If the waiter comes, order some wine."

If the waiter comes? I thought to myself in panic. The waiters here couldn't see me naked. What would they think?

I reluctantly took of the beautiful dress. Naked, I used the restroom to check my makeup and my hair, and then waited anxiously at the table. When I heard the door open, my heart stood still. I hoped it was Mark.

Ever unlucky, a waiter appeared from behind the curtain. I cringed, waiting for his reaction to my nudity. He only briefly paused and looked surprised. I watched his expression and knew he was consciously shaking off his shock. He smiled and greeted me politely.

"Good evening," he said, "and welcome to Haven. My name is Charles, I'll be your waiter this evening. The chef has a lovely dinner planned for you. Would you like something to drink?"

"Yes... please..." I stammered, blushing. "Um... could you ask Chef James to recommend a nice bottle of wine? I'm sure whatever he chooses will be perfect."

"Of course," said Charles.

Mark came back just a minute after Charles left. He carried a long black bag. My anxiety level increased immediately. I knew if a bag was involved, Mark had much more than just a romantic dinner planned.

He crouched by the side of my chair and pulled out a pole and a large vibrator. Screwing the vibrator onto one end of the pole, he looked at me. But he didn't say a word or smile. I squirmed nervously.

Mark ducked under the table. He pulled my chair closer to the table, and pushed my legs apart. I felt him place the vibrator directly against my clit and heard a 'click'. I realized he had the vibrator propped up between the base of the table and my cunt.

He popped back out from under the table and smiled at me. Rummaging around in his bag, he pulled out two large cuffs. In an instant, my ankles were secured to the legs of my chair. He walked behind me and I heard him doing something underneath the chair.

"This room has some unique hooks in convenient places. Your chair is secured in place. I'd hate for you to struggle so much that you topple yourself over. So – don't worry."

"OK," I whispered.

"Just two more ties," he said. Using thick, soft rope, Mark tied my waist to the chair. Next, he looped a rope between the vibrator pole and my thighs, and tied it tight around the seat. My entire lower body was completely secured – I tested the ties and found I could barely move at all.

Mark sat in his chair beside me, stroking my thigh. His hand felt the tip of the vibrator against my clit, checking to make sure it was in place.

"Good," he said, satisfied.

Our waiter appeared with a bottle of wine and two glasses. He greeted Mark and set the glasses in place. I was thankful for the tablecloth to hide my pussy and vibrator from his view, but knew as he walked around the table that he could see I was tied to the chair.

When Charles asked Mark if he needed anything else to drink, Mark flicked the switch of the vibrator and the unmistakeable humming sound filled the quiet room. I groaned audibly as the vibrations send waves through my clit, then clamped my mouth shut. The waiter looked at me, then back to Mark.

"Nothing else for now, thank you," said Mark.

I wanted nothing more than to shrink down in my seat, but the ties kept me firmly in place.

"This brand of vibrator is particularly strong," Mark said, ignoring my embarrassment. "I imagine you'll be close to cumming rather quickly."

I moaned. I was close, he was right.

"Ohhhh, sir," I said softly. I felt my back arch and I tilted my head towards the ceiling. I came hard, biting my lip to keep from crying out.

Mark got up and stood behind me. He grabbed both of my hands and held them firmly behind the chair. The vibrator was still on and I gasped and trembled, trying to move away from the buzzing on my sensitive clit.

"Please, sir, I'm done cumming sir," I said, frantic. I tried to pull my hands away from his grasp so I could turn the vibrator off myself. He held me tight.

"Don't worry about keeping quiet, Heather," I heard him say behind me. "As long as the door is closed, this room is soundproof."

"Sir, please!" I pleaded. I felt my body give in and I exploded into a second orgasm, this time crying out.

"Aghhhhhh," I moaned loudly. I was sweating now, struggling hard against the ties on my legs and against Mark's hold on my arms.

"Please, I'll do anything, please turn it off," I begged.

"One more for now," Mark said.

Nothing was on my mind anymore except for the huge discomfort of having such a strong vibration on my sensitive clit. I bucked against the chair, trying as hard as I could to get away. But my body still reacted to the vibrator, and I screamed out as the third orgasm coursed through me. It felt like strange pain more than pleasure.

"Oh oh oh, please sir," I said as he released my arms. He quickly reached around me and turned off the vibrator.

"This," he said as he sat down, "is going to be fun."

My cunt was twitching against the vibrator. Though off, it still was firmly in place. If I shifted even slightly, my pussy would rub against it. My whole body shuddered.

"Orgasm aftershock," said Mark. He was looking at me, clearly amused.

I took a sip of the red wine the waiter had brought us. I couldn't remember what kind of wine he said it was, but barely cared.

"Careful with the wine, Heather. You'll just have one glass tonight, then water. I want you to stay hydrated."

"For what?" I asked.

"Remember when you asked me about forced orgasms? And I told you the story of my slave who came over and over at my hand until she nearly fainted?"

"Yes, sir," I responded. I looked down at the table. Was he going to make me faint?

"After I told you that story, I felt your pussy. I know it turned you on."

I blushed. "But, sir," I said, "I don't know if I can take it."

"You can. I thought about doing it in the comfort of my apartment, but I think I'll rather enjoy a nice meal in my favorite restaurant while I watch my slave squirm."

Our waiter returned with appetizers and Mark turned the vibrator back on. My clit had some time to cool off since orgasm number three, and I willed myself not to cum quickly. I knew once I came my sensitive pussy would continue to feel the torture of the vibrator.

Charles took his time setting down the plates of food. I closed my eyes and imagined the picture he saw: my naked, sweating body so close to orgasm.

Thinking about that sent me over the edge and I threw my head back and cried out. I frantically reached for the vibrator, hoping to turn it off before Mark held me back.

"No." Mark said loudly. "Put your hands on your thighs."

I did as he said and gripped my thighs hard, my entire body tense as the vibrator continued its assault on my pussy. I knew the waiter was just standing there, waiting for us to finish so he could safely open the door. I breathed deeply, trying to make my brain force my pussy to not feel a thing.

This was of course no use. My body ripped into another orgasm. I felt like screaming after I came for the fifth time in under a half-hour.

"Pleeeeeease, Mark, please," I begged. I couldn't keep myself from reaching for the vibrator. Mark grabbed my hands and held my wrists tight.

"Please sir, I can't take it," I cried.

"Breathe, Heather," he said. His voice was firm.

I inhaled and exhaled quickly, trying to calm myself down. Mark held my wrists in one hand and used his other hand to massage my breasts, flicking my nipples lightly. Every part of my body felt so much more sensitive than before, and his light touch on my breasts sent me into another orgasm.

I felt the vibrator turn off but continued convulsing slightly.

"Thank you for waiting, Charles," said Mark after I stopped

moaning.

"Certainly, sir," he said, slipping out of the room.

I can hardly remember what we ate for our final course. I do remember eating hungrily and being interrupted constantly by the vibrator. Mark told me later that he had taken care never to turn it on if I was chewing because he was concerned I might choke. He also informed me that Charles was wearing an earpiece so he knew he wouldn't open the door to the rest of the restaurant while I was crying out.

When Mark took me home, he carried me into my apartment. He took off my dress and laid me down on the bed naked. I was exhausted and my pussy was dry, but I submitted willingly when he pressed his cock into my cunt. He looked deep into my eyes as he fucked me. After awhile, he slowed down, but I knew he was close. His eyes sparkled and he opened the drawer of my nightstand. When I saw what he was looking for I nearly screamed.

Instead, I whispered, "No, Mark..."

The familiar sound of the buzzing made my whole body tremble. I knew he could feel me shaking, but he pressed my vibrator against my clit anyway and started fucking me hard.

I cried out as I came one last time for the night. He came with me, groaning loudly as he slammed into my cunt.

Mark and I both lost track of how many times I came that night. My body had never felt so completely exhausted. For days after, anything brushing up against my clit made me shudder as I recalled cumming for him, over and over again.

Chapter Seventeen
SLAVERY

Michelle and I made sure to have lunch together at least once a week, usually at the cafe across the street. When we had time, we drove to a new restaurant or even on a few occasions made a picnic at the park downtown. We helped each other with any problems or questions we had in our respective relationships. In February, Michelle sulked into my office one morning, tears in her eyes.

"Can we go out after work?" she said so softly I could barely make out what she was saying.

"Sure, hun," I said. "What's wrong?"

"I'll tell you later. I have to finish up some stupid paperwork for my last case."

We finished at the office around seven and made our way immediately to a nearby bar and grill. I was famished and ordered a hamburger. Michelle wouldn't even look at the menu.

"Jack and coke," she said sullenly to the waiter, not looking up to make her order.

"OK, what's up?" I asked with a somewhat demanding tone. She *never* acted like this; she was nearly always completely cheerful.

"Stephen..." she said, her voice quivering. She burst into tears just as our drinks arrived. "Just give me a minute, OK?" She sucked down half of her drink in one long gulp.

"Sure." I said, my mind going over the possibilities. He must have broken up with her. I moved over to her side of the booth and held her hand. We sat silently for a long time. My burger arrived and she took the opportunity to order another drink. I ordered her a sandwich, not wanting to deal with a completely drunk *and* sad Michelle... which seemed to be where she was heading tonight.

"Stephen wants another slave," she blurted out.

"What?!" I said, surprised. They were so great together. As two.

"I mean, I've always known this was a possibility. But I just feel like he is bored with me. I feel like he wants to replace me. And I know... I know that's not true. But I can't imagine living with another slave. I mean, you know that I love to *play* with other slaves. I love playing with you," she paused, looking at me with fondness. "But, god, Heather, I don't think I want this."

"Is it... I mean, is he sure?"

"He said he's looking for her actively. He just hasn't found the right person yet. But yeah. It's final. He won't discuss it."

"That just seems so unfair," I said. I was a bit shocked. Two women serving one man reminded me the unpleasantness of my Mormon childhood.

Michelle looked at me, her face hard. "It's what we're doing, Heather. It's what we chose. We chose this lifestyle, and this is the shit that comes with it. Do you really think 'slaves' get an equal vote? Do you really think you have *equality* with Mark? You shouldn't, because you'd be fooling yourself. You have your safeword with play, but as far as big decisions go, you're not in charge. Ultimatums, Heather, are a part of our lives. With Stephen, he might consider my opinion, but in this case, it's irrelevant. I can accept his choice, or I can leave him. Those are my two options. *Compromise* is not one of them."

"I'm... I'm sorry, Michelle. I didn't intend to..." I stammered. Her tone was almost mean. I didn't really understand what she was saying, I couldn't wrap my mind around it.

"It's fine, Heather," her voice softening as she squeezed my hand. "It's just... this sucks."

Her sandwich arrived, interrupting our conversation. This time we *both* ordered another round. We were quiet for a long time, sipping our drinks, each of us deep in our own thoughts. I hadn't really considered the depth of Mark's control over me. I could always leave him, that was very clear. But I wasn't sure how I felt about him being able to make such huge lifestyle choices for me. I wouldn't want to share him with another slave. If we moved to Rock Creek, I wouldn't want to *live* with another slave. What if he loved her more than me? Or what if she didn't like me at all and worked to whittle me out of their lives?

I shook myself out of that frame of mind. Mark didn't want another slave. He'd never mentioned it, and we'd been together for nearly a year now.

I wished I could speak with Michelle about Rock Creek. Mark had sworn me to secrecy regarding the community – I wasn't to talk with anyone but him about it. Even Mr. Richards, who knew I knew about Rock Creek hadn't said a word about it at work. But I wondered what she would think about it.

I looked at her and my heart nearly broke. She looked so sad. I put my arm around her and gave her a half-hug.

"Do you know what you're going to do?" I asked.

"No..." her voice was so small, so different from her usual strength. I was normally the one who needed advice or comfort, not her.

"You could always just... try it. To see how it goes. If you don't like it, you can leave," I offered.

"I can't... then..." she began to cry softly. "Then Stephen will have someone and I'll just be... I'll be so alone. I can't live without him, Heather. I don't want to go back to the life I had before. I just can't imagine... I can't imagine life without him. Without a Master."

"Oh, honey," I said, wishing I could comfort her. "That's the thing with relationships... *any* relationship, Master-slave or just normal vanilla girlfriend and boyfriend. Husbands and wives... it always hurts to end things. Sometimes it's so painful that people can't imagine going on with their lives. But they do. People break up. It's the biggest risk of having a relationship. But sweetie, you'll never be alone, OK? That's what friends are for... among other things, of course. I'll be here for you, whatever you decide."

"Oh, thank you Heather, you're so sweet," she turned to hug me tight. "It's just... it's hard."

When I asked Mark about Stephen's decision, he nodded. "Yes, he told me about that."

"Um, sir?"

"Yes?"

"You... do you want another slave?" I asked timidly.

"That, my dear, is a discussion for another day," he said. I frowned and crossed my arms.

"Do you have a problem with that, Heather?" he asked, his eyes narrowing.

"Well I don't see how you can keep information like that away from me. I want to know. I deserve to know, it affects me." I couldn't help but snap at him a bit as I said this. I felt so sorry for Michelle, and it all just seemed so... *unjust*.

"Your actions also affect what happens to you, slave. You don't *deserve* to know anything."

I stomped my foot against the floor with frustration. "It just isn't fair," I said.

Within two seconds I was thrown across his knees, my skirt flipped up and my ass exposed to him.

He spanked me hard. I bit my lip, determined not to move out of place or make any sound. I didn't want him to get the satisfaction of hearing my cries that day. It was the first time I felt angry about my place in our relationship. It was the first time I doubted my decision to become Mark's slave.

Mark wasn't stupid. He saw right through my resistance. He stopped his assault on my ass.

"Get your fucking ass up," he said gruffly, half throwing me off his lap. I leaped to my feet, rubbing my sore butt with my hands. I glared at him and he glared back at me.

"Get on your knees and crawl. Go get my wide belt, and bring it back in your teeth. GO!"

I fell to my knees as he shoved me down to the ground and quickly crawled away from him in an effort to avoid any 'encouragement' on my already burning ass. I was so angry and confused. Should I use my safeword and leave?

I couldn't. I couldn't leave. Mark... I had to trust him. Maybe he had a reason for not being upfront with me. Maybe not. But I had to hold strong. He had been training me for the past year. My trust ran deep. Perhaps today was just a speed bump. Maybe he didn't even want another slave.

I found his belt in his closet and placed it between my teeth.

A deep sense of dread flowed through my veins as I slowly made my way crawling back to him. Mark had never – *would never* – hurt me. But I hadn't ever seen such anger in his eyes. In fact, I'd never seen *any* anger in his eyes at all before now. All of his previous discipline had been planned. This was in reaction to my insecurity. A reaction to my distrust. I knew it wouldn't be pleasant. I knew he'd break me; he'd make me cry out.

Mark was seated when I returned with the belt, staring straight ahead. I knelt in front of him as he had taught me: my ass on my heels, my knees spread far apart, my hands behind my head, breasts jutting forward. I offered him the belt in my mouth.

He took the belt from me and laid it across his knee. His eyes were narrow. His gaze was focused on something distant, far from me.

"Heather, do you know why I'm upset with you?" he asked me.

"I think so... I'm not sure..." I responded softly. All the anger I'd felt had disappeared. Now I felt sorrow. And fear.

Mark stood up and folded the belt in half.

"Stand up," he commanded. "Strip. Then bend over, with your hands on the wall. Arch your back, and present your ass for a beating."

I gulped and did as he said. My skirt and top came off, and I placed my hands on the wall. I spread my legs wide as I knew he'd like, and arched my back so my ass was on display for him.

Mark moved close to me and said sternly, "You will have faith in me, in my decisions, *always*. My tolerance for disobedience is very low, as you know. And guess what, Heather?"

"What?" I said softly, trembling. His tone was strong, and his anger was obvious.

"I have *zero* tolerance for distrust." He pinched my nipple as he said that, making me cry out in pain.

"Please, Master, please, owww!" I cried, begging him to stop. He twisted my nipple so hard I nearly fell to the ground in pain.

He let go and continued, speaking into my ear, "I'm going to beat you, you silly little cunt. And this is a beating you will never forget. One neither of us will enjoy."

He stepped away from me and my world stood still. I knew I couldn't beg my way out of this punishment. Forgiveness would come, but only on his terms. My arms shook with fear.

"Please, Master. Tie me down. I don't think I can do this," I began, pleading for help. I knew with enough pain I wouldn't be able to hold myself in position for him.

"Shut up, you fucking whore!" he said loudly, kicking my legs farther apart. I clasped my mouth shut and prayed he would take pity on me.

"I will be giving you fifty lashes of the belt. You'll count every single fucking one. On every tenth lash, you'll turn around and do a thirty second wall-sit while I either ignore you, torture your tits, or spank your cunt. Do you know what a wall-sit is, slave?"

"No, sir," I said, my voice quivering. I was so scared I was near tears.

"You'll turn around and sit against the wall. Your calves and thighs will stay at a ninety degree angle, your back flat against the wall. Your feet and knees will be more than shoulder width apart. Got it?"

"Yes, sir."

"After the wall sit, you will beg me to let you up and give you more lashes. Understand?"

"Yes, sir," I said, a tear slipping down my cheek.

"If you fail to count even one lash, we start over. If you fail to complete a wall-sit, we start over. If you safeword, I'll stop immediately – and we'll talk – and, if you want to continue being my slave, guess what, slut? *We'll start over.* In other words, you'll finish this session if you want to be mine. If you don't, you should walk out the door right now. It will save us both time, and it will save you a great deal of pain."

Mark paused, and my brain went into overdrive. It was just as Michelle had said: I wasn't free to make my own decisions in this relationship. It wasn't my place to decide how he should punish me. If he felt that this was what I needed, I had to accept it. I had to accept his decisions, even when I wished they were different.

My stomach was queasy with the thought of what was coming next, but I did what I knew I had to do.

"Please, Master, punish your slave. Please. I'll take what you know I deserve." I bowed my head down and braced myself, and I heard Mark suck in his breath. I had said the right thing.

I felt the cool leather of the belt against my skin, and then its absence. It was coming.

Whoooosh! CRACK!

"Aghhhhhh!" I cried out loudly as the pain swept through me, bringing the tears I was holding back to my eyes. "Ohhhhh god, one sir," I counted dutifully. "Thank you, sir."

"No need to thank me. Just keep count."

"Yes, sir," I agreed meekly.

Whoooosh! CRACK!

"Aghhhhhh! Fuck!" I bolted upright and grabbed my ass with my hands, squeezing it to ease some of the pain. I looked over to Mark with fear.

"I don't expect you to hold your position. But keep your fucking hands off your ass," he said through gritted teeth as he slapped my hands away from my butt. "Count!"

"Ohhh God, two, sir," I said, placing my hands back on the wall.

With each stroke I cried out loudly until we finally got to ten. I gratefully turned around and positioned myself for the wall sit. I didn't think I could make it to 50 strokes, but I definitely knew I wouldn't make it without any breaks. I knew the wall sits wouldn't be comfortable, but at least my ass would have 30 seconds to recover. I pushed my back against the wall and bent my legs to 90 degrees, then looked to Mark for his approval.

He nodded slightly. I shuddered, looking at his expression. His face was cold, his eyes were narrowed.

"Time starts now," he said, and crouched down in front of me. "I expect occasional disobedience, Heather. I expect you to make mistakes. But I do not expect *defiance*. Do you understand me?"

"Yes, sir," I choked out as tears ran down my face.

Smack! Smack! Smack! Smack!

Mark used his palm to firmly slap my pussy. I cringed with each slap, willing myself to keep my legs apart for him. For his punishment.

"Not surprisingly," Mark said, his tone somewhat condescending, "your pussy is sopping wet."

I sobbed audibly, unable to understand why my body could possibly be turned on by this.

"But don't worry," he growled into my ear. "Your mind will not enjoy this, even if your slutty cunt does."

Mark stood up and grabbed the dreadful belt. "Your time is up. Beg."

"Ohhh Master please continue to punish me with your belt. Please punish my ass some more. Please sir, give me what I deserve," I bubbled out anything I thought he might want to hear as the tears rolled down my cheeks.

"Get up, cunt. Into position."

I jumped into place and braced myself for the next ten.

Whoooosh! CRACK!

"Aghhhhhhhhhh!" I cried out in pain. "Eleven, sir."

Whoooosh! CRACK!

"Twelve, sir. Oh sir, please..."

Whoooosh! CRACK!

"Ohhhhhh fuck, thirteen, sir."

"Don't count the next seven, Heather. Stay silent. Concentrate on the pain."

I did as he said, stroke after stroke hitting my ass like lightening to a tree. I knew I would bruise; I wondered if I would bleed. I desperately wanted to please him and take my punishment well. Another part of me wanted to end it, to say my safeword and walk out the door.

Whoooosh! CRACK!

Whoooosh! CRACK!

I fell to the floor after the last two strokes from the set crashed down on my upper thighs. I wanted to rub out the pain so much, but I knew I had to obey. I clutched my knees and curled up on the floor at Mark's feet, sobbing uncontrollably.

"Up, Heather. Wall-sit, now." Mark's voice cracked a bit and I looked up at him in surprise, then horror as I saw a tear run down his cheek.

He hated this.

A new strength set over me as I became determined to make this less painful on him. I had to be strong. Sobbing at Mark's feet wasn't helping.

I took my position against the wall. Mark knelt by me again and looked straight at me, through me, boring holes in my eyes and into my inner soul.

He grabbed both of my breasts and kneaded them roughly, making me squirm though I firmly held my position. While one of his hands continued the assault on one breast, the other worked on twisting and pulling my nipple so hard that I nearly screamed.

He went back and forth, torturing one of my nipples while kneading or smacking the other breast. My legs were shaking in exhaustion. My body was covered in sweat.

"Please, Master," I begged, trying to hold back my sobs. "Please, it hurts so much..."

When I didn't think I could take any more, Mark stood up and announced time.

My begging shifted to what I had been instructed. "Please continue to beat me, sir. Please let me get up. Beat me with your belt."

Mark nodded at me and I slowly put myself into position once again.

"Count," he said.

Whoooosh! CRACK!

"Ohhhh... twenty-one, sir."

Whooosh! CRACK!

"Twenty... twenty-two, sir," I choked out, trying to be strong.

Whoooosh! CRACK!

"Twenty-three, sir."

Whoooosh! CRACK!

"Ohhhh owwwww!" I couldn't tell where the strokes were landing anymore, each one just added another slash of pain to my ass. "Twenty-four, sir"

Whoooosh! CRACK!

"Aghh!" A particularly hard stroke. "Twenty-five, sir."

"Halfway, Heather. Do you have anything to say to me?"

Mark set down the belt and stepped away from me, waiting. Expecting something.

I began rambling a long, long apology for my defiance, for not trusting him.

"Stand up, look at me," he said.

I stood and turned to him. He half-smiled, which sent a flood of relief through my body and soul. I couldn't take the look of his stone cold face; I'd rather be beaten until bloody than lose his smile. And kindness.

My sobs renewed as I was unable to control my sense of relief.

Mark sighed. "Let's get this over with."

I took a deep breath and turned back to the wall.

Whoooosh! CRACK!

"Twenty-six, sir," I said quickly.

Whoooosh! CRACK!

"Twenty-seven, sir."

Whoooosh! CRACK!

"Ohh.... twenty-eight, sir."

Whoooosh! CRACK!

"Twenty-nine, sir."

Whoooosh! CRACK!

"Ohhhhh god.... thirty, sir."

"Wall-sit, slut."

Mark waited until I got into position, then left the room.

I was alone.

Without him, in the middle of this awful punishment, I felt oddly very lonely. I'd rather have him hurting and abusing me then be alone. Alone, I began to realize that my thighs were becoming very sore. I struggled to hold my position, knowing if I faltered we'd have to begin anew. Between the aching pain on my ass and the burning in my thigh muscles, I felt weak. Like I wouldn't make it. I doubted myself, without him.

Just as I considered shifting my position a bit to help ease the stress on my thighs, Mark returned.

"It's so hard, Mark. My thighs... they can't take it."

"They better fucking take it." He stood back, watching me.

My legs trembled. I knew I was close.

"OK, Heather. Beg."

"Please, Master," I said automatically. "Please let me up and continue punishing me. Please beat me as you see fit."

"Up."

"Master..." I said tentatively, placing my hands on the wall. "Do you think... can you... can I not count this time?"

I just wanted him to beat me, to get it over with. Counting made it hurt more. It made it last longer. It made me totally aware of every single lash.

"You'll count. If I don't want you to count, I'll let you know. You know that, slut. These will all be on your thighs." His tone was hard and unyielding.

I half-moaned, half-groaned as I braced myself for the next set.

Whoooosh! CRACK!

"Aghhhhhhh!!" I shot up from the pain, a new burning on my thighs instead of my ass. I clenched my hands in front of my body to keep myself from grabbing my thighs to ease the pain. I hopped up and down, any thought of what I must look like long gone from my concern.

"Thirty-one, sir," I cried out loudly.

"Back into position, slave."

Whoooosh! CRACK!

Each of the strokes in this set burned into me, making me break position every single time. He wasn't going easy on me, wasn't letting up at all. He was fully thrashing me as hard as he possibly could. Submissives, Mark had told me, sometimes cross this line when in 'play'- where the pain becomes pleasure and the world changes, if only temporarily. This wasn't happening for me, but something similar, though clearly different, was happening with Mark. I looked at his face halfway through the set, and his eyes, while still slightly cold, were *different*. He knew what he was doing, he was in full control. He was set in his decision to punish me, and he was carrying it out, without faltering.

Whoooosh! CRACK!

"Ohhhh gaaawd," I bubbled, a mixture of spit and tears rolling down my chin. "Forty, sir."

"You know what to do," he responded firmly.

When I took position, Mark kicked my feet a little farther apart, making different muscles feel the strain of the wall sit. He grasped the belt by the tip, leaving just 8 inches or so free.

"This is your last wall-sit, slave. Hold position. I don't want to have to do this again."

I held myself firmly in place, closing my eyes as the inevitable began. He struck my pussy over and over with the belt, each slap making me gasp in pain. I repeated a silent mantra in my head, demanding from myself some inner strength.

So close, Heather. Just get through this.

Mark wasn't letting up, each slap a little harder.

"Open your eyes," he demanded.

I obeyed, looking at him. Pleading with him with my eyes. Then, suddenly, as the intensity of the slaps kept increasing, I yielded. I felt the pain, but my will to obey took control. My eyes stopped pleading, and just gazed at him. Submission.

"Good girl," Mark said softly. He helped me up, gently turning me around towards the wall. "Last ten. Don't count."

Whoooosh! CRACK!

Whoooosh! CRACK!
Whoooosh! CRACK!

Mark continued my beating. With each stroke I held my position, only letting out a small gasp of pain.

Whoooosh! CRACK!
Whoooosh! CRACK!
Whoooosh! CRACK!

Somewhere in the back of my mind I knew we were both going through a transformation. I didn't understand it, but I was sure I could do anything for him. I could take any pain or punishment he had to give, and I would do anything he asked me to do.

Whoooosh! CRACK!
Whoooosh! CRACK!
Whoooosh! CRACK!

"Last one, Heather." He took a step back.

Whooooooooosh! **CRACK!**

The last stroke lifted me off of my feet, the intensity and force so high that I nearly toppled over. I cried out softly, but put myself back into position.

Mark pulled me away from the wall.

"It's over," he said softly. "Shhhhh..."

I collapsed into his arms, sobbing. He held me silently and gently. After some time, he scooped me up in his arms and carried me to his bathroom.

He set me down carefully and began drawing the bath. Looking back at me, he asked, "How do you feel?"

I couldn't believe I had tears left in my body, but I started crying again as I threw myself down to his feet. "I want to be yours, Master. Please, I'm so sorry. I want to be your slave."

I repeated this over and over, my head on his feet, my sore ass against my heels. I didn't care about the pain anymore. I wanted his acceptance. I needed it.

Mark sat on the edge of the tub and ran his fingers through my hair, petting me.

"Shhh, shhh, sweet slave. You are mine. You are mine."

He lifted me up to my feet and motioned for me to get into the tub. "Get on your hands and knees."

I climbed in. The rising water was warm and soothing. Mark washed me softly, using a soft cloth and mild soap.

His touch was so different now, so caring. He washed my back, my neck, then down around my bruised breasts. Gently, he lifted them, moving them to wash under every curve. I winced as he washed my ass and whined a bit when he spread my cheeks to wash my asshole and pussy.

"Shush," he warned me quietly.

He washed my legs, my feet, in between all of my toes. My armpits and arms. Every so often he scooped warm water over me to rinse off the suds.

"Close your eyes," he whispered, pulling me up to my knees. I felt the warm cloth on my face, wiping away any remnants of my tears.

He lifted me out of the tub and wrapped me up in his robe. He turned me towards the mirror and slowly combed through my hair, straightening out any tangles before pulling it up into a loose ponytail.

Taking my hand, he led me to his bedroom. He paused at the foot of the bed, turning to face me.

"I'm proud of you, my sweet Heather," he said sincerely. "Do you know what happened today?"

I thought about it for a few seconds. I did know. I nodded.

"Tell me."

"I accepted... *this*. Before... it was role-play, to me. A fun game. I mean, I took it seriously... But, god, Master, I *need* this. I *am this*. I am a slave. I'm your slave. Thank you."

"Good girl." His hands on my shoulders, pushing me down slightly, told me what he wanted next. I dropped to my knees, eager to please him for the first time as *his*.

I pulled out his sweet cock and lightly grazed it with the tip of my tongue. Sucking softly on the sensitive, soft head I looked up at him as he gazed down at me. I swirled my tongue around his shaft, going slow, savoring his treasure, feeling him harden in my mouth.

He moaned as I took his balls in my mouth, one at a time, sucking softly. I replaced my mouth with my hand, tickling his balls and returned my oral attention back to his cock. Slowly I moved my head back and forth, fucking him with my mouth, my lips suctioning around his shaft providing pressure and pleasure.

His hand held the back of my head, not forcing me, but moving along with my rhythm. I quickened my pace, tightening one hand around the base of his cock while the other continued massaging his balls.

"Good, Heather, keep going," Mark groaned above me. Both of his hands now held my head, encouraging me to speed up. I twisted my hand at the base of his cock and he moaned loudly, forcing himself deep inside me and cumming. His cum fill my mouth. He pulled out of me slowly and I caught my breath, swallowing down his load and looking up to him, smiling.

He smiled back at me. "Good slave. Now, take off the robe and go lie down in the bed. Face down. I'll be back in a few minutes."

I pulled down the covers and gratefully collapsed into the bed. I was physically and emotionally exhausted, but felt peaceful. Sleepy. As soon as my head hit the pillow I drifted off into my dreamland.

I awoke only for a few minutes as Mark was carefully

applying some sort of cream to my swollen ass. When I winced and looked back at him, he explained, "This will help you heal faster. Now, go to sleep my sweet slave. Rest well tonight. Dream." He kissed my forehead and tucked a sheet around me, leaving me to sleep.

Chapter Eighteen
CLIMAX

After that day, our relationship changed significantly. I never found myself hesitating any order Mark gave me. Whatever he demanded, I did without second thought. Mark was pleased with my smooth progression into submission, and I found myself happier than I had ever been before.

I discovered that I couldn't talk with Michelle about it. I mentioned what had happened, and she looked at me almost scornfully.

"Well, good for you," was all she said. She canceled our lunch date for that day — she said she was just too busy. But I knew better than to bring it up again. When I asked her what she was going to do about Stephen's decision, she just muttered, "Well, what *can* I do? I'll just wait to see if she works out."

"Has he found someone? Someone right for you both?"

"No," she said. "Not yet. He goes out without me though, now, to clubs. To hunt. He said my attitude only turns women away. He's... I think he's pulling away from me."

At work, I became a bit distracted, though I still did fine with my casework and kept up with my workload – as well as helping Erik with his. Since being with Mark, Erik and I had actually developed a friendly working relationship. We were always ready to help each other out with our workloads, and more often than not it was me helping him. I didn't mind though. Conversation was easy between us, and I was lucky to share an office with someone as kind and friendly as him.

The week after my 'awakening' – I wasn't sure what to call it – Erik noticed me tapping my pen against my desk while staring into space.

"What's up, Heather?" he asked.

"Oh. Sorry." I put the pen down.

"No problem. But what's up? You seem to be thinking about something."

"Ah, it's nothing. But hey, Michelle can't eat lunch with me today. Want to fill in?"

"Gee, thanks. Replacement lunch date."

"Pretty much," I said, grinning.

Erik and I had so much fun at lunch – we'd never spent time together away from the office – that we decided to do it more often. I told Mark I had more friends at work, and he was happy to hear about that.

One Sunday, at Mark's apartment, he approached me with a serious expression.

"Heather. I want to talk with you."

"Yes, sir," I said, putting down a file I was working on.

"I've spoken with Mr. Richards about you. He says you're one of the top members of his team."

I smiled. Mr. Richards had always given positive feedback to me, but I was proud that he said this to Mark.

"He says," Mark continued, "that it might be possible for you to get a serious promotion. And pay raise. And put on the track for partnership."

I gasped.

"...If you switch to the Rock Creek branch."

"Wait a minute... the Rock Creek *branch*?" I asked, confused. "I thought Mr. Richards worked for two firms. I didn't know... What am I missing?"

"Heather, your law firm is much bigger, and much more powerful, than you have been led to believe. You're working at a very small branch of a very, *very* large firm. Your branch exists to allow the partners and leaders of the firm to identify the rising stars. You, Heather, have been identified as a star. Since you already know about Rock Creek, well, Mr. Richards is pleased. It is extremely difficult to find good lawyers who are willing to represent Rock Creek; usually we need to find them internally. You'll be one of the few who has been selected for their skills, rather than the simple fact that you accept the lifestyle and live in the community."

I stared at Mark, speechless.

"Anyway," he continued, "Mr. Richards would like to meet with you tomorrow about this. At Rock Creek. He's checked your current cases and will begin to reassign them with your permission. If you're even willing to consider this, I'll take you there tomorrow. Heather, this could be an excellent opportunity for you. It would definitely be a way to expedite your acceptance into the community. I won't make you do this; this is your decision. But I hope you decide to at least consider this change. It would mean..." he trailed off.

"It would mean we could be free," I finished his sentence. I had thought often about Rock Creek since the day on the hill, looking over the houses and community with Mark. It could be paradise.

"Well, I'd love to speak with Mr. Richards about this," I said. "And I'd love to see Rock Creek. I'll be honored to go there with you tomorrow, Master."

Mark grinned at me. "Oh, Heather. This is exciting. Calls for a celebration! Go pick out some wine and make a nice snack. I'll be back in a bit, I want to show you something. To help you prepare."

He stood up and made his way down the hallway and I scurried to the kitchen to prepare the wine and food. I made a platter of olives, brie cheese, smoked salmon and some artisan homemade crackers. I looked through the wines he had in his kitchen – he had taught me a bit about wine since my first flop with serving him cheap white wine in a juice glass. I selected a pinot noir, poured two glasses, and set up the platter in between them on the coffee table in the living room.

I knelt on the floor and waited patiently for his return, my mind racing as I tried to imagine what it would be like at Rock Creek. I also considered whether it would be weird to speak with Mr. Richards there. We hadn't even spoken of the fact that we had this mutual secret. I decided it would be fine. Mr. Richards was, after all, a professional. He had much more experience in the lifestyle than I.

Mark returned with a large folder that he set near me, and a thin black box which he set on the opposite end of the table.

"Come sit up on the couch with me," he said, patting the cushion beside him. I sat next to him as he opened the large folder and pulled out a thin booklet. I peered at the title.

Community Guidelines, Version 545.1, RC X74P2

"Version five hundred and forty five? Really?" I asked,

amazed.

"Point one. Yes, really. X74P2 is the official name of Rock Creek. These guidelines apply only to our branch, though they share many attributes with the other communities around the world. Anything inside that is italic is unique to us. You won't be able to read it all today, but it will give you an idea. Go on, flip through it."

I opened the booklet carefully. The book was letter-sized, and the print was small. The paper was thin, reminding me of whatever is used in standard Bibles.

The first section was a list of regulations for members in the community. It was long, and the wording was very legal. I read a couple paragraphs before moving on, but it did cross my mind that the average person in the community must have higher intelligence than normal people; this stuff wasn't easy reading.

The end of the first section had a few phrases in italics, mostly referring directly to the community's interactions with the closest cities. The following section pertained to the various sections of the community; the 'family-friendly' side was section A, the other called section B. Within A there were three sub-categories, within section B there were seven sub-categories. These appeared to be roughly defined.

"Which... what neighborhood, or whatever, are you in?" I asked Mark.

"Well, various. But the house I hope to move you to is in B-4."

I flipped to section B-4 and scanned it. Each section had letters on top to signify what types of members populated it, for the most part. B-4 was *M/f, F/f, Poly, M/m and F/m.*

"What's it mean?" I asked.

"Well, you know that the capital letters represent tops. So B-4 has mainly female submissives and slaves. Male subs are fine, but just not usual in the neighborhood. They usually only exist in poly households, where there are also female slaves. 'Poly' refers to polyamory – a lot of the households develop relationships with each other. Some households have more than one Master, or more than one slave."

I looked at him, hoping for more information. He just shrugged. I looked back at the book.

'Most households have agreements in which Masters and Mistresses have certain rights over slaves. In absolutely all cases this must be predetermined among the Tops before actions are taken to play with, punish, discipline, or perform sexual acts with any slaves. Tops' choices regarding their slaves can vary from 'anything goes' to 'off-limits'. New Masters and Mistresses must prove themselves as trusted community members before being granted any slave access. Seasoned and trusted community Masters and Mistresses are generally given rights to slaves in B-4.'

I looked at Mark, pointing to that paragraph.

"Heather, this lets people understand what they're moving into. A Master who was very possessive and jealous of any time someone else spends with his slave would prefer a different neighborhood. He could just tell everyone his slave is off-limits, but the general dynamic of the neighborhood is such that this type of possessiveness... well, it's not common. B-4 is actually the most sought out section. Slaves are submissive to all the tops; just as you are with Stephen. If, for example, I see my neighbor's slave sneaking a smoke outside, and I know she's not allowed to smoke, I can discipline her a bit and then turn her in for more punishment when he gets home. On the lighter side, when I'm taking my morning stroll, I'm welcome to smack her on the ass as she's taking her morning crawl. Get it?"

I gulped, nodding. I had a hard enough time behaving for Mark. I wondered how it would feel having more than just his eyes watching me.

He continued, "Masters and Mistresses don't take advantage of their position. No one is given any rights at all, to any slave, until they know the person well. Most of us actually attend a meeting, once every two weeks, to discuss any changes or anything we want for our slaves. If I ever need to leave town, I'll bring that up at the meeting to be sure someone watches over you. We work together.

"And, the slaves get together often as well. In B-4, as you'll read later, there is a mandatory monthly meeting of slaves and submissives. There is always a Master or Mistress present during the meeting, but it is run by the slaves themselves. They discuss problems, fears, or whatever is on their minds."

"Huh," I said, flipping the pages to browse other sections. They were mainly separated by kinks. B-1 was Daddys and Mommys with their little girls and little boys, and B-2 was disciplinarians and spank-os. B-3 was like B-4, but more male submissives than female. B-5 was for exclusive couples who, besides occasional exceptions, didn't play with others or do a lot of exhibition play. B-6 had a focus on 'switching', and more on play than the lifestyle.

"I thought you said there were seven sections," I said, looking for B-7.

"There are. You'll learn about B-7 later. And, don't forget, the sections are simply a helpful tool. But in every section there are always people who either change, or make exceptions. Within the entire B area, nudity and public play are acceptable. It's just that, in B-1 you're more likely to see someone getting a paddling while wearing a little girl's outfit. And in B-3 you'll see more men crawling around then women. And, when I want you to get a big spanking but don't want to administer it, guess where I'll send you for your punishment?"

"B-2," I said softly.

"You've got it. There are several men and women in B-2 who publicly list themselves as disciplinarians, and help the Masters and Mistresses out with keeping all submissives and slaves properly disciplined. Ever hear of the 'walk of shame' in college?"

I smiled. The walk of shame was when girls walked back to their house the morning after a night out at a bar. It was so named because the girls had on their slutty makeup and clothing from the previous night, and everyone knew they had just put out. "Yeah," I said, nodding.

"Well, it has a whole new meaning at Rock Creek. You'll commonly see a woman walking naked back to her Master's house, her ass bright red and her eyes puffy from tears. Sometimes she'll even be carrying a sign, an added humiliation to the walk of shame. It might say, 'I've been a bad girl'. Or, 'I've just been punished. Please give my ass another spank.' That way, any master who knows her will bend her right over in the street, inspect her butt, and smack it once more, hard, before sending her on her way."

I swallowed, not so sure I wanted to think more about any of this. I put the booklet down and took a sip of the wine.

"Ohh... it's good," I said, savoring the flavor and hoping to change the subject.

"It is," Mark agreed, looking at me. "Does it turn you on at all, thinking about Rock Creek?"

I looked down at the ground, embarrassed with his direct question. "I don't know... I think so, maybe."

He rolled his eyes at me, pushed my legs apart and roughly groped my naked cunt. "Open your mouth."

I obeyed and he put his fingers in my mouth, wet from my own juices. I sucked him clean.

"Slave, does it turn you on to think about Rock Creek?" he

asked again.

"Yes, sir," I said softly.

"Good girl. I'm glad."

He turned to pull out a satellite map from the folder. "This is where one of my houses it," he said, pointing to the map. "See how the houses form a circle around the backyards?"

"Yeah," I said, looking at the map closely.

"The backyard area is a place for play. It is all grassed and kept very clean by a gardener we employ full time. We host parties there for other members of the community – the dog show is one, and the slave olympics is another. Often, people from Section A will come over to play."

"Are there... wait, where is your road?" I asked. There appeared to be several sidewalks on the front side of his house, but I couldn't make out any cars or roads.

"B-4 is car-free. Much more pleasant that way. Our parking lot is here," he said, pointing to a large space on the other side of the circle of houses.

"How many homes are there in B-4?"

"About fifty. The circle has twenty-five homes, meaning that shared backyard is pretty large. The other twenty-five homes are scattered around the circle. Quite a few are earth homes, built partly in the ground, so they are less visible via satellite. Of those, ten are rentals for members who aren't residents. Jasmine and Rose rent one home there a few times a year; they have it reserved for the special events."

I cringed, thinking about the last time I saw Jasmine.

Mark noticed me cringing and smiled. "If you end up living at Rock Creek, I'll be lending you to Jasmine whenever they visit. She loves playing with you."

"As you wish, sir," I said softly, knowing that's what he expected me to say. "She's sadistic."

"I know," he said. He pulled the map from me and put it back into his folder. "Do you have any questions, Heather? To help you prepare yourself for tomorrow?"

"I don't know. I have so many questions but I doubt the answers will help me prepare mentally for tomorrow. Luckily, Mr. Richards knows me. He must value my work. I have to admit, I'm kind of excited to see the place. Where will I meet him? What section?"

"The firm is in section A. You'll meet him there. I've gotten permission to show you section B in the afternoon, after your meeting. Whenever there's a new guest on site, all residents must be notified at least one week prior."

"You've known about this for a week?" I asked, my tone expressing my annoyance. Mark slapped my thigh, hard.

"Ask that again," he said sternly. I repeated my question, fixing my tone.

"I have known about this for much longer than a week. I tell you things on *my* time, not yours."

"Yes sir," I said meekly. I snuggled up close to him. Whenever he was stern with me I felt both guilty and aroused. He put his arm around me and we sat silently for awhile, both deep in thought.

"Kneel at my feet, Heather," he said, breaking our silence.

I slid off of the couch and took my place by his feet, looking up at him for more direction. He picked up the long black box and opened it.

"I want you to wear this tomorrow," he said, pulling out a woven silver chain.

It was a beautiful, thin collar.

Mark continued, "You are mine. This, my dear Heather, represents that. When I move you into Rock Creek, I will hold a collaring ceremony to celebrate my ownership of you. But, in the meantime, you must never forget that you belong to me. Your actions, good or bad, reflect back onto me. Your words, your tone, and your behavior. Do you understand, slave?"

"Yes, Master," I whispered.

"I have not collared many slaves, Heather. I do not take this lightly. I trust you understand the deep meaning of our bond, and you will respect and honor it."

"I will, Master. I'm honored you have taken me as yours," I said, a tear of joy sliding down my cheek. He reached down and clasped the chain around my neck. When he withdrew his hands, I felt the weight of the collar against my skin; the physical weight was nearly nothing but the psychological weight was immense. I struggled to hold back my tears.

Mark ran his hand through my hair, petting me gently. I wanted to stay there, at his feet, forever.

"Tell me that you trust me, Heather."

I looked up at him, surprised. "Oh, Master, of course I trust you. Completely."

"Good." He stood up. "Let's get some rest. Tomorrow will be a big day."

Chapter Nineteen
RED CHECKERED TABLECLOTHS

Mark picked out my outfit the next morning. A tight black skirt that came to just above my knees, with a slit in front that would show off my right thigh as I walked. He paired it with a blood-red blouse, also quite tight, and a sleek black jacket. For my feet, simple three-inch heels. I admired myself in the mirror as I pulled my hair up into a professional looking bun. Mark was good at selecting clothes that would show off my body.

We were both quiet on the drive out to Rock Creek. My mind was moving fast, fueled by nerves and anticipation. I wondered who I would meet, what I would see, and if I would feel comfortable. I glanced over at Mark often, considering asking him one of the hundreds of questions I still had, but always thought better of it. His gaze was concentrated straight ahead on the road, also deep in thought.

I noticed the road we had turned off on months before when Mark brought us for a picnic. We were close.

"You'll meet quite a few people today," Mark said, breaking the silence. "Mostly, everything will be casual. But you will be respectful and submissive to every single one of them. If you are asked to do something, you will do it."

"Yes, sir." I fidgeted in my seat, suddenly even *more* nervous then before.

"Don't worry," he said, noticing my unease. "You'll make me proud."

The road curved and as we moved forward I kept my eyes fixed on the buildings ahead, eager to see the community. Mark slowed the car down and pulled off the highway, taking a right on a dirt road.

"Where are you going?" I asked.

"There is no paved road to enter from this side. It just makes it easier. We don't want a lot of people driving in by accident. There are small convenience stores and gas stations at either entrance, outside of the gates, for drivers who spot the buildings and assume they can fill up their tank. But the stores don't get a lot of traffic. See?" Mark pointed to the left and I noticed the unassuming gas station and sandwich shop.

"Interesting," I said.

I could see the wall surrounding the community very well now. It was large, over twelve feet tall, and made of beautiful stone. Whoever built this place was able to invest quite a bit of money for the sake of privacy. We approached the gate and Mark slowed by a small building. A man came out to greet us, and Mark pulled some papers from the glove compartment.

"Mark Doston. I have a guest with me today, she's been approved. Heather Green," Mark said, handing the man his ID and the paperwork.

"Certainly Mr. Doston, just a moment please," he said, disappearing into the building. He reappeared seconds later with a plastic badge. "This is for Ms. Green. Go ahead."

"Keep that on you," Mark said, handing me the badge. It had my photo on it, along with what looked like a computer chip and a bar code. I clipped it to my blouse.

The large, black metal gate opened as we approached, giving me my first up-close glimpse of Rock Creek. I stared out the window, completely in awe. It was just like a small town; so totally *not* what I had expected. I wasn't sure what I *had* been expecting, to be truthful.

"This is Section A. I don't spend a lot of time here, so let's see if I can find the office where you'll meet Mr. Richards without getting us lost," said Mark.

We pulled into a part of Section A that was like the quintessential sort of small-town American Main Street. There was a quaint little street with pretty storefronts, diagonal street parking, and wide sidewalks on either side of the road. Trees were planted along the sidewalks, providing a nice canopy of shade. A few people were out, some obviously going to work, dressed in suits, while others were dressed casually and holding shopping bags or paper coffee cups. It was all so completely normal I nearly forgot that this was a kinky community. It was like a movie set. Mark pulled into a parking spot.

"Well, ready or not, here we are," he said.

We entered an unmarked building and made our way to the second floor. A receptionist greeted us warmly and within seconds Mr. Richards was out to meet us.

"Heather! Mark! So great to have you here." Mr. Richards smiled at us, shaking our hands. It was odd, I somehow felt like I hadn't seen him in a long time even though I saw him just last Friday.

"Let me give you a little tour," he said. "Mark, are you going to join us?"

"No, Mr. Richards, thanks. I'll pass. Just give me a call when you're done," Mark said. "Be good, Heather." He kissed my forehead before zipping past us down the stairs.

Mr. Richards led me down the hall, pointing out a library, a conference room, and several private offices. It was an impressive size, at least as big as our office in the city.

"This, Heather, would be your office," he said, opening a door towards the end of the hall. A large mahogany desk sat at the center of the room. Behind the desk, a huge window overlooked a park. Two bookshelves graced the walls on either side of the office, and at the corner of the room by the door was a small bar.

"I'd have a bar?" I asked, a bit giddy.

Mr. Richards laughed. "It's a sign of success when your office has a bar, no?" He reached behind the bar and pulled out a bottle of scotch, pouring us both a drink.

I walked behind the desk, my fingers trailing along the smooth wood as I imagined making this huge change to my life.

"Well, it certainly is a beautiful office."

"It is." Mr. Richards sat down in front of the desk and sipped his scotch. "Have a seat. Let's talk logistics."

Over the next two hours Mr. Richards explained more about the legal work behind Rock Creek. I was truly amazed at how complex the system was, though once he went through the details it all made perfect sense. Residents were required to sign many contracts before joining the community. Land and home ownership had special clauses, and there were small but important differences between ownership in the two sections. Families with children had even more contracts to sign for the agreements of the community. Democracy had a strange role at Rock Creek. Voting determined a lot of the community decisions, which explained why the handbook had undergone over five-hundred revisions.

"Your job," Mr. Richards said, "would start off as sort of a training program for you. You'll handle small legal disputes within the community. As you get comfortable with the framework, you'll move up the 'corporate ladder,' so to speak. I'd like you to eventually take over my position within this branch."

"Really?" I felt honored. I had no idea Mr. Richards had so much faith in me and so much trust in my work.

"Yes, really. But, that's years out. We'll start with the basics. Salary-wise, you'll start at double what you're making now. Your health benefits will be the same, though you'd see doctors in the community. They're better here, anyway."

My heart thumped with excitement. *Doubling* my salary!

"In the top drawer of your desk there is some paperwork and a contract. I'll leave you to read it through. Any questions, before I go?"

"Yes, well, just one. The only reason I know about this place at all is because of Mark. What would happen if we were to separate, and I move out of the community?"

"Part of your contract is that you'll be living here at Rock Creek. In the event that you separate, you would rent a home or apartment here. In the event that you want to leave Rock Creek, we would terminate your contract. It is possible I could reassign you to another firm, but Heather, I'm counting on you to stay on board here. And that means being *here*. Lawyers who live and work at Rock Creek are compensated heavily for their time and the value they provide us. You know this is a huge promotion. I'm not doubling your salary because your workload will increase; I'm doubling it because I want to be able to depend on you."

"Of course, Mr. Richards. I understand."

"Call Mark before you sign anything. If you have any more

questions, come find me."

I browsed the contract. It was quite similar to my current contract, with added statements concerning community privacy and internal branch security. I poured myself another glass of scotch and turned my desk chair around to look out the window. The park was very beautiful. Like a plaza, there were sidewalks surrounding a large green area in the middle. Benches spotted the walkways, with flower beds in between them. Beyond the park were more buildings, similar in style to this one; double storied businesses. I could just make out the beginning of apartments and residences a few blocks north of the park.

"Oh, Heather, what should you do?" I asked myself out loud. The decision seemed so obvious, yet I felt internal conflict. Signing the contract meant moving out of my apartment and leaving behind my life in the city. Yet what would I really be leaving? It wasn't as if I had a huge social life. I'd miss lunches with Michelle, and chatting with Erik – but that was no reason not to take a huge raise.

I tried to see it without the BDSM aspect. Even if Mark didn't exist, I'd be stupid not to take this job. With the salary, I could work for a few years and retire early if I wanted to. I *had* to sign.

I called Mark and told him about the meeting with Mr. Richards.

"Does the contract look right?" he asked.

"Yeah. Everything is correct. I want to sign, Mark."

"Good girl. I'm proud of you. I'll take you and Mr. Richards out to lunch to celebrate – I'll be there in an hour or so."

I read through the contracts again, signing where it was needed.

Afterward, I found Mr. Richards in the front of the office, chatting with the receptionist. Handing him the paperwork, I nodded. I was in.

"Wonderful! Hey, listen, I started your official residency application process a few weeks ago in anticipation of this meeting. I should be able to expedite the process considerably."

Why was it that everyone knew about this meeting so far in advance, except for me?

"And I have a surprise for you. Come with me."

I followed Mr. Richards to an office, where he knocked a few times lightly before opening the door. My jaw must have been near the floor as I gasped loudly.

"What? How...?" I stammered. I was speechless. Sitting at the desk in the office was Erik. He grinned at me.

"You just thought I was your semi-stupid office mate, eh?" he said, laughing at my expression.

"What were... were you *spying on me*?" I asked, somewhat incredulously. This was too much.

"Did she sign?" Erik asked, ignoring my question and directing his attention towards Mr. Richards.

"She did."

"Good."

"Heather, Erik is here to answer any questions you have and show you the ropes of working at this branch. You'll report to him daily for the first two weeks with your progress."

"I'll *report* to *Erik*?" I asked.

"Watch yourself, Heather," Erik said. "I'm actually a pretty damn good lawyer. And I've got permission from Mark to discipline you as needed. You'll show me respect. Got it?"

I felt my face burn red and I looked down at my feet. I had certainly not expected this.

"Yes, sir," I mumbled.

"Good. See you tomorrow morning, then."

Mr. Richards led me back to reception, chatting about

where we would eat lunch as if the conversation with Erik hadn't even happened. Mark was waiting for us.

"Congratulations, my beautiful," Mark said, kissing me. He turned to Mr. Richards. "Did she meet Erik?" he asked.

"Yep – we just finished talking with him," said Mr. Richards.

"Heather, I think you'll find having him here to keep an eye on your behavior quite rewarding. You're such a productive worker already, just think of how well you'll do with a little motivation." Mark's eyes were sparkling.

"You... you knew too? About Erik? Spying on me?"

"Of course."

We walked to the restaurant Mark chose. It was an Italian place, a couple of blocks from the office. A few tables adorned with red checkered tablecloths and set with wine glasses and breads sat outside. I found myself incredibly pleased with just how quaint this little downtown area was. We chose a table and Mark ordered a bottle of wine. The waiter returned promptly and filled our glasses.

"A toast," said Mark, raising his glass, "to Heather's first day at Rock Creek. To a new beginning for her, a new job. I'm so proud of you, Heather."

We drank and we ate. Mark pulled his usual trick of asking the chef to serve us what he wished. The food was rich and plentiful: spinach and ricotta homemade ravioli served with beautiful slices of roasted duck. Another bottle of wine arrived with the meal and I felt slightly tipsy from the combination of the good mood at the table and the alcohol.

When he paid, Mark showed me his card. "Everyone here has an account. I fill mine every month and you'll do the same. It means no one needs to carry cash," he explained as we stood to go.

"Well, thanks so much for lunch and conversation. I should get back to work," said Mr. Richards, shaking our hands. "See you soon, Heather. Congratulations."

"Thanks Mr. Richards," I said sincerely.

"All right, my dear," said Mark. "Time for Section B."

Chapter Twenty
ROCK CREEK

We drove through part of the Section A neighborhoods first so I could finally see the homes. Not surprisingly, they were very normal looking. Some houses were bigger than others. They were all well-kept. Some homes had toys in the front yard.

"Where are all the kids?" I asked. I had expected to see children playing outside.

"Where do you think? It's the middle of the day, Heather. They're at school."

Of course. Mark turned left onto a long stretch of road.

"This is the road that connects the two sides internally," he said. "It's the only one that's passable by cars. There are two foot bridges crossing the river on either side of this road as well."

We came to a gate, where a man popped his head out of the small building on the left to check the car quickly before opening it for us.

"He's checking for minors. Sometimes kids will, out of

curiosity, try to get to Section B."

"What do parents tell their children?"

"Depends on the family. The ones I know usually just say that Section B is a private community that doesn't want outsiders."

I kept my eyes glued to the window, waiting to see anything unusual or kinky.

"Try not to look like a tourist, eh?" Mark said, smiling at me. I did my best to make my posture and expression casual.

He drove slowly through the various neighborhoods. For the most part, it was just like Section A. But there were obvious signs of the lifestyle, and occasional glimpses of people mid-play. I knew we were in B-1 when I saw a tall, slender woman dressed in nothing but a diaper, crawling around her front yard. Her breasts were small and her hair was pulled into two pigtails – she really did look like a little girl.

"We're getting towards B-2 now," said Mark. I couldn't help but stare when I saw a young woman, naked, walking down the sidewalk with her hands behind her head. Her ass was bright red and spotted with bruises.

"Freshly punished," he commented. "Hey, look here!"

Mark pulled over. I turned to see what he was looking at and my stomach turned as I realized why he had stopped the car. Across the street, in the front yard of a particularly large house, a young man sat in a large, straight-backed chair. In front of the yard was a sign: "Today – free spankings!"

Mark grinned at me. "That looks fun! Go on, get yours," he said. He waved at the man and opened his window. "Hey Danny, how are ya?"

"Pretty good, Mark. I was hoping you'd stop by with the new one!"

I forced myself to get out of the car and crossed the street.

Thankful that I had at least a little bit of alcohol in my system to calm my nerves, I smiled at the man. Danny. He was thin and tan. His wrinkles made it obvious he'd spent a lot of time working outdoors. He wore a plaid shirt and blue jeans.

"I'm Heather," I said shyly.

"Nice to meet you, darlin'. Have you had a spanking yet at Rock Creek?"

"No sir."

He grinned. "Well, bend on over honey, let's break you in!"

I awkwardly bent over his lap, the tight skirt making it difficult to put myself in position gracefully. Danny put one hand on my waist, holding me in place, while the other spent some time rubbing my ass. I squirmed under his hands, wishing he would just get started. I looked over to Mark, who was watching from the driver's seat. He looked amused.

Smack! Smack! Smack!

Danny spanked me lightly. I imagined the sight and shuddered under him with humiliation – the new lawyer bent over a lap in the middle of a neighborhood. I looked around to see if anyone could see me and noticed the girl who we had seen walking. She had stopped and turned around to watch. Her eyes met mine and she smiled slightly. I turned away, embarrassed.

"You can barely feel this with that skirt on. Stand up, darlin'."

Danny looked to Mark for approval, then turned back to me. "Scootch that skirt up. Hurry up now, I've got other customers."

I turned around and saw a couple standing on the sidewalk, watching me and waiting for their turn.

"Oh, god," I said with shame. I yanked my skirt up and practically threw myself over his lap, wanting this to be over as fast as possible.

Smack! Smack! Smack!

Danny wasted no time now and began spanking me in earnest. I squealed under him, not expecting such a hard onslaught. He held me tight and I tried my best not to move, not wanting to provide more of a show for the onlookers.

Smack! Smack! Smack! Smack! Smack!

He paused for a minute, rubbing my ass to ease some of the sting.

"What do you think, Darlene?"

"Is she the new one?" The woman in the couple, who I assumed to be Darlene, spoke up from the sidewalk.

"Yep."

"Well, then, cut her a break. She's so embarrassed, just look at her face. It's more red than her ass!"

I covered my face with my hands, groaning.

"Heather, you're off the hook. Get on up."

I scrambled off of his lap and pulled my skirt down. "Thank you for the spanking, sir."

"You're welcome. And, hey, welcome!" Danny smiled at me. He had a friendly face.

I half-ran to the car. I tried to yank open the door and nearly fell to the ground – Mark had locked me out.

"Strip," he commanded through the open window. I looked over to the yard. Darlene had taken her place over Danny's lap but he hadn't begun spanking her yet. All eyes were on me.

I shimmied out of the skirt and unbuttoned my blouse with shaking hands. I folded both items carefully and then unsnapped my bra, adding it to the clothes. I pass them in to Mark through the window, and heard the blessed sound of the automatic lock clicking out of place. I hopped in the car as fast as I could.

Mark smiled at me. "I love that I can show off your body in public now. You're beautiful, my little slave."

"Thank you, sir." My heart was beating fast and I was a little out of breath from moving so quickly. Mark started the car and we continued, leaving the free-spanking yard behind.

We drove in silence and I took in the sights around me. It was obviously an inactive day; it was, after all, a work day. But I noticed one couple gardening naked. One woman was leading around a man by a leash. We passed a jogger wearing a sports bra and a thong, with "SLAVE" written across her ass.

"You get kind of used to seeing this stuff," Mark said when we passed her. "Not that it ever becomes totally normal... but it becomes... well, *somewhat* normal."

He pulled into the parking lot that I recognized from the satellite photo.

"This," he said, gesturing to the block of houses in front of us, "is B-4. Go over to the grass and kneel. Don't speak."

I got out of the car and did as he said. Kneeling on the soft grass I found myself looking around, hoping I wouldn't see anyone. I looked over to Mark, waiting for his direction. He was on his cell phone, ignoring me.

A woman walked up behind me, startling me.

"Oops, sorry! I didn't mean to scare you. I'm Mandy. Are you the new girl?"

I nodded, smiling up at her.

"Welcome to Rock Creek. I'm one of the people who helped with your stuff today. It took forever, but we did it!"

What? I wasn't allowed to speak with her, but I was desperate to ask her what she was talking about. I pointed to my lips and shrugged.

"Oh, you can't talk can you? Well, see ya around!"

What was she talking about? Why did everyone always seem to know something I didn't know?

Mark finished on the phone and came over to me.

271

"Follow me," he said. "On your hands and knees."

He walked ahead of me and I scrambled to keep up. I looked around, amazed with how beautiful B-4 was. Without having a road, all of the yards sort of melded into one. It felt like I was crawling through a lush green park.

"OK, slave. Here we are."

I looked up. His house was a beautiful, two-story building with wooden siding and white painted trim. Vines crawled up the sides of the house, framing it nicely with greenery. The porch was large, with a table and benches set out for company.

A man dressed in a black suit sat on one of the benches, waiting for us.

"This is her?" he asked Mark.

"Yes. Heather Green."

"Heather, come here please."

I looked to Mark who nodded. I stood and walked over to the man.

"My name is Arthur. I actually work for your firm. Welcome to Rock Creek."

"Thank you," I responded, a bit confused.

"I have some paperwork here for you to sign. Mr. Richards was able to pull some strings and get you approved for membership and residency. I've just added some contractual stuff about you needing to complete a medical evaluation within the week."

"Wow," I said, surprised. "I thought this process was supposed to take months."

"Well, they've been recruiting you for months already. So, you're different than the normal case. By far. Plus with Mr. Richards, Mark, and Erik all vouching for you... plus... well... This was just easier than it is for other potential residents."

"Oh. Well, all right," I said, looking through the papers he had handed me.

"Sign them, Heather," said Mark from behind me. His tone was strong. Set.

"But I haven't read them," I said.

"Yesterday, I asked you if you trusted me. What was your response?"

"I trust you, sir," I whispered. I looked at Arthur, then back to Mark, and then to the papers in front of me. "OK."

Arthur pointed to each line I was to sign. When it was all complete, he stacked them together and stood to go. "It's nice to meet you, Heather. Welcome." With that, he briskly walked away, leaving me with Mark on the front porch of his house.

Mark reached down for my hand and I took it, standing next to him in front of the door.

"Ready to see your new home?" he asked, smiling down at me.

"Yes, sir."

"Go on, then. Open the door."

I tentatively reached for the door, pulling it open and stepping inside. Instantly I fell in love with the home's interior. It was tastefully decorated with beautiful furnishings. Beautiful, yet livable. The wood floors were covered with gorgeous woven rugs, the walls painted with light colors and trimmed with barn-red wood.

"It's wonderful," I said quietly, looking around. Mark still stood behind me in the doorway.

"Well, you can walk around if you like," he said, his voice playful. "Actually, I'll give you a little tour." He slid past me and led the way.

The kitchen was huge, like a dream kitchen from a magazine.

I'll really need to learn how to cook, I thought to myself, lightly touching the surface of the counters. The marble was cool to the touch.

Mark chattered on while he led me around the house.

"There are three full baths and four bedrooms. The basement is finished, of course, but you'll only get to see that if you're *very* good... or very bad. Every bed, chair, and table in the place is equipped with hidden tools to turn it into a piece of bondage furniture. And, you'll notice the ceilings..."

I looked up and saw strategic hooks hanging from various parts of the ceiling. *Interesting.*

"But all of that is hardly necessary here. Why play inside when you can play outside?"

He opened the patio door and stepped out onto the deck. "This is the shared backyard I was telling you about."

I peered outside. The area was *huge*, at least the size of a half football field. On one end was a pool and hot tub area. The other end was equipped with various pieces of 'furniture'. I stayed inside, not wanting to expose myself to the backyard just yet.

Mark chuckled, and closed the door. "OK, upstairs we go. The bedrooms. There is a surprise waiting for you. Two, actually."

He led me upstairs and into a large room with a king-size bed. The room was painted a dark shade of maroon. A small window overlooked the front yard of the house. "This is your room," he said.

I looked around, my eyes wide, and gasped.

"This... these are all my things," I said. A few boxes were stacked by the door, but I saw most of my personal possessions unpacked around the room. My shoes piled up in the corner. My painting on the wall.

"These are *most* of your things. Your old apartment still has some things I didn't really think were necessary. If you discover you're missing anything, I'll send someone for it."

"But I..." I was speechless. I didn't know what to say. He hadn't even *asked me* what I would want to bring here. I felt as if I'd been manipulated.

Suddenly feeling queasy, I pulled out the desk chair and collapsed onto it.

"Heather," Mark's voice grew stern. "You already know that slaves don't take part in some of the decisions regarding their lives. Now, come. One more surprise."

He held my hand as we made our way to another room. Turning to me, Mark looked deep into my eyes.

"This..." he said, taking a deep breath. "This is a surprise that I expect you will not immediately enjoy. Which is why I didn't tell you about it to begin with. But, you'll adjust and learn. Slave, you *will* keep an open mind, and you *will* be respectful. Is that very clear?"

I paused slightly, disoriented, before nodding. "Yes, sir, it's clear."

He stood behind me, reaching around me to open the door. I felt pressure at the small of my back, his hand urging me to step into the room.

I entered the room and immediately staggered backwards, stumbling onto Mark who caught me and held me up.

"Hello, Heather."

Rebecca.

Rebecca. What was my college friend doing here now?

She was wearing a black corset. A small black g-string covered her cunt, and long black stockings ran up her legs. She wore black gloves that nearly went up to her armpits, and high-heels that made her already tall frame seem gigantic; Amazonian.

"Heather," said Mark, softly speaking into my ear. "Say

hello to my wife. Your mistress."

My world tumbled around me as my brain immediately began to put things together. The sudden call from Rebecca, out of nowhere, leading to our night out. Meeting Mark. The law office, Erik, Mr. Richards.

It had all been set-up. Coordinated.

My mind flew with feelings of confusion and betrayal. I looked from Rebecca to Mark, then back again. I only recognized one action I could take.

I dropped to my knees, bowed my head, and whispered, "Hello, Mistress."

ABOUT THE AUTHOR

Sadey Quinn is a fiction and non-fiction writer who lives on a small farm with her partner.

Her erotica work is based on her ongoing real-world experience as a submissive as well as her rich fantasy life and imagination of a future where submissives can be free to submit.

~~~~~~

Sadey Quinn's website, with book information
and her blog: http://sadeyquinn.wordpress.com

OTHER WORKS BY SADEY QUINN

Social Service
Heather's life at Rock Creek continues in this sequel to Quinn's debut novel, *Under Order*

Spanktastic
A collection of short spanking stories set in Rock Creek, a kink-friendly community.

Slaves on Pertz
Alien abduction leads to a group of humans creating their own anarchic society.

SOCIAL SERVICE

An Excerpt from Chapter One

I was standing at the shuttle stop, trying not to think about my skirt which had been unceremoniously yanked up around my waist just a moment before. Mark smiled mischievously as he bared my ass to anyone who cared to look. My face was hot with shame.

I wished he let me wear panties. Or a thong. Or a g-string. Any simple scrap of modesty would have been appreciated.

"The collar you wear has a small chip in it," Mark said. "Your location will be known and tracked at all times."

I nodded, barely hearing him. I was tired and confused. Just last night Mark had torn my world apart. Now I was on my way to work. I wished I could curl up in bed and sleep for hours. Ignoring what was happening to me seemed like a better plan than anything else.

"I've granted all of the high-level dominants rights to play with you," he continued. "I expect you to obey them. If I find that you've been punished for disobedience, I will punish you again when you return home."

"Yes, sir," I said automatically.

"Because you're new you will find that a lot of attention is paid to you. This is common, and shouldn't last more than a few months. Soon you'll blend in just like everyone else. Any command you receive today must be followed by the word *linda*. If you don't hear the word, you don't need to obey the command. I highly doubt anyone would try messing with you without my permission. If it happens, you must tell me. Playing with a collared slave without permission from the owner is a serious crime here. Clear?"

"Linda?" I asked. I was more confused than ever and slightly nauseous.

"It means 'beautiful' in Spanish," Mark said. He sounded impatient. "Do you understand that you are to obey anyone who says that word in your presence?"

"Yes, sir."

"Good."

We waited silently for a moment. I stared into space and let all of my thoughts race through my head. Rock Creek. Signing contracts. New job. Mark. Erik.

Rebecca.

How could they do this to me?

"Heather, I'm proud of you," said Mark. "You will adjust and feel more at home every day. This is just... well, as you know, this is all moving very fast. For all of us. There was pressure from your firm and of course our own impatience to consider. But I know you well, and you will be fine. You'll be great today, I promise." He lifted my head to face him directly. I looked into his eyes. They were kind, compassionate and full of grace.

I marveled at how his eyes could always make me feel right and at ease.

"Thank you, sir," I said sincerely.

"Today will be good for you, Heather. I'm glad you're going to work. Focusing and being by yourself will help you. But remember, Heather, you are never alone. You are *never* on your own," Mark said. His voice went from kind and smooth to a rough growl, making a shiver run up my spine. "You're here because of a number of reasons, but above all, you must never forget that you are owned."

"Yes, Master. I understand," I said.

"You are reporting to Erik this morning, is that correct?"

Mark asked. His fingers traced lines above my ass.

"Yes, sir," I said, quivering under his touch. His kind eyes turned to stones and were impossible to read.

"Very good, my pet. I am sure you will have an interesting day. If you have any trouble or need anything, I'll have my phone with me. All of the people who have permission to play with you know your safeword, and know more about you than you could even imagine. They also all know that this is your first day of work, and your first full day here at the community. You'll mostly be left alone."

"Yes, sir. Thank you," I replied, feeling slightly relieved. Just then the shuttle van pulled up. I checked my watch: eight o'clock exactly.

"Good girl," he said, smiling at me. I turned to step into the van, but before I could move Mark's arm wrapped around my waist. He quickly bent me over and smacked me hard four times on my bare ass. I yelped more from surprise than pain.

He righted my posture, pulled my skirt into place, and pushed me towards the van.

"Have a good day," he said.

I climbed into the shuttle, my face burning red. I fished my new account card out of my purse and handed it to the driver. He was grinning.

"Where are you going?" he asked.

"Downtown, Section A."

He swiped the card and handed it back.

Six other people were on the mini-bus with me. I was relieved that none of them really even looked at me when I took my seat. I gazed out the window, watching the houses fly by as we made our way to Section A, making various stops along the way.

Over and over my mind repeated, *"Mark and Rebecca. Mark is married. Mark and Rebecca."* I just couldn't believe I'd been manipulated in so many ways over the last year. I felt slightly queasy thinking about Rebecca. Last night, when I arrived, I was so exhausted and confused that I didn't really process the entire situation I had just been introduced to. I was Mark's slave yesterday. Today, I belonged to both of them. And Mark wasn't my single suitor. He wasn't my exclusive master. He was Rebecca's husband.

The shuttle halted to a quick stop and a young woman climbed on board. She slid in next to me.

"Hello, Heather," she said, placing her hand on my leg.

I shifted a bit, moving away from her. "Hello," I replied.

"Don't move away, darling. You are, as they said, quite *linda,*" she said. When I heard the magic word I froze, unsure what to do next.

"My name is Mistress Lacy," she said. "Rebecca told me about you. You're even more beautiful in person than she had described."

I looked around us, wondering if anyone was listening in as she spoke.

"Thank you, Mistress Lacy," I replied respectfully.

She ran her fingers up my torso, stopping to play with my nipples through my blouse. "Rebecca and Mark seem to think you to be quite a novice at submission. Is this true, Heather?" she asked, pinching each of my nipples lightly.

"I... I guess it is," I said.

"Hmm," she drawled, making circles around each of my nipples which were now poking out against the fabric of my blouse. "Well, I'm thrilled that we will share the bus in the morning. On the way out, you see, we're on Section B rules. When we get to the gate, we must behave. But for the next few minutes... I think I'd like to see you without your shirt on,

Heather."

I wanted to cry, I was so ashamed. Everyone else on the bus was studying their newspaper or listening to headphones. None of them were engaging in anything at all sexual. But I knew I was expected to obey. I knew I must do as I was told.

"Yes, Mistress Lacy," I whispered. My shaking hands unbuttoned my blouse until it fell open, exposing my breasts.

"All the way off, silly Heather," she said, helping me pull my arms out of the blouse. "You have such pretty breasts. Round and full, a nice big handful. What are you, 34-B?"

I nodded.

"Very pretty," she said.

"Want her up here?" called the driver from the front. Startled, I looked to what he was referring to. He pushed down a small padded seat in the front that faced the entire bus. My stomach turned with dread.

"Not today, Stu. Thanks." Mistress Lacy turned to look at me. My nipples were both rock hard from a combination of her stimulation and the chill of the morning air.

She watched me as I sat quietly until we pulled up to the gate, where she handed me my blouse and told me simply, "Put it on."

For the rest of the ride she didn't engage with me, neither with conversation nor touch. She got off a few stops before downtown and ignored my attempt to say good-bye.

Feeling more confused than before, I decided to get off the bus a stop early in order to get more of a feel for Section A and the neighborhoods around the office building. I walked through the park that I knew I could see from my personal office, enjoying the breeze and the fresh air. I loved the feel of the quaint downtown; it was like a mainstreet of a small mid-western town. There was no evidence at all of kinky activities. Around the corner I found a little coffee shop, and using my new account card I ordered myself and Erik a latte. Unless he had been deceiving me about his tastes, I could order for him better than nearly anyone else in my life.

At the door to my law firm, I took a deep breath before walking inside. *Be calm*, I said to myself. I knew in my heart I'd do fine. I would excel here as I had at the city branch. But starting anything new always comes with a feeling of uncertainty. Especially considering Erik's new role in my life.

Inside, the receptionist greeted me warmly.

"Good morning Heather," she said, handing me a couple of file folders. "I'm Steph. I can help you with any basic questions you have today. Also, a few of us are going to lunch together. If you want you're welcome to join us." She smiled at me.

Though I'd seen her yesterday, today I really looked at Steph for the first time. She was a beautiful woman. She had dark skin with jet black hair that fell in tight curls down past her shoulders. Her face was long and thin and her features were sharp.

"Thanks, Steph," I said.

Erik was in his office speaking on the phone. He motioned me inside. I took a seat in front of his desk and slid his latte over to him.

His office was the same size as mine, more or less, and furnished fairly equally as well. It was clear from how much stuff had accumulated that Erik had been working here for a long time.

After a few minutes, he hung up the phone and looked at me. His arms were folded casually across his chest, his tie loose. I was curious how he would act, who the *real* Erik was. Just a week ago, he was my casual office-mate at the other branch. There, he was almost a friend. I felt hurt to find out that he deceived me. He had been spying on me, making sure I was right for this branch.

"You know, Heather," he began, "I'm still the guy you knew at the city branch."

"But… it's different," I responded, my voice cracking and betraying my emotions.

"Yes, it is. You'll adjust. Go close and lock the door."

I stood, my legs shaking, and shut his office door. The click of the lock sent a shiver down my spine. I turned around, staying put near the door, waiting for further instruction.

Erik still sat at his desk, watching me carefully. "What do you think would help you learn your place here, Heather?" he asked.

"I don't know," I replied softly, staring at my feet.

"Strip, *linda*," he said, his voice steady. My stomach turned and I looked over to him, searching his expression for a clue. When Mark gave me an order, his face became stern and hard. With Erik, his face gave nothing away. No emotion, no lust.

I slipped off my skirt and unbuttoned my blouse while Erik watched. I knew I had no choice. Disobeying him was the same as disobeying Mark. The consequences for direct disobedience would be severe. I wondered how many times Erik had imagined this day as we worked together for so many months.

"Step out of your shoes, too," he said. His voice was quiet. Calm.

I slipped off my heels. I folded my clothes and placed them on the seat of a chair by the door. Shrugging away my instinct to cover up my body, I stood before him, my hands by my side, completely naked.

Erik rose and walked over to me. I had always thought of us as the same height, but without my heels he seemed to tower over me. His face was close to mine, three inches away at most. He placed his hands on my waist.

"Heather, you are a slave. You are also a very talented lawyer.

It will, at times, be difficult for you to grasp how to manage these two very different worlds. I think it became difficult for you at the city branch these last few weeks. Would you agree?"

I nodded. A month ago I had finally begun to see the role of slave as real. Before that it was sort of a game. Role-play. But Mark had helped me understand myself. I was a slave.

"You may address me as sir, Heather," Erik said, his grip tightening around my waist.

"Yes, sir," I whispered.

"So," he continued, "these feelings present an interesting problem that I think we can tackle together. First, you will be subject to regular corporal discipline here at the office. Most of the team here is BDSM friendly. You'll learn who you are expected to submit to with time. Of the people here who practice BDSM, the majority are dominant. This shouldn't come as a surprise, considering our field. I will be the main person who you will report to, and I will be the one dishing out the majority of your discipline. But in the event that I'm unavailable, you will retain utmost respect for the others here who demand your obedience and submission. Is this clear?"

"Yes, sir."

"Good. Secondly, you must never forget that, even though you are a lawyer, you are more importantly a slave. You will have humility. You will not balk at any task, no matter how trivial. You are not too good for anything."

"Yes, sir," I said, swallowing hard.

"Good. Finally, I will require that you submit to me, at the end of the day, at least one thing you could have done better. I don't care if it's something small. We are all working on self-improvement, and you will improve *daily*. This will help both your service and your humility. Is that clear?"

"Yes, sir."

Erik let go of my waist and stepped back. His expression finally changed, his calmness giving way to lust. I watched as his eyes wandered over my body.

"It will be a pleasure to put you in your place, Heather. Though you never said it directly, I knew you thought you were a hot-shot lawyer back at the city branch. And of course, you *are* a remarkable lawyer. But god... I can't wait to humiliate you to your fucking core."

My stomach turned when Erik said this, though I felt the familiar tingle in my pussy. My mind ran over the possibilities of what he might do to me, or what he might make me do. My heart was beating hard. What had Mark given him permission to do with me? Would Erik fuck me? Make me give him a blow job? I felt helpless.

"Lay on the floor, on your back," he said, walking over to his bookcase and opening a drawer. His floor was tiled, but near the desk was a pretty woven rug. I lay down on the rug, stretching out. He returned to my side.

"Knees to your chest."

"Yes, sir," I said, groaning inwardly. I pulled my legs up to my chest knowing that my ass and cunt were exposed to Erik's eyes.

"Spank yourself," he said. He pulled a chair up beside me and sat down, waiting.

"Wha... what?" I asked, confused.

"Use your hand and spank yourself on your ass, Heather. This isn't rocket science."

My face burned red imagining the view he was getting. I began to spank myself with my right hand.

"Harder," he urged. "This only ends when I think you've been well spanked. And I don't plan on helping you."

"Oh, Erik... please," I moaned, wanting to disappear.

"Address me with respect, slave," he said, glaring down at me. He leaned back in his chair, fondling his cock through his pants as he watched me spank my own ass.

I closed my eyes and continued smacking my butt, wondering how long he would make me do this. I wished he would just spank me himself... that would have been humiliating enough. I was kind of annoyed. He was probably doing this simply to prove that he could make me do whatever he commanded.

"My arm is so tired, sir," I whispered after what felt like forever. I hoped he would consider my bottom well-spanked.

"OK. You may use this, now," he said, handing me a flat wooden spatula. "You'll be able to spank yourself just as hard but using less arm strength. And Heather, you need to give yourself a very firm spanking. I want your butt to be red for the better part of the morning. If I need to assist you, you'll be a very sorry little girl. So spank yourself, *hard*."

I choked back tears. The pain on my ass was nothing compared to the embarrassment I felt. I spanked myself in earnest, praying that the slapping sound of the wood against my skin wasn't able to be heard outside of his office. Finally, just when I felt like I wouldn't be able to raise my arm again, Erik grabbed my wrist.

"That's enough. Get dressed."

I stood up awkwardly and put on my skirt and blouse. Erik took the seat behind his desk and began leafing through the folders I had been given by Steph.

"Thanks for the latte, Heather," he said, smiling up at me.

"You're welcome, sir," I replied, pulling on my heels. I looked around for a mirror.

"You look fine," he said. "So, for today, I need you to take a look at these contracts. They're for some of our newer applicants. Contract law is a bitch, Heather. And it's some of the most important work we do. I also want you to look through our main contracts that we use for home and land ownership and community relationships. You need to be *extremely* familiar with them, and you need to be able to explain the gist of them to any prospective homeowners or residents."

I nodded. Our boss, Mr. Richards, had already explained that a lot of my work would be in contract law. And, like Erik mentioned, I knew it would be tough work. That was why they were paying me so well.

"I'll expect you here every morning at nine sharp. You will leave every day at five, checking in with me before you go. We don't have our lawyers work ridiculous hours here, unless we have some extreme priorities. You, Heather, are not *allowed* to work late unless you get specific permission."

"Yes, sir," I mumbled. My workaholic personality would have a tough time adjusting to the hours. Erik had to know that; he very rarely worked later than me back at the city branch. I was accustomed to over seventy hour work weeks. Cutting back by nearly half would be a struggle.

"OK. Get to work." Erik turned to his computer, dismissing me.

15985928R00176

Made in the USA
Lexington, KY
01 July 2012